WHEN LOVE IS ENOUGH

Laura Landon

TENTH ANNIVERSARY EDITION

PRAIRIE MUSE BOOKS INC

2020

This is a work of fiction. Names, characters, places, and incidents
either are the product of the author's imagination or are used fictitiously.

WHEN LOVE IS ENOUGH
Copyright © 2020 by Laura Landon
First published 2010
Paperback Edition
ISBN: 9781937216313

Prairie Muse Publishing
Lincoln, Nebraska 68520

www.lauralandon.com

Dedication

To my mom—
who is the most special mom in the world.
Thank you, Mom. I love you!

CHAPTER ONE

London, England
October 16, 1853

The carriage slowed in front of the Earl of Etherington's town house. Before its three occupants could disembark, Gabriel Talbot shot his arm out and braced it against the door.

"No one move," he demanded, preventing his best friends from exiting. "What did the two of you do to earn this command audience with your father?"

"I can't imagine," Austin Landwell, the younger of the two brothers said, sinking back against the cushions. "Everything was fine when we left the house this morning. Wasn't it, Harrison?"

Harrison Landwell, Viscount Rundmoor, and heir to the Etherington title, released a heavy sigh before swiping his hand through his thick dark hair. "I *thought* it was—well, as fine as things can be with Father's constant concern over money issues."

"Do you think this is over money?"

Harrison and Austin looked at each other. "I can't see how discussing money would be important enough to call us home in the middle of the day. And Father commanded *your* presence too. So this doesn't involve just the two of us."

Gabriel considered what Austin said. "I'd like at least a

little warning about what to expect before we have to face your father. I *was* going to request a meeting with him tomorrow to offer for Lydia's hand."

Smiles broke out across both brothers' faces and before he could protect himself, Austin and Harrison's arms shot out and punched him on opposite shoulders.

"About time," Harrison said on a laugh. "I wasn't sure how much longer Austin and I were going to survive competing with your near-perfection. When Lydia isn't walking around with that syrupy moonstruck look in her eyes, she's extolling your godly virtues to everyone within earshot. I swear, sometimes I feel like I should bow when you walk into a room."

"It's disgusting," Austin teased. "Just the other morning I was foolish enough to mention the trouble cropping up in the Crimea and heard a ten minute dissertation on the reasons you think we'll end up in a war over it. I thought women only cared about shopping and balls and the latest fashions. Look what you've turned our Liddy into—a woman with a mind."

Gabriel smiled. He'd hoped he'd concealed how much Lydia meant to him, at least until he could ask for her hand. Austin's next statement told him that ship had already sailed.

"Bloody hell, Gabe. You've got it as bad as Liddy. You should see the look on your face. You'd better not wait until tomorrow to speak with Father. You'd better offer for our sister today."

Gabriel moved to the edge of the seat. "Maybe I will. After we find out what's so important your father has commanded our presence."

Gabriel jumped out of the carriage and strode up the slate walk a short distance behind Harrison and Austin.

Ruskins, the Etherington butler, held open the door, then took their hats and gloves when they entered.

"Lord Etherington is in the library, my lord. Mr. Landwell, sir," he said with a moving glance that included each of them in turn. "He asked that the three of you join him as soon as you arrived."

"Are there clouds on the horizon?" Harrison asked the austere butler. If anyone was privy to the prevailing mood of his employer, Ruskins was the perfect judge.

"Lord Etherington asked not to be disturbed after you joined him," Ruskins answered and Gabriel felt a hitch in his breathing.

Harrison and Austin must have felt the same foreboding, because a worried glance passed from one to the other.

"Well, then, we'd best face the lion and see what we can do to calm the beast," Harrison said, taking the lead across the foyer's parquet-tiled floor. A footman scrambled to open the door and Gabriel followed the two brothers into the room.

"Good afternoon, Father," Harrison and Austin both acknowledged somberly.

"My lord," Gabriel said with wary apprehension.

"So, what's so terribly important that you called the three of us away from the sale at Tattersall's?" Austin jumped right into obviously troubled waters.

No one could coax a smile from someone in a foul mood better than Austin. No one was better company when you needed a friend to cheer you. But on the opposite side of the coin, no one needed a friend to watch over him more than Austin did. Although Gabriel was fond of both of Liddy's brothers, he felt a special kinship toward Austin. He always had.

"There was a beautiful stallion just going up for bid that Cummings and Rothman were both determined to own. Harrison and Gabe put their money on Rothman, but I thought Cummings looked more determined to—"

"Austin," the Earl of Etherington interrupted. "Perhaps you could cease your chatter long enough to greet our guest."

They turned in unison to where Etherington's gaze was focused at the back of the room. A man Gabe didn't recognize stood in the shadows. He didn't step out when they looked at him, but only lifted his shoulders and faced them with a pompous air that seemed to come naturally. For no reason he could explain, Gabe felt an instant stabbing of dislike.

"Chisolmwood, you remember my eldest son, Harrison, Viscount Rundmoor. Harrison, the Duke of Chisolmwood."

"Your Grace."

Chisolmwood nodded slightly.

"And my second son, Mr. Austin Landwell."

"Your Grace."

Chisolmwood barely greeted Austin. His attention was already focused on Gabriel.

"And may I present Gabriel Talbot. Talbot is—"

"I'm well aware of Talbot's lineage. You are Baron Talbot's son—his...*third* son."

Gabriel tried to ignore the condemnation in the duke's voice and raised his chin. "Yes, Your Grace. I am my father's...*third* son. Are you acquainted with my father?"

The duke's expression hinted that Gabriel's question was a blatant affront to his elevated station.

"No, Talbot, I've never met your father."

Since Gabriel couldn't remember the last time his father had come to London, he knew it was highly unlikely Chisolmwood and his father were acquainted. And since his two older brothers were content to stay in the country with their wives and children, he doubted Chisolmwood was acquainted with them, either. If it weren't for Harrison and Austin—and of course, Lydia—Gabriel doubted he would have spent the last several months in London or met half the people to whom he'd gained introduction.

"I'm sure you didn't call us away from Tattersall's because His Grace came to call," Harrison said to his father, his voice carrying a note of wariness that matched the unease sifting through Gabriel. "Has something happened?"

"Yes," Etherington said, slowly rising from behind his desk. He paced four steps toward the open window then stopped and turned. "I called you here because His Grace has come with an offer. An offer that affects all of you."

Gabriel stood rooted where he was, unable to move. The fact that he'd been summoned was warning enough. The worried frown on Etherington's forehead reinforced the concern eating at him. That the Duke of Chisolmwood was at the center of the issue tripled the danger.

Etherington clasped his hands behind his back and looked at Gabriel.

"His Grace has come with an offer of marriage."

The earth shifted beneath Gabe's feet. He clenched each hand in a grip that sent waves of pain up and down his arms and he forced himself to take one breath after another.

"An offer of marriage?" Austin sputtered. "For whom? Lydia?"

Harrison took a step forward. "You can't be serious. For God's sake, Father. Surely you aren't considering His Grace as a husband for Liddy?"

Etherington slammed his fist against the corner of the desk. "Enough. Both of you. His Grace isn't offering for himself. He's offering for his son, the Marquess of Culbertson."

Gabriel felt the air freeze in his lungs, yet he somehow kept breathing as if Lydia's father hadn't just spoken words that had the power to destroy his future. He knew he had to do something to stop this from going further or he'd lose her.

"Lord Etherington," he said, stepping deeper into the room. "Lydia and I have already come to an understanding concerning our future together. I do not claim to have His Grace's wealth or influence, but I'm not without means. Nor am I without a future. Lydia will never lack for anything. On that you have my promise."

Etherington looked uncomfortable. And defeated.

"That isn't the issue, Talbot. Surely you can't expect me to consider any proposal you might make when I am presented with the chance for my daughter to become a duchess?"

Gabriel's jaw clenched. "Have you asked Lydia her wishes? Perhaps she doesn't wish to become a duchess."

"That doesn't matter. You and I both know she's too young and too impressionable to know her mind."

Gabe couldn't stop the smile that lifted the corners of his mouth. "You don't know your daughter nearly as well as you think, my lord." He paused. "Or perhaps you don't care nearly so much for her happiness as you do for how her marriage to a duke's son can benefit *you*."

The color drained from the Earl of Etherington's face and the earl staggered back a step before he caught himself against the chair behind his desk.

"I want what is best for *all* my children," the earl said, and Gabriel heard something in the earl's voice he hadn't recognized before—an absence of hope.

"Then you will at least consider my offer for your daughter's hand."

"No, he will not," the Duke of Chisolmwood said from behind them.

Except for their frosty meeting, Chisolmwood had been ominously silent. Gabriel recognized the challenge in the duke's words but refused to let him dominate. He turned to where the duke stood and faced him.

"For months now, neither Lydia nor I have made a secret

of our feelings for each other. Out of all the eligible women to consider for your son's bride, why have you chosen someone whose heart is already taken?"

The duke's eyebrows shot up. "My reasons for choosing Lady Lydia are none of your concern."

"They are when you've chosen the woman I love."

"Then you'd best choose someone else to love because you will *not* marry her."

"I hardly think that's your decision to make, Your Grace. Lady Lydia has a father to see to her best interests."

"The woman's father has already made his decision. Haven't you, Etherington?" Chisolmwood's voice was commanding enough to stifle any argument.

All eyes turned toward the Earl of Etherington.

"What does His Grace mean?" Austin asked. "How can you have already decided who Lydia marries?"

"Would you like to tell them, Etherington? Or shall I?"

The Earl of Etherington sank into the chair behind his desk and buried his face in his hands. Gabriel thought how old he suddenly seemed, how pitifully weak.

"Tell us what, Father?" Harrison stepped forward. He stopped and his gaze rested on a bundle of papers lying on the top of the desk. He stared at the papers before tentatively picking them up. One by one he sifted through each sheet, the frown on his forehead deepening with each flip of a new page. "What are these?"

"They're every note your father has ever signed," Chisolmwood said, stepping out of the shadows to be the center of attention. "And found himself unable to repay." He cleared his throat and elevated his chin. "They are all now paid in full."

"By whom?"

"By me."

Austin snatched the packet of papers out of Harrison's hands and shoved them toward Chisolmwood. "We don't need you to pay our debts. All our creditors have agreed to wait until the *Guardian Angel* docks. The profits from the tea it's bringing from China will—"

"The *Guardian Angel* sank going around the Cape nearly a month ago. Its cargo and most of its crew were lost."

A deafening silence enveloped the room. Gabriel knew how much Lord Etherington as well as Harrison and Austin had been counting on the profits from the delivery of the tea. Austin had told him that all three of them had borrowed as heavily as they could to finance the venture. Now, to have it lost…

"Then we'll find a way to pay you back," Harrison said, the bravery Gabe knew he strove to achieve in his voice faltering. Chisolmwood knew it, too, and a sinister smile crossed his face.

"The amount is over one hundred thousand pounds, Rundmoor. A sum even I find staggering."

"How long before you demand payment?"

"Tomorrow."

"Tomorrow! You can't be serious."

"But I am. Your father intends to sign the papers agreeing to a betrothal between his daughter and my son in exchange for the complete payment of his notes."

"If Liddy refuses?" Austin said with a defiant look on his face.

"My man of business will seek out the authorities. You will all be in debtors' prison by week's end. And your sister with you. Is that what you want, Etherington?"

The Earl of Etherington looked into the faces of his two sons then dropped his gaze to the empty desk before him.

Chisolmwood took a threatening step closer to Lydia's father. "I didn't think so."

Chisolmwood placed a single piece of paper in front of the

earl. "Sign this and consider your debts paid in full."

"You can't, Father," Harrison said. "We can't sell Liddy to pay for our debts. She'd never forgive us—"

Chisolmwood held up his hand and Harrison broke off his sentence. "What would you have them do, Talbot? Would you encourage Etherington to withhold his signature?"

Chisolmwood paused as if giving Gabriel time to consider his question, then paced a small area in front of them as if he were an orator giving a lecture. He stopped and fired another question Gabriel couldn't answer.

"Or better yet, perhaps we should call in Lady Lydia and let her make the choice." He leveled his gaze at Gabriel. "Which do you think she'll choose, Talbot? Marriage to you, or keeping her father and brothers from ultimate ruination?"

Gabriel tried not to react. Instead, he stared at the paper in front of Etherington. The paper that had the power to take Lydia away from him forever.

His mind didn't want to consider the answers to any of Chisolmwood's questions. Neither did his heart. Deep inside he knew he had no choice but to face the nightmare that was unfolding. Once Lydia understood what her marriage to him would cost her family, he knew the choice she'd make. She loved her father and her brothers too much to see them ruined.

Yet, how could he give her up?

"What answer would you give him?" Chisolmwood repeated.

"We'll find another way, Gabe," Harrison declared. "You and Lydia love each other."

A similar declaration came from Austin, even more resolute. He was ever the one to search for the bright side to every problem, ever the one to refuse to admit the hopelessness of a situation.

"Choose, Talbot," the duke demanded.

Austin stepped forward. "We have until tomorrow, Gabe. Maybe we'll find a way by then to—"

Gabriel shot him a harsh look and Austin's words died unspoken.

"Sign the paper," Gabriel said to the Earl of Etherington.

"Gabe, no," Harrison and Austin both protested as if there was another possibility.

"Sign it," he repeated. The second the words were out in the open, a pain exploded inside his chest that nearly took him to his knees.

How could he live his life without her?

Chisolmwood smiled. "I'm glad to see your pride is exceeded by your wisdom. Rest assured, though, I am not totally without feelings. I will make your sacrifice well worth any inconvenience it might cause you."

Before Gabriel could think better of his actions, he stepped so close to the Duke of Chisolmwood he could have wrapped his fingers around the bastard's throat and choked the air from his body.

"I'll not take one shilling from you, and you have my promise now. If I ever have it in my power to destroy you, I won't hesitate to do so."

For an instant the smug, self-confident expression on the duke's face fell away. Gabe was glad that Chisolmwood understood his meaning. If ever given the chance, he would more than destroy him. He'd kill him.

Chisolmwood faltered, then with an inborn aplomb, he recovered.

"I'm waiting," the duke said to Etherington.

Etherington lifted his gaze, first to Harrison, then to Austin. And finally to Gabe.

The older man's features were tightly drawn over pasty white cheeks. His lifeless blue eyes clouded with guilt and regret and something more. Despair.

"What choice do I have?" he said softly, the question lacking hope, his expression beseeching one of them to offer a solution.

No one did because there wasn't a solution.

Then, with trembling hands, Lydia's father picked up the pen from his desk and condemned his daughter to pay for the debts his reckless spending and poor investments had created; he condemned her to live a life unlike the one they all knew she desired.

Unlike the one Gabriel had dreamed of from the day he'd met her.

When the paper was signed, the pen fell from Etherington's fingers and the earl sank back against his chair, a broken man.

The Duke of Chisolmwood folded the signed document and secured it in his pocket. "I'll see myself out," he said and walked from the room.

No one said anything for several long minutes after he left. How could they? What was there to say? The damage was done and no words could change what had happened.

Gabriel waited until his legs were steady enough to carry him from the room, then walked to the door. Harrison's voice stopped him.

"*You* have to tell her, Gabe."

Gabe clutched his hand around the brass knob on the door. What could he tell her? What words were there to explain why he couldn't marry her that wouldn't leave her hating him? Hating her family? Hating the man she'd eventually have to marry?

Gabriel spun around. "*You* tell her. I've sacrificed enough for this family."

"I know you have. More than any of us. But you can't let her think you still have feelings for her. You have to convince her you no longer love her."

Gabriel dropped his head to his chest. It was suddenly too

heavy to hold up. "I could never do that. Never."

"If you feel anything for her, you won't let her go through life thinking you still love her. It would be kinder to sever any ties today."

There was a softness in Harrison's voice that pulled at Gabriel's heart. Was Harrison right? Would it be better if she forgot what they'd shared so she could be happy with someone else? Was disgust and disappointment better than a broken heart?

He sucked in a deep breath that burned in his chest. He would make his break swift and clean. Maybe it would be less painful that way.

Except he knew the pain he felt now would never go away.

"Where is she?"

"Probably in the garden. Down by the lily pond. It's where she always goes when she's upset or needs to be by herself."

He walked across the room to the multi-paned glass door that would take him outside. Austin's voice stopped him before he left.

"Gabe?"

He didn't turn around. He couldn't face any of them. He needed all his courage to face Lydia.

"I'm sorry," he heard Austin say as he threw open the door.

They seemed empty words to Gabriel Talbot, who knew it was he who would regret this day for the rest of his life.

❦

He crossed the terrace, then made his way along the flag-stone walk, each step echoing a plea that she would survive the pain he would cause her. He had to be cruel, final. He couldn't let her think he still loved her or that there was a chance he would come back to her.

Harboring such hope would be unfair to them both.

He took the path to the right of the gazebo and walked a few feet. He saw her ahead of him looking out over the small pond and stopped. Fingers of dread clenched about his heart.

God help him. He couldn't do this. He loved her too much to lose her. But if they married and she found out their love had ruined her father and brothers, she'd hate him forever. And herself.

He willed his heart to turn to stone. Unfeeling, unemotional. As cold as ice. He walked toward her. She turned when she heard him.

"Gabe!"

Her dainty hand flew to her mouth. She ran to him and threw herself in his arms.

He saw the fear on her face and held her, but not close enough to feel her warmth. If he weakened now, he knew a part of him would die when he had to let her go.

"Oh, Gabe. I've been so afraid."

"Afraid? Why?"

He pushed her away from him before her body left an imprint that would last a lifetime.

"Didn't Father tell you? The duke wants me to marry his son, the Marquess of Culbertson! I refused, of course. I told Father I loved you and we were going to marry."

She leaned into him and wrapped her arms around his waist. His flesh burned from her touch. Every protective instinct raced to the forefront. He wanted to take her somewhere far away from here. Someplace where they would never find her. Someplace where he could keep her safe, keep her to himself.

"What are we going to do, Gabe?"

God help him. He wasn't going to survive this.

He placed his hands against her upper arms and separated her from him. The desperation in her deep blue eyes was nearly his undoing. He forced another layer of ice to form around his heart before he looked at her.

"Did you tell them?" she asked.

"Tell them what?"

"That we love each other. That we intend to marry."

She stared at him, her expression darkening with concern. He didn't want to say what he knew he must. He didn't want to see the pain he would cause her. But—

"Oh, Liddy," he said, tapping the tip of her nose with his finger. "What a silly goose you are. Surely you realized all along we couldn't marry. I'm not titled. My future is with the army. I'll never earn enough to support you."

She stiffened in his arms. "You know the money doesn't matter. I've never cared whether you were rich or titled. We wouldn't need a great deal. We'd get by on whatever you could provide. And I have Southerby Manor that my maternal grandmother left me. It would be enough."

"No, it wouldn't. If I married you without your father's blessing, you'd come with no dowry."

She separated herself from him. "And that…that matters?"

He laughed, and the sound of it splintered his heart. "Of course it matters. Even *you* have to realize it matters."

She stepped back another step. "Is that why you wanted me? For my dowry?"

"Well, I just naturally thought…"

She stumbled again. Her voice broke when she spoke. "No, Gabriel. Don't do this to me."

The pain in her eyes shot through to his soul.

"Ah, Liddy. Don't look so shocked."

"You said you loved me. You said you wanted to marry me."

He forced himself to smile. "A man says many things when he *thinks* he's in love. I would have promised you the moon but you know I couldn't have given it to you."

She shook her head, the shock, the disbelief, the pain evident in her eyes. "Why are you doing this?"

"I'm doing nothing. Only being practical. We need money to live, and you, unfortunately, will come with none."

A vast chasm of silence separated them until she spoke, her voice hesitant, filled with pain. "Did you mean anything you said to me? Even one word? Or was everything a lie?"

"Darling Liddy, of course I meant it. Every word." The icy shield around his heart cracked. Her face began to soften and he knew he had to drive the wedge wider. "At least I did when I thought you'd come with a dowry."

She opened her mouth to say something but no words came. He filled in the gap. "I wouldn't be satisfied living the rest of my life in poverty, Liddy. And neither would you. In time, you'd resent me because I couldn't provide for you as you're accustomed. And I'd come to resent you as well."

"You know that's not true."

"But it is. Without money we'd end up hating each other."

She slapped his hands away from her and stumbled back to put more distance between them.

"Who are you?" she asked, the horror on her face plain to see. "You aren't the Gabriel to whom I gave my heart."

Another layer protecting his heart shattered and fell away.

"You aren't the man who had no care for riches or the title he'd never have. Nor are you the loving and caring man I would have been content to spend the rest of my life loving. What have you done with him? You aren't that man."

The final layer surrounding his heart crumbled, exposing his vulnerability. He struggled to protect himself with the thin barrier left around his emotions. "Of course, I am. I'm just more practical now. I'm the same person, only now I've had time to realize the obstacles we'd face if your father refused to give you a dowry. Now I realize I could never be content with just your love."

She shook her head. "No, you're not him. I could never have loved someone as greedy and selfish as you."

His heart died inside his chest. "Surely you're aware of how important money is to someone who has none."

"Get out," she whispered, her voice harsh. "Go away and leave me alone."

"Liddy—"

"Go!"

He stood, unable to move for several seconds.

Finally, he forced his body to turn and his feet to go forward. He walked away from her. But it was only his body he took with him.

He left his broken heart behind because he knew he would never love again.

CHAPTER TWO

Crimean Peninsula
April 16, 1855

The stench of death permeated the air so that Gabe could hardly breathe. The moans and screams of the injured and dying echoed in his ears. There was no escape from it. Death was all around him, a part of him. Even if he survived this madness, he knew the sights and sounds of the suffering and inhumanity would haunt him for the rest of his life. And the nightmares would stay with him until he drew his last breath.

Major Gabriel Talbot sucked in as deep a breath as his injured body would allow, then prayed to God he wouldn't die here. Not in this hellhole, fighting a war that had no purpose and would gain nothing for Britain when it was finished.

Blood dripped steadily from his fingertips and he clutched his hand over the blood-soaked bandage wrapped around his upper arm. Just his damned luck. The bullet was still lodged in his flesh. Now he'd have to let those filthy butchers cut on him to get it out.

Every soldier in the Crimea knew they had a better chance of surviving on the battlefield than in an army hospital. And Gabriel knew the wounds he'd suffered tonight were too severe to keep him from going under the surgeon's knife.

He dragged in a shuddering breath and fought a pain so

intense he could barely stand up under it. The dead Russian general responsible for his injuries lay lifeless at his feet and Gabriel tucked the papers he'd taken from him into a secret pocket in his jacket. Papers that outlined the Russian plan of assault. Papers that contained information that would save thousands of lives and affect the outcome of the war. He had to get the information to General Simpson.

Gabriel pushed himself away from the crumbling wall that surrounded the town of Sebastopol, the Russian stronghold that protected their naval port. From here the Russian army received food, arms, and the replacement troops they needed to rain down destruction on the allied forces. He'd received a coded message that informed him about the Russian general who'd be carrying the secret papers, but he'd been forced to venture far into enemy territory before he had an opportunity to take them from him. Now he was in more danger than he wanted to admit.

He took the first tentative step on his wounded leg and fought the pain that knifed through him. The Russian general had been a far more threatening adversary than he'd looked, and Gabriel suffered the wounds to prove it. He just prayed that neither the sound of the Russian firing his gun nor his dying screams had drawn any attention.

He swiped his hand over the beads of perspiration running down his face, then stumbled into the open. The sounds of enemy shelling echoed in his ears. The screams of the wounded, the moans of the dying—he ignored them all.

Bloody hell, but he wanted this to be over. He wanted to be home, even though he wasn't quite sure what awaited him there.

Certainly not the wife he'd thought he'd have.

Certainly not the future he'd envisioned.

A picture of Liddy's sun-kissed feminine beauty appeared,

as if conjuring her graceful elegance could somehow give him the strength he needed to survive. Dark, laughing eyes looked up at him, brimming with the vibrancy and life he chose to remember when he thought of her, instead of the deep blue pools spilling tears of hurt and betrayal that were more reminiscent of the way she'd looked the last time he saw her.

It was best if he concentrated on getting back to safety rather than on what he'd left behind in England. That part of his life was lost to him forever.

He took his next step forward and tripped over the lifeless body of another soldier. He waited while white-hot stabs of pain gripped him with an intensity that stole his breath, then he pushed himself to his feet and continued to move.

Every lift of his mud-caked boots was heavier than the last, but finally, he topped the ridge. The British encampment was within view. Soon General Simpson would have the papers in his possession and Gabriel could sleep.

He brushed his hand across his face, wiping away a trickle of blood burning his eye, then forced himself to make his way through the tangle of corpses that littered the battlefield. Just a little farther and he could hide himself in the trenches. Just a little farther.

He took another step and stopped short. The thundering of horse's hooves echoed in his head. He turned. An armed Russian rider raced toward him, his saber drawn.

Before he could move, the rider was on top of him.

Gabriel spun away, but not soon enough.

An unbearable fire knifed through his arm and he looked down to see the sleeve of his jacket separate and the frayed edges turn crimson.

He lifted his rifle, but before he could get off a shot, the rider leveled the barrel of his own gun. Gabe twisted to the side, but knew he would not be fast enough.

A rush of smoke spiraled from the tip of the soldier's rifle and Gabriel's chest exploded in an inferno that took him to his knees. The last sight that flashed before him was the broad-shouldered man in an enemy's uniform, bearing down on him, his sword drawn and the confident look of victory in his eyes.

Gabriel felt the slash of the enemy's rapier cut his flesh from his shoulder to his waist and his world went black around him. The papers that could save thousands of lives were still tucked inside a hidden pocket of his jacket.

❦

"Gabe! Gabe!!"

Captain Austin Landwell stumbled amidst the mass of human carnage in search of his friend and fellow officer. Every time he saw a body that looked to be over six feet in height with a large frame and hair as dark as midnight, his heart lurched in his chest. Gabe was out here somewhere. Austin could feel it. They'd gone through so much together that sometimes Austin felt as though they shared each other's pain. And the pain he felt right now was so intense he swore it was his own.

The gray dawn was lightening the sky, the sun beginning its ascent. A dusky haze hung over the battle-scared earth, the dead and dying still lying where they'd fallen. Austin walked from corpse to corpse, turning the bodies over, praying the face would not bear Gabe's familiar features.

Sixty thousand Russian troops had launched the massive attack, the losses staggering on both sides. Upwards of five thousand Russian soldiers were dead, along with hundreds of French and Sardinians. The British fared better this time, most of their troops having not been in the thick of the battle. But Austin knew Gabe was out there—knew he was among the wounded.

He would not think he was dead. He couldn't be. Austin pushed forward, wending his way through the inert bodies.

Then he saw him.

He knew before he reached the unconscious form that it was Gabe. He raced over the rough, uneven terrain and came to a blinding halt. Even though the body was face down on the cold, hard ground, Austin didn't doubt it was his friend.

He looked down at Gabe's twisted, mangled arms and legs and felt the air leave his body. "Don't let him be dead," he whispered in prayer, dropping to his knees at his friend's side. "Please, God, don't let him be dead."

Gabe didn't move but lay still as death, his left hand still clutching his sword, his blood turning the earth an unholy black. Austin's heart thundered in his chest as he reached out a trembling hand and touched Gabe's blood-stiffened jacket.

"It's me, Gabe. I'm here. I've come to take you home."

Ever so gently, he turned Gabe over, easing him onto his back. Blood pulsed from a gaping hole in the upper right side of his chest. Austin swallowed hard, his breaths coming in harsh gasps. "Oh, damn, Gabe," he whispered, staring into Gabe's ashen, gray face. "Oh, bloody hell. What have they done to you?"

Austin swiped the back of his hand across his cheeks to wipe the salty wetness away, then leaned down, praying he'd hear Gabe's heart beating.

Nothing.

He held his hand over Gabe's nose, praying he'd feel air.

Nothing.

He placed his palm over his mouth.

Perhaps. He couldn't tell for sure. But Gabe was still warm.

He placed his palm to the dirt-encrusted, ashen cheek, then lifted Gabe's hand. It was limp. Surely that was a good sign. Surely that meant something.

"Stay with me, Gabe. Don't you dare die."

He knew he had to hurry. Knew he had to get him back to camp. He ripped open Gabe's jacket and shirt and stared at the torn flesh of his chest. Austin's stomach revolted and he turned his head, then forced himself to concentrate on taking care of his friend. He ran to the nearest dead soldier and removed his shirt. The material tore easily, most of the uniforms little more than rags.

"I'm going to get you back to England, Gabe. The doctors will take good care of you there. You'll be fine."

Austin worked as quickly and carefully as he could, but the minute he pressed the cloth against the massive wound, Gabe threw his arms out and fought him.

"Gabe. Lie still. You're hurt."

Gabe's eyelids fluttered. "Austin?"

"I'm right here. I'm going to get you help."

"No…"

"You are *not* giving up. I won't let you. We promised each other," Austin said, binding Gabe's wounds as best he could. "We took an oath when we landed in this hellhole that we'd leave together. And I'm holding you to it. We're going home together."

Gabe shook his head but Austin ignored him. He couldn't think of leaving his friend here. He had to get him home. Back to England. He concentrated on nothing else until Gabe's fingers clamped around his wrist, bringing his frantic movements to a halt.

"In my…pocket. Papers."

"You can give them to me later." Austin worked harder to stop the bleeding in Gabe's chest. Nothing he did was helping. He looked around. Where the hell were the soldiers who combed the fields after a battle to retrieve the wounded?

"Now…" Gabe whispered on a moan. "Take them. Important."

Austin reached into the secret pocket of Gabe's jacket and pulled out the papers, then stuffed them into his own pocket.

"I'll take care of them," he whispered, pressing the cloth harder against Gabe's chest. "But you stay with me. Don't you dare die on me, Major, or I'll haunt you to the ends of hell and back." Austin watched more color drain from Gabe's face and heard his breathing become more labored.

"Too…late," he whispered, then closed his eyes and sank back into unconsciousness.

Austin lifted his gaze, frantic to find someone to help.

In the distance he saw two soldiers bearing a stretcher and he called out to them. They both hurried forward, the looks on their faces expectant, as if they were relieved to finally find a soldier who was still alive. Heaven only knew they'd seen enough dead ones.

"Help me get him back to camp," Austin said, prying the sword out of Gabe's hand.

The two placed the stretcher beside Gabe's body and one of the two men leaned over to look at him. "Is that Major Talbot?" one soldier asked.

"Yes."

The two men looked at each other and Austin knew they didn't think it was wise to move him. Knew they thought Gabe would die before they got him back to camp. Only one had the courage to say the words out loud.

"He's hurt real bad, Cap'n. Mayhaps it'd be best if we left him be. At least the end will be more comfortable-like if we don't move him."

"He needs to get to the surgeon. Now!"

"But—" the other soldier started, then stopped short when Austin gave him a stinging look.

"Right away, Cap'n. We'll get the major to the surgeon right quick, we will."

The two men picked Gabe up and moved him onto the stretcher. He moaned and Austin's heart lurched in his chest. His friend looked more dead than alive.

"We're going home, Gabe. Just like we promised. We're leaving here together. Both of us."

Austin walked beside the stretcher as they made their way through a battlefield littered with dead.

He'd give General Simpson the papers. Then he was taking Gabe home.

CHAPTER THREE

London, England
June 1, 1855

What a crush! What an absolute crush!

Lydia pasted a smile on her face and made her way from one group of longtime friends to another. She reminded herself for the hundredth time that this is what she'd have to learn to love about London—the endless rounds of balls and parties and social gatherings, buying new gowns, getting dressed up, and staying out nearly all night. There must be plenty of good reasons to enjoy the excitement, invitations, and laughter.

London during the height of the season should be her favorite time of the year.

So why did she wish this night were over?

She walked through Lady Puttingsworth's exquisitely decorated ballroom and told herself it was no wonder she was reluctant to jump back into the whirl of social life. Gabriel's cruel rejection of her, followed by her father's unexpected death only weeks later had delivered a doubly harsh blow. Austin's abrupt departure to follow Gabe and fight the war in the Crimea had prompted her to spend a year of mourning in quiet solitude at Southerby Manor. After the peacefulness of the country, the number of people here tonight was a bit overwhelming.

From the moment she walked through the door, she was inundated with greetings to welcome her back from her long absence. She wanted to blame her desire to escape on the number of well-wishers vying for her attention, but she knew that wasn't it.

Coming here tonight forced her to leap back into a world that no longer held Gabe.

She made her way to the room the Marchioness of Puttingsworth reserved for her lavish array of foods and refreshments and took a glass of spiced punch from the table. The tangy liquid was still relatively cool and Lydia welcomed the relief it provided. For the first time in her life she felt like an outsider stepping into unfamiliar surroundings. How odd, since this was the life she'd been born into, the life she'd been raised to expect, the only life she'd ever known—until Gabe let her glimpse a life that would have been different.

She felt a heavy weight press against her chest and pushed the hurt away. In the last twelve months she'd become expert at replacing the pain with an emotion that was limited in the feelings it recognized. It was a trick she hadn't mastered completely, but was getting better at each day.

She didn't hate him yet, but she would—soon.

She pushed all thoughts of him far from her mind. It had taken her a year to recover from the hurt. A year to realize that the promises he'd made had all been empty, that he'd only wanted her for the money he thought would come with her. It had taken a year to accept the fact that he was never coming back, and even if he did, it wouldn't be to her. Because she wouldn't have him.

When he'd first left, she doubted she'd survive. Now, she knew she would. She'd not only survive, but she'd have everything from life she'd always dreamed of having—marriage to the perfect husband, a home with children to nurture and care for, an enviable position in Society.

Everything Gabriel took away from her.

She lifted the glass to her lips and took a small sip, blaming the tartness of the liquid for the burning in her throat. She swallowed hard and looked up, her gaze focusing on the open doorway.

Her heart gave a startled leap at the man walking toward her. He was a breathtaking sight—tall, golden blond, with perfectly chiseled features. Probably the most sought-after catch of the Season. Except he wasn't interested in any of the debutantes falling at his feet. He was already linked to her.

Lydia looked up at the Marquess of Culbertson and smiled.

"Lady Lydia, you can't imagine how surprised I was to hear you'd finally returned to Society."

"I came with Harrison. He convinced me it was time."

"He was right. You've been in mourning long enough. Your father wouldn't have wanted you to give up any more of your youth to grieve for him."

"No, he wouldn't have," she added, although it wasn't only her father's death she'd mourned for the past year.

"I can't believe there isn't a horde of eager young men vying for your attention." He raised his thick, golden brows in an enchanting gesture. "Or have you come to get something to drink to escape your press of admirers?"

"Of course not," she said. "I simply needed a glass of punch to quench my thirst."

Culbertson took the empty glass from her hands and smiled. "Perhaps you'd like to step outside on the terrace for a breath of fresh air?"

Without giving her a chance to refuse, he turned her toward the open patio doors and ushered her out into the cool, crisp London evening.

She didn't mind. In fact, she'd anticipated having a conversation with the Marquess of Culbertson tonight. He'd been far more than patient with her. After all, a year had passed since his father had been to see her father. The Marquess of Culbertson had been her father's hand-picked choice to be her husband, but when he'd come to make his intentions known she'd been too distraught over Gabriel's rejection to see him. Then, only weeks later, her father had died in a hunting accident and she'd welcomed her year of mourning.

Now, however, the year since her father's death had passed and it was time to resume her life. Now that she'd reentered Society, she'd let her relationship with Culbertson proceed at whatever speed the marquess determined.

"I intended to send a note to inform you of my return," she said, "but Harrison told me you were gone from London on business."

"Yes. Estate business takes up a great deal of my time. I regret that I wasn't here. We could have spent several weeks in each other's company."

Lydia waited for the rush of heightened anticipation to warm her blood. The thought of spending time with Gabriel always set her heart racing. Culbertson's announcement, however, caused no reaction. *Damn Gabriel.* If the opportunity ever arose, she'd make sure he paid for what he'd done to her.

"Are you enjoying yourself?" he asked, walking at a leisurely pace as they exited through the open doorway and into the cool spring evening.

"I am. The Marchioness of Puttingsworth can't be outdone when it comes to entertaining. It would have been foolhardy to turn down one of Society's most coveted invitations."

"Perhaps that's why there's such a crowd."

"Yes. There's always a crush at her balls. Such a throng of people makes it all the more exciting."

"And the perfect event to mark your return."

She smiled as she walked beside him.

He led her to the far side of the terrace and held her hand to help her sit on a curved stone bench.

"I must apologize," he said, sitting beside her on the edge of the bench.

Lydia brought the skirts of her peach satin gown closer to give him room, then looked into his face. "For what?"

"For not commenting on how stunning you look tonight. You stole my breath the minute I saw you. But I was so pleased to see you here that my manners escaped me."

Her cheeks warmed. It had been so long since anyone had noticed how she looked. It had been even longer that she'd cared. "Thank you."

"If I had known you were going to attend tonight, I would have asked permission to escort you." He turned his head and looked at her. "Would that have been agreeable?"

She knew his question implied more than escorting her here tonight. It meant being her escort through the remainder of the London Season. She took a deep breath and smiled.

"I would have been delighted."

"I'm glad." The marquess rose. "I don't know if anyone told you, but I came to see you shortly before your father's accident. I'd just discovered your father and mine had planned our futures. I thought it might be prudent to see if their plans met with your approval."

"I appreciate your concern."

The marquess paced a small area in front of her. "I wanted you to know that I had no part in their matchmaking."

She sensed the marquess's unease. "Would you have rejected the arrangement if you had known about it?"

He stopped and looked at her. "I would have made sure you

were open to such an arrangement before any details were discussed. As I remember, all of Society thought there would be
a match between you and Talbot. Even your brothers seemed
certain of it."

"Well, they were wrong."

"May I ask what happened?"

"That was a long time ago. I've forgotten."

Culbertson arched his brows. "Have you?"

Lydia saw the open question on his face. He deserved an
explanation. "Anything that might have existed between
Captain Talbot and myself was finished the day he left."

"Talbot's a major now. Did you know?"

Her heart tripped. "If I did, I'd forgotten. Thankfully, my
father saw *Major* Talbot's true nature and exposed him. I'm
grateful to have escaped marriage to him before it was too late."

Culbertson clasped his hands behind his back. "Then I see
no reason to avoid pursuing our relationship. My father is quite
insistent upon a match between us, and I certainly have no
objection. You are beautiful beyond measure and you come
from a very prestigious family. Your brother, Lord Etherington,
has a reputation for being an astute man of commerce with a
keen intelligence. The improvements he's made to the Landwell
holdings in the last year are remarkable."

Lydia realized she hadn't paid the slightest attention to the condition of their estates. Before her father's accident, she'd thought
they might be in financial difficulties, but since money was never
a topic that was discussed, she had no way of actually knowing.

"And your younger brother," Culbertson continued, "is
already a captain in Her Majesty's Army. He's received acclaims
too numerous to mention. Is it any wonder, then, that only the
bravest of men would dare to compete for the sister of not
one, but two brothers with such remarkable attributes? Not to

mention the fact that your name was closely linked with Major Gabriel Talbot. The standards he set are quite daunting."

"I wouldn't know," Lydia interrupted with a little more sarcasm than necessary.

She didn't want to hear of Gabriel's bravery, or his accomplishments. She didn't want to hear anything that would remind her of him. She only wanted to get on with her life. A life that would never include him again.

"You haven't heard the tales of his heroism?"

"I'm hardly interested in anything Major Talbot does." She lifted her gaze and stared at Culbertson. "You sound as if you're intimidated by the major. You needn't be."

"I'm not intimidated. Perhaps a little in awe, though."

"In awe?"

"Who wouldn't be?" He sat down beside her again. "The major is already rumored to have saved hundreds of lives. His valor on the battlefield is renowned, as if he defies death with the risks he takes. Who wouldn't wish to be half so brave?"

"Then you wish to be part of the military?"

He sighed. "Taking a post in the military was never an option for me. I'm the only son of the Duke of Chisolmwood. I can hardly risk getting killed and allowing the Chisolmwood title to pass down to a distant cousin now, can I?"

"No, I imagine not. But if what I've heard is correct, you've contributed more than most titled nobility where foreign affairs are concerned."

"Oh, really? Just what have you heard?"

"Nothing much." She noted his reaction, one of surprise. For some reason it puzzled her. Maybe because she expected a denial and didn't receive one. "Just that you are included in many of the meetings where our military objectives are discussed."

Culbertson laughed. "Oh, that. Yes, well, I've found that rank has its privileges when it comes to being included in military strategies. I've always been fascinated with the military, and being the son of the Duke of Chisolmwood allows me to satisfy my fetish. Luckily, I've found if I sit quietly and offer no examples of my ignorance, those in command allow me to stay." He looked at her and smiled. "I always remain the silent observer, I assure you."

"You make the role you play sound very insignificant."

"Oh, I promise you, I play no role. Neither Lord Fenton nor Lord Rediger of Her Majesty's Foreign Service would put much credence in anything I might be foolhardy enough to offer. They tolerate my intrusion because my father is one of the military's largest supporters. It's all about money, my dear. Everything is, you know."

Lydia studied the serious expression on Culbertson's face. The marquess was much more complicated than she'd imagined. But he was right in one thing. Everything was about money. Wasn't that the reason Gabe had wanted her? Because of the dowry she would bring with her?

Wasn't the lack of it the reason he'd given her up?

At least money wasn't the reason the Marquess of Culbertson wanted her. Everyone knew his father was one of the richest men in England.

Lydia smiled. Perhaps Culbertson *was* the perfect match for her.

"I intend to take a carriage ride through Hyde Park tomorrow afternoon," he said, taking her hand. "Perhaps around five o'clock. It would be my pleasure to have you accompany me if you aren't otherwise engaged."

His eyes gleamed with a keen intelligence she admired and his mouth lifted slightly.

Lydia waited to feel the surge of warmth that had always engulfed her when Gabriel touched her. It didn't happen.

She paused.

What did that matter? This was the man her father had chosen for her. The man to whom Gabriel had gladly given her over. As she pondered his invitation, she realized that even though she didn't experience a stirring warmth when he touched her, neither did she find him unappealing.

"I'd be delighted," she said, knowing she'd just taken the first step in showing Society that she'd accepted Culbertson's declarations.

"Very good." Culbertson rose and held out his arm to help her to her feet. "The air has a definite chill to it. We'd best go inside before our absence is noticed."

"Of course."

She placed her hand on Culbertson's arm and walked back into the crowded ballroom. So what did it matter if her fingers didn't tingle when she touched him? So what if a shiver of expectancy didn't race down her spine when he looked at her? So what if her blood didn't thunder in her head when he held her? There was more than love to any marriage.

Everyone knew that.

❦

"Lydia."

She turned from a group of friends with whom she'd been conversing to see her brother walk toward her. It was impossible not to notice the anxious expression on his face.

"What is it, Harrison? Is something wrong?"

"I have to leave. I just received a message from Austin. He's home. Here in London."

Lydia clamped her hand over her mouth to stifle her cry of elation. "Austin's home?"

"Yes. I'm leaving immediately, but you can stay if you'd like. Lady Henshaw said she would see you home."

"Don't be ridiculous." Lydia placed her hand on Harrison's arm. "How could you think I would want to stay?"

Her brother laughed as he escorted her to the door. "I can't wait to tell Austin his arrival caused his sister to cut short her first ball in more than a year."

She ignored his teasing remark and kept pace with him as they walked up the stairs of the ballroom. They said their fare-wells to the Duke and Duchess of Puttingsworth, then made their way to the foyer.

"Did you know Austin was coming?" she asked while they waited for their carriage to be brought round. "I thought he couldn't come for months yet. Do you think something's wrong?"

Harrison smiled. "Austin always said you were the most curi-ous female he knew."

Lydia stepped up into their carriage when it arrived, but she couldn't erase the unease. "You haven't answered my question. What do you think it means that he arrived so unexpectedly?"

"That they transported him on the first available ship and he didn't have time to write us."

Lydia turned to look out the window as they made their way down the quiet London streets. "Or that he wasn't able to write us."

"Don't borrow trouble, Liddy. We'll find out soon enough. We're almost home."

When the carriage came to a halt in front of Etherhouse, Harrison dismounted before the groom had the carriage step in place. He helped her to the ground and they both raced through the door the butler held open for them.

"Captain Landwell is upstairs," Ruskins said as he took their cloaks.

Lydia raced across the foyer and looked up. Her breath caught. "Austin?"

Austin stood above them, his hair mussed and his clothing still dirty and wrinkled from weeks of travel. But he was whole and healthy, with all four limbs intact. He leaned against the balcony railing as if he needed support, then pushed himself away and staggered before taking his first step.

She ran up the stairs and into his arms.

"Austin!" she cried, touching his stubbled face and mussed hair. "Are you all right?"

"I'm fine."

His voice was little more than a whisper and he pulled her to him again and held her so tightly she could barely catch her breath.

"Oh, Liddy. I didn't think we'd ever get here."

"But you did. You're home now."

When he finally released her, she looked into his face. There was a dark, hollow emptiness in his gaze, nothing that even resembled the laughter in his eyes that had twinkled with mischief and merriment before he'd gone to war.

Huge black circles rimmed his eyes, bespeaking long, agonizing days with little sleep and a weariness that went bone deep. He looked as if he was ready to collapse.

He tenderly touched her cheek, then looked over her shoulder to where Harrison stood.

"Welcome home, Austin."

Tears filled her eyes when her two brothers embraced. After several moments, they stepped apart. They both swiped their hands across their faces to erase the dampness on their cheeks.

"I'm sorry I didn't let you know I was coming, but there wasn't time."

"It doesn't matter. You're here. That's all that's important."

"I didn't come alone. I brought..."

Austin's words halted, then he shifted his gaze to where she stood. A knot tightened inside her stomach.

"I brought...Gabe."

Her heart lurched in her chest and she looked over her shoulder to the empty hallway as if she expected Gabriel to be there. "Where is he?"

"He's in the guest room. The one next to my room. Matthias is with him."

"Matthias?"

She looked toward the room where Gabriel was. Matthias was one of the Earl of Etherington's most trusted servants and had been with them for years. Everyone knew he was better at healing than most doctors. "Why did you bring him here? You should have taken him—"

"He's hurt, Liddy. I don't think he'll..."

Austin looked to the ceiling as if he couldn't finish his thought. "The doctor wanted to take off his leg but I wouldn't let him."

She placed her hand over the railing and squeezed until her fingers ached.

Gabriel was hurt. Austin didn't think he'd live.

Blood roared inside her head and thundered against her ears. With waning strength, she pushed herself away from the railing and moved toward the room where he was.

"Liddy, don't."

Some force she didn't understand drew her to his room. Even Austin's warning didn't stop her. Her heart pounded harder with each step she took, and try as she might, she couldn't force her legs to halt their journey to his room.

"Liddy, no." Austin stepped in front of her to stop her. "Don't go in. Gabe wouldn't want you to see him like he is."

She lifted her gaze. She wasn't sure what she felt, wasn't sure if the emotion was concern, devastation, fear, or hatred. She wasn't sure why she needed to see him, wasn't sure if she was afraid he'd live and she'd have another memory of him to try to forget—or afraid he'd die and she'd have to grieve for him all over again.

She looked beyond Austin to the closed door and knew she still had the choice to walk away—until she heard him.

His muffled cry pierced her soul, the sound of his pain was so agonizing it stole her breath. She tried to ignore his call, tried to turn away from him, but his anguish was so all-consuming it was as if the demons of hell tortured him.

On legs that trembled beneath her, she stepped around Austin and reached for the latch. A part of her feared what she'd see when she pushed open the door. Another part of her needed to know.

Despite Austin's final warning and his attempt to stop her, she opened the door and stepped inside.

"You shouldn't be here, my lady," Matthias said over his shoulder as he worked on the figure lying on the bed.

She ignored the warning and stepped closer. Inch by inch Gabriel's battered and bruised body came into view.

She wasn't sure what she expected, but she wasn't prepared for this. Wasn't prepared to see the man she'd once loved with all her heart a mere shadow of what he'd once been.

She reacted as if some traitorous force took control of her emotions. The light from the lamps at Gabriel's bedside revealed his features in a clarity more vivid than she wanted. Her gaze rested on his face, on the part of him that night after night had haunted her dreams.

His eyes remained closed, but even in his unconsciousness she saw the strain of agony in his features. Deep, heavy furrows lined his forehead. His lips were pursed, lips she remembered pressed against hers, lips that were warm and vibrant and intoxicating.

Thin bony fingers of pain and grief reached in and wrenched her heart. The tightness inside her chest gripped until she had to gasp for air.

She hurt for him, ached with a pain so agonizing she wasn't sure she could survive it. His face was devoid of color, his features gaunt and sallow, so different from the healthy bronzed tone she'd always known. His cheekbones were still high and pronounced, but the flesh beneath them had hollowed to deep, empty pits. The strong, determined jaw she'd always admired was locked tight, as if clenching his teeth was the only way he could keep the screams from escaping.

Another torturous stab of agony twisted her heart.

He shifted, not much, just enough that his movement forced him to release a sound so filled with pain she nearly doubled over. Matthias placed a hand on Gabe's shoulder to hold him down and he sagged back into the mattress with a soft moan—a moan that stole the warmth from her body.

"*Liddy,*" he moaned, as if her name was a plea for help.

Her breath caught and she wrapped her arms around her middle to keep from reaching out to him.

No other man would have survived the wounds, or the long, arduous ocean voyage home, but he had. Perhaps only to die on English soil. Perhaps only to torture her with one last painful memory of him.

She looked around the room, her eyes darting from Harrison's damp eyes, to the tears that streamed unabashedly down Austin's cheeks, then back to the prone figure on the bed fighting to stay alive. He called out her name again. *"Liddy."*

She staggered back as if she'd been struck by a boulder.

"Damn you, no," a voice whispered, and she realized the voice was hers.

"Damn you," she said again, then spun away from him and fled the room.

She managed to take three steps before the weight of having him near her again crashed down around her. Every muscle in her body trembled.

She ran from the room as if some threatening peril was after her. She couldn't care whether he lived or died. If she did, he'd destroy her life a second time.

CHAPTER FOUR

The house was finally quiet. Servants no longer raced past her doorway talking in hushed whispers as they carried water, bandages, and anything else the doctor needed as he worked on Gabe. Even though everything seemed peaceful beyond her four walls, she couldn't control the feeling of dread inside her.

She pressed back against the corner of the window seat and waited in solemn silence for someone to come to tell her he had died.

Even the doctor predicted he wouldn't survive the night.

With a deep sigh, she wrapped her arms around her legs and tucked her knees closer to her chest. The logs in the grate were little more than glowing embers, the room taking on a chill she would have loved had she been buried beneath her covers. But she couldn't sleep. How could she when he'd come back into her life as if there was a place for him. There wasn't. The only emotion she would ever feel for him again was—nothing.

She huddled closer and held her breath, her ears straining to hear the faint sounds of his pain that the thick oak doors couldn't muffle completely.

Or the ominous silence of his passing.

An agonizing moan escaped from deep inside her, a cry to ease the pain gnawing at her heart.

She tried to forget the tortured look on his face but she couldn't. She would always remember the pain written on his features.

She rose to her feet and clutched her hands to her churning stomach. She didn't care what happened to him; she wouldn't allow him to be important to her ever again. But if he wasn't going to survive, she didn't want him to die alone. And if he was going to survive, she wanted to do everything in her power to ease his suffering.

As if she no longer controlled her own actions, she walked across the room and out the door. Her legs trembled beneath her with each step, and when she finally reached his room, her hands shook as she reached for the doorknob.

The room was dark now with only one lit candle flickering on the table beside his bed. She paused. Heavy breathing and the faint crackle of dying logs in the fireplace assaulted her senses. Gradually, her eyes acclimated to the darkness and she looked around the room.

A large oak armoire stood at an angle in the corner to her right with a small dressing table and mirror close beside it. A marble fireplace took up most of the opposite wall, its low flames a gentle wave of muted light that didn't quite reach to the center of the room.

Austin reclined in a padded leather wing chair, his feet propped on an ottoman and stretched out before the fire, his exhausted body wrapped in a blanket.

She stepped around him and walked to the bed.

Her gaze lowered to Gabriel's prone body and for the first time since he'd left her, she allowed the emotions she'd locked away to surface.

She needed to face how she felt and deal with it. Conquering any leftover affection she harbored for him was the only way to prove she no longer cared for him. If she was ever to give her love to another man, she needed to extinguish every ember of emotion she felt for him. She couldn't risk having one spark of the former love she possessed for Gabriel come to life.

Her gaze rested on his face. Soft shadows outlined his still form beneath the covers. She listened, fearing she was too late and he'd died alone. Then he moaned as if in agony, and she hardened her heart to make sure that any love she'd ever felt for him was dead and buried so deeply there was no way to unearth it. She was wiser now than she'd been before, more prepared.

"Never again," she whispered with a bitterness that shocked even her. She would never care for him again.

She forced herself to watch his shallow breathing. With each small rise and fall of his chest she reminded herself that *he'd* been the one who'd abandoned her.

She stood without moving, her eyes taking in his battered body, her mind coming to grips with his nearness, her heart refusing to recognize the place he once occupied. Satisfied that he was as comfortable as they could make him, she turned and—

"Don't...go."

His pathetically weak voice cut through the silence as forcefully as if his words had been a command, and she stopped.

For several long seconds she didn't turn around—*couldn't* turn around. It was one thing to be near him when he didn't know she was there, but more troubling to be with him when he did.

"It's late," she said and continued toward the door.

"Please ..."

She halted, then slowly turned.

His eyes remained closed. His head rested on the pillow.

She didn't know how he'd realized she was there, but she wasn't surprised. It had been uncanny how attuned they'd been to each other, how they'd always known when the other was near.

With her resolve firmly in place, she slowly walked back to the bed. "Can I get you anything?"

"Water. Please."

She filled a glass with water. "Here." She placed one hand beneath his head and lifted him.

She raised the glass to his lips and he took only one sip before he sagged back into her arms. Her blood turned warm and thundered in her head but she refused to allow her mind to consider that he still had the power to affect her. She eased his head back onto the pillow and straightened.

His face had no more color than it had earlier and she heard a catch in his breathing followed by a heavy sigh.

"Do you need something for the pain?"

He shook his head.

"Go back to sleep, then. You need to rest."

"There'll be...plenty of time for that...later."

She pulled back and glared at him. "You're *not* going to die, Gabriel. So just get that thought out of your head."

He didn't answer her, but the corners of his mouth twitched as if he were trying to smile. "I'll...do my...best."

"You'll do more than that. My brother didn't work as hard as he did to keep you alive only to have you die on him now that he has you home. You need to rest so you can get better."

She turned again but his voice stopped her.

"Do I still have...my legs?"

A sharp pain stabbed through her chest and she went back. She knew what it would mean to him if one or both of his legs were gone. She couldn't imagine a man more unsuited to being confined inside, a man who enjoyed riding and being out of doors more than Gabriel. She looked down to the bottom of the bed, then back to the vacant look in his eyes. "Yes, you still have your legs."

His eyes closed for a long second. "They say you can...feel them...even when they're not there."

"They didn't take them off. Austin wouldn't let them. You can thank him for your pain."

"I'll thank him later."

She stood quietly and watched him breathe. He wasn't asleep, but there was nothing more to say. She turned to see Austin walking toward her. A frown covered his face.

"You shouldn't be here."

"I came to make sure you didn't need anything."

"Go. Being here won't help you or Gabe."

She stared at the determined look on Austin's face, then lowered her gaze to where Gabriel lay. "You can't care for him by yourself, Austin. You're going to need help. Show me how much laudanum to give him. He'll need something soon for the pain."

"I've cared for him since we left."

"Which is probably why you look like you're ready to collapse."

She straightened the covers on the bed, watching while Austin mixed the dark liquid in a small glass of wine. When he finished, he raised Gabriel's head and let him drink.

"It will be better soon," Austin said, lowering Gabe to the pillow.

Within minutes he was asleep. But Lydia was afraid to shift her gaze from the shallow rise and fall of his chest. There'd been something so final about the way he'd spoken. She stood next to the bed and watched him.

Austin remained by her for several long seconds, then shoved his hands in his pocket and walked to the window.

She couldn't see her brother's face but knew there were

worry lines etched in his forehead.

"If there had been anyplace else to take him, I would have, but even the hospitals aren't—"

He left his sentence unfinished and walked back to check on Gabriel.

"It doesn't matter, Austin. As far as I'm concerned, Gabriel Talbot died a year ago."

Austin smiled. "I think he tried to make that a reality. He risked his life more times than any soldier over there. There was a joke among the officers that he'd infiltrated the enemy's camp so often the Russians thought he was one of their own."

Lydia tried to ignore the surge of pride and fear that washed over her.

Austin patted her hand, then gave it a gentle squeeze. "Go to bed so you get at least a little sleep before it's time to get up."

She looked at Gabriel's sleeping form. "Will you be all right?"

"I'll be fine. He's resting now."

She gave her brother a quick hug, then left the room.

When she stepped out into the hallway, she stopped long enough to fight the tears that blurred her eyes. He'd live. She prayed he would. But that didn't change anything.

To her heart he was still dead.

❧

"Lie still, Gabe. You'll tear your stitches open."

Gabe heard Austin's voice but couldn't follow the order. He had to escape the mêlée, the violence and bloodshed. The pandemonium and confusion were unimaginable. Bullets flew all around him. Sabers swung through the air. The ground thundered as if a thousand cavalry mounts bore down on him. But it wasn't a thousand. It was only one. And there wasn't a human sitting atop the giant destrier. The rider was a monster with fire raging from his nose and mouth, with lightning flashing from his eyes.

The sword in his hand was long and wide, felling dozens of innocent men, women, and children with each fatal swoop. Gabriel knew he couldn't escape the demon. Knew there was no way to avoid death. He no longer wanted to. It was time. He'd fought long enough. Endured enough.

"Gabe, no! Wake up, Gabe! Fight, damn you! Fight!"

Gabriel turned to face his enemy. He braced his feet wide and held his arms out from his sides. He had no sword with which to defend himself, nor a gun with even one last bullet, but it didn't matter. He wouldn't die cowering like a frightened child. He'd face death as boldly as he'd gone into every battle, knowing what the outcome might be.

Gabriel took one last gasping breath and…

"Gabe, no! Liddy, help me!"

Austin's voice shattered through the hazy fog, then...*hers.*

"Gabriel, come back. Right now!"

He walked steadily onward, toward the bright light in the distance. If only he could reach it, he was certain he wouldn't feel the pain anymore. If only he could reach it—

She called out to him again. *"Don't you dare give up!"*

He hesitated, then looked again to the light. It was still there but not quite as bright. He had to hurry or he wouldn't reach it.

"Gabriel, open your eyes! Look at me!"

It was Liddy. Her touch. Her hand clutching his. Her pleas calling him back.

"Gabriel, don't you dare leave me. I'll never forgive you if you do."

Then her voice became a gentle whisper that brushed against his cheek.

"Don't you dare leave me. Please, don't leave me here alone. I couldn't bear it."

Something wet ran down his cheek. A tear? He was hardly deserving of her tears. Another drop hit his cheek.

He heard her soft cry and moved his gaze from the light. When he looked back, the light was gone and he knew he'd missed his chance to escape this misery.

"Don't...cry."

"I'm not crying. I cried over you once. Never again."

A small slit of light invaded the shadows and he focused on her. In his mind's eye he knew how she'd look. He'd imagined her likeness every hour of every day since he'd left her. But he didn't remember her eyes being so blue. Or her hair so golden. Or her features so lovely.

She had the face of an angel, one more beautiful than any artist could paint. Her complexion was as clear as porcelain, her cheeks flushed pink, her lips full and silky smooth, as if they'd been made for kissing. And her eyes.

A man could get lost in those eyes, huge and deep blue, with long, velvety lashes. Except the warmth he remembered was absent. A coldness sat in its place, a bitterness he knew he was responsible for creating.

He breathed a ragged sigh.

"Liddy?" he whispered, wanting to hear her voice once more. But she didn't answer him. She was gone.

"That's for the...best," he said to himself.

But inside he felt a loss exactly like he'd felt when he walked away from her in another lifetime.

CHAPTER FIVE

She was like a moth drawn to the proverbial flame.

She'd managed to stay away from him for over a week now, but she was weakening and couldn't find the strength to help herself. Worry consumed every hour of her day and the desire to go to him was like a cancer that ate away at her.

It was suddenly important that she recall every hurtful word he'd spoken to her the day he'd walked out of her life—every reason he'd given her for not wanting to marry her. She encouraged the anger she felt for him to smolder hot enough to fuel her temper. She could never forget what he'd done to her. Never forget how he'd so callously toyed with her affections, pretending to love her, allowing her to open her heart to him, when all he'd wanted was her dowry.

Every time she remembered how she'd run to him after he'd spoken with her father, expecting him to tell her he'd convinced her father that he loved her with a passion equal to hers, she felt another bitter stab of humiliation.

To add to her embarrassment, she remembered his condescending manner when he'd tapped her nose and called her a silly goose, as if she were a child. As if she were some stupid imbecile who should have known his declarations of love had purse strings attached to them.

She couldn't believe she'd been so naïve.

She bolted to her feet. She would never let any man take advantage of her like that again.

Her angry steps carried her to his room and she turned the knob without hesitation. She fully expected to find Hannah, who'd been Lydia's maid and was now Major Talbot's nurse, keeping vigil while Gabriel slept soundly. What she saw stopped her feet from moving forward.

Hannah rushed from one side of the room to the other, hurrying to change the linens on the bed, while Austin and one of the servants, named Morgan, lifted Gabriel's shoulders and turned his torso.

His pain was obvious. From the deep furrows that etched his forehead and the heavy sheen of perspiration that covered a face already void of color, his torment was evident. His lips were pursed tightly as if to cut off a scream.

She couldn't care. She wouldn't *care.*

"Hold on, Gabe," Austin said, his face flushed from exertion. "Hannah's almost done. I have your medicine ready for you."

"Bloody...hell...Austin," Gabriel uttered through clenched teeth. He breathed a jagged sigh when they laid him back down.

"All finished, Major," Hannah said, her ample bosom heaving as she took in several ragged breaths.

Lydia watched as Gabriel collapsed against the covers. The sight of him in such pain wrenched her stomach. Austin must have felt it too. He bent at the waist and braced one hand on his knee while he anchored the other against a bedpost at the foot of the bed.

"Are you all right, Gabe?" he asked.

Color slowly returned to Gabriel's face. "Of course," he sighed. "You keep telling me I've already survived the worst of it."

"So I do."

"I'm not fooled. You do this because you enjoy seeing me suffer."

A smile crossed Austin's face, but his lopsided grin faded when he turned his head and saw her. "You shouldn't be here, Liddy."

She waited until Hannah and Morgan left, then put on a determined air of bravado and walked into the room. "Of course I should be here. This is my home. The major is our guest. Surely you don't expect me to avoid him forever?"

"That's exactly what I expect."

She ignored her brother's caustic remark and covered the distance to the bed. "Hello, Gabriel."

"Lydia."

He'd been washed and shaved, probably by Austin's valet, and his bedclothes had been changed. Her heart stuttered inside her breast.

He was still the most handsome man she'd ever seen. Not handsome in the same way as the Marquess of Culbertson, with his blond good looks and his aristocratic features. But handsome in a different way—in a darker way.

He should have appeared weak, lying on the bed unable to move by himself. Instead, his rugged features and sculpted muscles made him appear strong and vibrant.

His dark hair was brushed off his forehead, and hung longer than he usually wore it. Her hands wanted to reach out to touch it. Her fingers ached to feel the weight of it. She pulled her hands back and clutched fistfuls of the material of her muslin day dress to anchor them at her side.

What was wrong with her? Her purpose for coming wasn't to admire the traits she'd always loved in him. It was to prove to herself and to him that there was no longer anything between them—to prove that when he rejected her, he'd killed whatever feelings she'd had for him.

Lydia raised her chin to assume that regal posture she'd been taught from her youth and lowered her gaze to the bed.

"Everyone tells me you're improving by the day. I came to see if there's anything you need."

"There's nothing. Thank you."

She should leave. She knew Austin wanted her to, and perhaps even Gabriel did. Instead, she lowered herself to the chair beside the bed and clasped her hands in her lap in a relaxed posture, as if being this close to him was the most natural thing in the world.

"When you're better, you and Austin can go riding. Harrison still has that big gray you used to ride. No one's ridden him since you left and he desperately needs the exercise."

Gabriel smiled. "He was a beautiful horse."

Austin held out a glass of wine laced with laudanum but Gabriel motioned it away.

"But not as fast as Hercules," Austin said.

"You can tell Austin longs for the country," she said. "He hates the city nearly as much as you used to, although I can't understand why. The entertainment here is endless."

"Do you...enjoy London now?" he asked, his voice still faltering a bit from his general weakness.

She snapped her gaze to where he lay on the bed watching her. She knew what he meant by his question. There'd been a time when neither of them could wait to set up a home far away from London. A time when neither of them enjoyed the noise, the filth, or the smell. A time when they both shared the same hope.

Until he'd shattered her dream.

"Yes. I *love* the city."

She rose from her chair and walked to the window. She pretended the need to adjust the drapery as an excuse not to look at him. "There's never an end of things to do." She looked over her shoulder and focused her gaze on Austin. "Did I tell

you I'm attending the Biltmore Ball tonight? The Marquess of
Culbertson has invited me to accompany him."

"Liddy, don't," Austin said, but she ignored his warning. It
was important for Gabriel to know she'd picked up the pieces
of her life and had moved on. That she intended to have the
future she'd dreamed of having—without him.

She released her hold on the fringed drapery and turned to
face the bed. "You don't mind listening to my plans, do you,
Major? You never used to."

"I'd be...delighted."

"Well, the Biltmore Ball is one of the most prestigious affairs
of the Season. Everyone will be there."

"And you enjoy the...crush?"

She gave him her broadest smile. "I adore it. Especially when
I'm in such pleasant company as the marquess." She turned
back to the window. "This isn't the first social function to which
I've accompanied him. Night before last we attended a dinner
at Lord Westmore's. Next week Lord Culbertson has asked me
to accompany him to the Kennsington Ball."

Lydia put a tie around one of the lightweight inside linen
panels that still fluttered at the window and took a step away
from it to evaluate her handiwork. "Lord Culbertson has been
such a dear to allow me this year of mourning, but he does
seem to have become quite a bit impatient of late. I daresay that
doesn't surprise you, does it? You knew marriage was what his
father intended when you handed me over to him."

"Ah, hell, Liddy." Austin took a step toward her but she
stopped him with a lift of her hand.

The major's face seemed paler. Lydia knew her attack was
unwarranted but she couldn't stop. Not yet. She wanted him
to hurt. Wanted him to ache with the same emptiness that had
eaten away at her for the past year—until she'd been able to

turn that pain to hatred.

"You remember the marquess, don't you?"

"I don't think...we've...met."

"Perhaps you haven't. Now that I recall, it wasn't Culbertson who was here that day you—" She stopped to let her silence emphasize her assault. "...*left* me, but his father, the Duke of Chisolmwood, *was*. Culbertson was probably at some important meeting at the Foreign Office."

She sat on the chair beside the bed and gave him the sweetest smile she could muster.

"I'm sure you'd remember if the two of you had ever met. He's ever so intelligent, and of course, rich as Croesus. Harrison tells me he even has the ear of the Queen. As the Duke of Chisolmwood's heir, he's bound to play an important role in the running of our government someday."

"That's enough, Liddy."

She shivered at the fury she heard in Austin's voice, at the threatening glare she saw on his face. He was angry and she suddenly felt the need to defend herself. "I want the major to know that if it hadn't been for Father's death and my year of mourning, I would already be the Marchioness of Culbertson. Thankfully, Father saw through the major's greed and refused him." She didn't try to hide the bitter resentment in her voice. "At least I know the Marquess of Culbertson isn't interested in me solely for my dowry."

"Leave," Austin growled in a low, hostile tone.

She rose from her chair before her brother removed her himself, but when she reached the other side of the room she stopped. Some vile, hurtful person had taken over her body. She didn't like who she'd become, but couldn't stop herself from flinging more barbed words in Gabriel's direction. "I simply feel it's important for the major to understand how necessary it is for a woman to be able to trust a man when he tells her he loves her. And to realize how much a woman detests being lied to and deceived. These were qualities the major didn't understand a year ago."

Lydia jerked the door open and stepped out into the hall. She didn't slam the door like she wanted to, but softly closed it behind her and walked to her room.

She wasn't proud of the way she'd behaved, didn't feel vindicated like she'd thought she would. And, for the first time since she'd discovered Gabriel only wanted to marry her because of her dowry, she'd come to terms with a fact she'd refused to face until today. She needed to hate Gabriel Talbot.

She hated what he'd done to her. She hated what loving him had cost her. She hated that he made it impossible for her to trust a man enough to give him her heart.

She needed to hate *him*. But there were times when she wasn't sure she could. And that frightened her more than anything.

She needed to reclaim her heart so she could give it to someone who would cherish the gift she gave him. Still, deep down she was afraid that might not be possible.

Because there was a part of her heart he still possessed.

※

"Drink it," Austin said, holding the glass to Gabriel's lips. "I don't know why you didn't take your medicine before. Not only would it have numbed the pain to your body, but maybe it would have dulled my sister's sharp tongue." Austin tipped the glass to let him drink. "I'm sorry, Gabe. She had no right to say what she did."

Gabriel took a long swallow of the laudanum-laced wine then dropped his head back to the pillow. There was a generous amount of the opiate in the drink and Gabriel welcomed the relief he knew would soon come. "Don't blame her," he whispered. "She didn't deserve what I did to her."

Austin threw the rolled-up bandage he'd been holding onto the table and walked away from the bed. "How the two of you have suffered because of what Father did. I know it's not much consolation, but Harrison estimates that in five years he'll be able to buy back the notes Chisolmwood used to blackmail Father."

Five years.

He tried not to think of all that would transpire in five years. Liddy and Culbertson would be married, she would have presented him with at least one heir, perhaps two. Society would clamor to receive invitations to Lady Culbertson's affairs, the same as they anticipated invitations to the Biltmore Ball. And perhaps, if he were lucky, in five years knowing what he'd lost wouldn't hurt so much.

"I know it's important to Harrison...to be able to pay off the debt. I'd feel the same. But the damage...is done."

Austin paced back and forth at the foot of the bed. "I've thought about this a lot, Gabe. What do you think was so bloody important about Lydia's dowry that Chisolmwood would force a marriage on his son? Southerby Manor is a fine estate, but not nearly worth what it cost him."

Gabriel had to concentrate on what Austin said. The laudanum was beginning to take effect. "I've wondered the same thing. Is there anything special about the land? Its location?"

Austin shook his head. "Southerby has been in my mother's family for hundreds of years. It was bequeathed to one of my maternal ancestors with the stipulation that it can only be passed down through the female line of my mother's family."

"So, even if the Marquess of Culbertson marries Lydia..."

"...he can never gain possession of Southerby," Austin finished for him. "It will go to Liddy's eldest daughter."

Gabriel let his body relax into the mattress. "There must be another reason he wanted the marriage then."

"Whatever the reason, it was something Father couldn't live with."

"You don't know—"

Gabriel heard the thud of Austin's fist as he hit the window casing.

"I *do* know," he said. "You forget. I was the one who found him. He didn't die in a hunting accident like Liddy believes. Father took his own life and Chisolmwood was as responsible as if he'd pulled the trigger himself."

Austin pushed himself away from the window and sat in the chair beside the bed. "I think Father couldn't live with the thought of Lydia married to Chisolmwood's son. Killing himself was the only way he could stop the wedding from happening. At least for a year."

Gabriel turned his head on the pillow and looked at Austin. His vision was hazy, which meant the laudanum was working well. "Has Chisolmwood's name ever been linked to any scandal?"

"No," Austin retorted, the frustration obvious in his voice. "In fact, I can't think of anyone more highly regarded."

"What about his son?"

"I wish I could say the praises Lydia extolled were exaggerations, but from what I've heard, even what she said doesn't do him justice. He doesn't simply have the Queen's ear, he's rumored to be instrumental in much of the government's policy-making."

Gabriel fought to keep his eyes open. "If the reason isn't Southerby Manor, then...that only leaves Liddy."

"Liddy?"

"Yes. For some reason the Duke of Chisolmwood chose Liddy for his daughter-in-law and did whatever it took to get her."

"But why would knowing his daughter would be a duchess be so difficult for Father to accept?"

"Did something happen...between Chisolmwood and your father?"

"Hell, I don't ever remember Chisolmwood's name being mentioned in our home."

"Maybe there was a reason...his name was...never mentioned," Gabriel said, knowing his words were slurred.

"If there was, I'm not aware of it. I'll ask Harrison." Austin was silent for several seconds, then said, "I received a message this morning."

Gabriel closed his eyes. "From whom?"

"From Thorn."

Gabriel struggled to open his eyes and fought to make his way back through the haze. "Why the hell didn't you tell me before you poured laudanum down my throat?"

"After Lydia finished with you I didn't think you could stand much more."

Gabriel fought to stay alert. Thorn was the agent who issued their orders. Whatever Austin received had to be important.

"I have to return."

"When?"

"The end of next week. There's a ship leaving on the twenty-third."

Gabriel experienced a wave of unease. "I'm afraid you'll have to make this trip by yourself."

Austin laughed. "Are you worried that I'll get lost without you?"

Gabriel answered him on a lighter note than he felt. "There's always that possibility."

"Hardly, my friend. If I do, Thorn will find me. He has that uncanny knack."

Gabriel blinked twice as the haze clouding his eyes grew thicker. "Do you know what I regretted when I thought I might not survive? That I was going to die without knowing Thorn's identity."

Austin laughed. "It's amazing, isn't it? For more than a year we've taken orders from a man we've never met." Austin leveled a serious expression at Gabriel. "Do you have any idea who he is?"

Gabriel shook his head. "All I know is...the man's phenomenal. He knows exactly where to send us and what we'll find when we arrive. He knows when every meeting is going to take place and what orders are going to come down before our commanding officers know. He's got to have connections."

"Do you think he's a member of the nobility?"

Gabriel had already considered the possibility and knew he probably was. "That would explain how he has access to information only a very few in England have."

"Is he the reason you knew about the papers the Russian general had?"

Gabriel nodded. "I got a note...with a thorn." He wouldn't be able to stay awake much longer. Austin must have realized it too. He reached over to squeeze Gabriel's shoulder, then stood.

"I'll give our mysterious Thorn your regards if we meet." He extinguished all the lamps in the room but one. "Now, get some rest. We'll talk more tomorrow."

Gabriel watched his friend take another step out of the room and stopped him. "Will you do me one favor before you sail?"

"Anything. What do you need?"

"A place...to live."

"You're not ready to leave. Harrison won't hear of it and neither will I."

Gabriel wanted to laugh but couldn't. "It won't be today, but—" He paused. "...soon."

"It's Lydia, isn't it?"

"Staying here isn't good for either of us."

Austin stepped back into the shadows on the far side of the room. "Damn Chisolmwood for what he did to you and Lydia. Damn Father."

"Things worked out for the best, considering. You and I would have gone to the Crimea. I would have come back...like I am." Gabriel rubbed the ache in his leg while he waited for the laudanum to completely take over. "At least now...Liddy will have a partner...to dance with at all those balls she's so fond of attending."

"And what will you have?"

Gabriel breathed a heavy sigh. "I have a small estate...brothers are managing while I'm gone. When I'm well enough...I'll go there. I always intended to...live in the country."

"But that was when you thought Liddy would be there with you."

Gabriel considered his solitary future and closed his eyes. "Get the hell out of here. That blasted poison you poured down my throat is clouding my mind...can't think straight."

Austin stepped through the door and closed it behind him.

When the room was dark and quiet, Gabriel drifted to that place the laudanum took him where nothing was quite as it seemed—even the pain.

Starting tomorrow, though, he swore he wouldn't need as much of the opiate as he needed today. And the day after, he'd need even less. He had to get well enough to leave here.

He knew he'd never be strong enough to stay under the same roof with her and not die a little every day because of what could never be.

CHAPTER SIX

Lydia sat on the window seat in her bedroom and looked out onto the small flower garden to the rear of the house without noticing anything in particular. She hadn't been to see him for nearly a month. Even when word came that the war was over, she hadn't gone to his room to tell him.

She wanted to forget him, but that didn't happen.

With a heavy sigh she leaned back against the cushions and dropped her hands to her lap. How many times would she have to relive his painful words, his brutal rejection, before she could exorcize him from her thoughts, her mind, her heart?

She squeezed her eyes shut in an effort to forget the emotions that continually surfaced. Even after all this time, he refused to fade from her memory. How could she allow him to consume her like he did? She had her future to consider.

She was promised to the Marquess of Culbertson. Even if the announcement hadn't been made public or the date set, the agreement her father had signed just weeks before his death was as binding as any legal document. As the future Duchess of Chisolmwood, she couldn't afford for there to be a hint of scandal associated with her name. She owed that to her family as well as her future husband.

Lydia looked down at the crumpled letter in her hand and felt an unquenchable burning inside her. The message arrived from Austin just this morning and he'd asked that they share it with Gabriel. But that didn't mean *she* had to deliver it. Harrison could. Or one of the servants.

She looked at the letter again. What was she afraid of? He meant nothing to her. Nothing! She intended to prove it—to herself and to him.

She bolted to her feet and turned toward the door. "Hannah," she called over her shoulder and her maid came in from the dressing room. "Come with me."

She walked down the hall and rapped twice on his door, then opened it when he beckoned. He wasn't in bed like she'd assumed he would be, but was sitting in a chair by the window. He looked much improved. Almost back to his former self.

Her heart raced the instant his gaze met hers. Dark lashes and brows framed his ebony eyes and although his bronzed complexion lacked the luster it had before he left, his handsome features still possessed a powerful pull that tugged deep inside her.

She stomped down her errant emotions and ground them beneath an imaginary heel before she crossed the room to where he sat. "You're out of bed."

He smiled. "I'm improving every day, thanks to your staff's excellent care. I'll be out on my own in no time at all."

She frowned. He was better, but she noticed he sat with his injured leg propped on an ottoman. He'd been rubbing his thigh when she walked in but lifted his hand to the arm of the chair as if he didn't want her to notice. "You won't leave until you're well enough," she said. "Harrison won't allow it."

His smile faded. It was almost as if he dared Harrison—or anyone, to stop him.

"How is your leg?"

"Improving."

"I'm glad." She sat down in a chair beside him. "I have a letter from Austin. I thought perhaps you'd like to hear it."

His head snapped to where she sat. "Yes."

She unfolded the letter and began.

> *November 22, 1855*
> *My Dearest Family,*
>
> *By the time you read this, the last details of the Paris treaty will have been executed and this dreadful war will finally be over for me, as well.*
>
> *I can imagine how you must have celebrated when you heard the war had ended, but Gabe alone will understand when I write that I cried. I wept not only for those who are fortunate enough to go home alive, but for all those who will never return. So many lives affected. So many families changed forever.*
>
> *The war lasted a mere twenty-eight months and according to the latest tallies, nearly a million men gave their lives for their countries. I will wager that two out of every three deaths were due to disease, starvation, or exposure. If nothing else, I pray to God we have all learned a lesson from such a travesty. If we have, our country will be the stronger for it.*
>
> *I wish I would be writing to tell you I am on my way home, but I am not. Her Majesty has need of me elsewhere, although I'm not at liberty to say where that might be. Just know that I am well and miss you more than you will ever know. Stay healthy and happy until I return.*
>
> *Forever yours, Austin*

*Gabe—Harrison tells me you are improving more
every day. When I return we will go to the country.
I do so long to be there.*

She lowered the letter to her lap and looked up at him. His eyes were filled with tears and it was nearly her undoing.

"I miss him terribly," she said, her voice husky with emotion.

"I know."

"Do you have any idea where they sent him?"

He shook his head.

"You and Austin aren't just ordinary soldiers, are you?"

She noticed a fleeting hint of detachment.

"We are both officers in Her Majesty's Army."

"And what exactly do you do that makes you and Austin so indispensable?" She folded the letter and placed it in her lap. "I know you relieved a Russian officer of some important papers that contained information vital to the outcome of the war. How did you happen to discover he had them?"

Gabriel remained focused on the scene outside the window. He obviously intended to ignore her probing questions. Except, she had no intention of giving up. "I overheard Austin say you were wounded in enemy territory. Are you and Austin spies?"

His brows arced. "We are soldiers," he said. "Now, if you don't mind, I'd like to discuss something else. Harrison tells me you intend to keep him busy every night this week attending one function or another. Who is hosting the ball you cannot miss tonight?"

"Lord and Lady Parness. It's their annual holiday ball and everyone who's come back from the country will be there."

"Does that include the Marquess of Culbertson?"

She didn't even try to keep the haughty tone from her voice.

"Of course. In fact, except for a short journey Geoffrey took a few weeks ago, I have been with him each night this whole month."

"How fortunate for you."

She smiled. "Yes. Last night we attended the theatre and the night before a musicale at Lady Plunkett's. And tonight, of course, we're going to—"

Lydia stopped. Gabriel's hand had dropped to his thigh and he clutched the muscles above his knee as if he'd been attacked. "Are you all right? Do you need something for the pain?"

"No, it will ease soon," he gasped, then rubbed the area harder. "It just chooses the most inopportune times to...remind me it's there."

She looked at his face. He was unbelievably pale. Her heart increased its steady pounding in her chest. She rose to her feet and poured some liquid from the only decanter on the bedside table into a glass. It wasn't the wine she remembered Austin using with the laudanum. This looked and smelled more like whiskey but maybe it worked better. "Where do you keep the laudanum?"

"I don't need...any," he said on a gasp.

He breathed heavier as his hand kneaded the top of his leg.

"You most certainly do." She yanked open first one drawer then another, searching for the small brown bottle she remembered. "Where is it?"

"I've had it...removed."

"Why?"

The corners of his mouth lifted as he attempted to smile through the pain. "You've obviously never been under the opiate's influence or you'd...know. It's not something...I could afford to continue to take...any longer."

"Then what do you take for the pain?"

"You have it in your hand."

Lydia poured a generous amount into the glass and handed it to him. He reached for the liquor with one hand but continued to rub his thigh with the other. His hand trembled.

"Here, let me." She held the glass to his lips.

He took two swallows then pushed the glass away.

"Enough, or I'll be in my cups before lunch."

She tried to smile but couldn't. He was in pain. Heavy beads of perspiration formed on his forehead and taut lines creased either side of his mouth.

An agonizing knot pinched the pit of her stomach. She couldn't bear to see him in such agony. The torture she saw on his face was unbearable. She dropped to her knees in front of him and massaged his thigh.

For several long minutes they both worked his muscles. Her hand burned from the contact. She knew touching him would be her undoing. It was.

His gasping breaths battled with hers, his nostrils flared as he fought the pain.

She worked as furiously as she could, pressing, rubbing, grinding, kneading. From his knee to high on his thigh she ministered to erase the grimacing pain on his face.

Her body flamed from a heat that was part exertion, part desire. She recognized the difference and fought to keep the two in balance. She lost the battle.

With rigid determination, she leaned into him and pressed harder. His hands pressed atop hers. A wave of heat more intense engulfed every inch of her body, spiraling from where his hands connected to hers, to the pit of her stomach—then lower.

In unison they circled the knotted muscles until the hardness eased. In unison they rode the waves of turmoil that ended when Gabriel sank back against the cushioned chair and dropped his hands to his side.

He slowly held out one trembling hand as a signal.

"Do you want me to stop?" she asked, lifting her gaze to look at him.

"I think you should never have started," Harrison's harsh-sounding voice said from behind them.

Lydia looked over her shoulder to see her brother standing in the doorway—with the Duke of Chisolmwood.

❦

Gabriel moved his gaze from the woman kneeling at his feet. He knew if he looked at Harrison he'd see anger at finding his sister here. But he wasn't interested in Harrison's reaction. He focused his gaze instead on the bastard who'd ruined his life a year ago, a man he'd hoped never to see again.

The two faced each other, the duke as pompous and arrogant as he'd been the day he'd taken away everything that was important to him. Except this time was worse. This time he wasn't even able to rise to his feet to face the man at an equal level.

"Lady Lydia," Chisolmwood said, turning his attention to where Lydia stood, still close to Gabriel's chair.

Gabriel took satisfaction in Liddy's reaction. She faced Chisolmwood with her head held high and not a hint of embarrassment or guilt on her face.

"Good day, Your Grace. What a pleasant surprise."

"Is it?" the duke answered with condescending politeness.

"Of course. I wasn't expecting callers."

"That much is obvious. You can imagine my surprise at finding you here alone in the major's room."

Gabriel gripped the arms of the chair. He was prepared to come to Lydia's defense but stopped when he saw her back straighten and her shoulders lift.

"I'm hardly alone," she said, nodding to where Hannah now stood beside her chair. "My maid has been with me the entire time."

"I hardly consider servants proper chaperones." Chisolm-wood stepped into the room, his pace slow and menacing. "And neither will most of Society." He locked his hands behind his back. "The last thing I will abide is a scandal involving the woman my son intends to marry."

"I assure you," Harrison said, "that no improprieties have occurred between my sister and Major Talbot."

"Of course they haven't," the duke answered, the glare in his eyes icy cold. "We all know how disastrous that would be. For everyone." He turned toward Harrison. "Especially you, Etherington."

Fire flashed in Harrison's eyes. His hands clenched to tight fists.

"Harrison?" Lydia stepped toward her brother. Several deep frown lines etched her brow. "I'm not sure I understand."

Gabriel clamped his fingers around the arm of the chair and struggled to keep from rising. If he were strong enough to make it to his feet, he'd hit the bloody bastard. And hitting him once wouldn't be enough.

He was afraid he wouldn't stop until he was dead.

Harrison dropped his gaze to his sister. "It's all right, Liddy."

The duke recovered smoothly. "Yes, there's nothing to concern yourself with, my dear. Just suffice it to say that we all understand how important it is to avoid even the slightest misunderstanding. And how imperative it is for you and my son to announce your betrothal. Soon."

Chisolmwood smiled at Lydia. "Perhaps avoiding the major altogether would eliminate any disaster and give you and my son ample time to make a decision."

"Of course," Lydia agreed, her voice sounding contrite and amiable.

Gabriel shot her a look. Agreeing so readily was totally unlike her. And yet...

Why wouldn't she agree with Chisolmwood? The man was going to be her father-in-law. His son was the man she was going to marry. She hadn't been there the day he'd threatened her father and brothers. She had no idea what he was capable of.

"Now," Chisolmwood said, giving Gabriel his full attention. "I'll get to the reason I've come. With the war at an end, news of the part you played in its conclusion is widespread. My son insists that your heroism needs to be acknowledged. He tells me it is my duty to host a gathering in which you will be given the accolades you deserve."

Gabriel experienced an explosive flash of anger. There had been nothing heroic in what he'd done. He'd simply followed the orders someone else had given him. If anyone needed to be honored, it was the man he and Austin had dubbed "Thorn". *He* was the one who had somehow ferreted out the information that led Gabriel to a meeting where the Russian general would in all likelihood leave with important papers in his pocket. All Gabriel had done was take them.

But even if he'd single-handedly brought the war to an end, the Duke of Chisolmwood was the last person he would allow to host a gathering to honor him. He rubbed his palms across the knot in his thigh that had begun to ache again.

"I'm sorry, Your Grace, but I doubt I'll be well enough to attend a function that *you* host any time soon."

Chisolmwood's brows arched. "I wouldn't refuse so quickly, Major. My son tells me that both you and Lieutenant Landwell are aware of several shortcomings concerning our military and the conditions our soldiers were forced to endure. Several very influential members of Society will be in attendance, as well as my son." Chisolmwood's chin lifted slightly. "If reform is truly your goal, you cannot ask for a better champion. Isn't that true, Etherington?"

Harrison nodded. "The Marquess of Culbertson would be the ideal person to sponsor reform." Harrison's look turned serious. "But the decision is yours."

Gabriel knew what he meant. Harrison knew how difficult it would be to give Chisolmwood the distinction Gabriel's presence would lend to his affair. He was torn between his hatred for the man and an obligation to make sure the men fighting under Britain's flag never had to endure the hardships the men in the Crimea had endured. Military reform was desperately needed. And yet...

He was being used by Chisolmwood. Since his recovery, he'd received more invitations than he could count to affairs at which he was to be the guest of honor. He'd refused them all. To give that privilege to the Duke of Chisolmwood turned his stomach.

"Come now, Talbot. The decision cannot be *that* difficult. Just think of the good that can come of it."

Gabriel considered his decision for a long moment more, then slowly lifted his gaze until his cold glare locked with Chisolmwood's. "Attending your gathering will involve a great deal of my time. Time that is very precious to me."

The expression on Chisolmwood's face turned to shocked surprise. "And what do you estimate one evening of your time to be worth?"

Gabriel paused then finally answered. "One note."

Chisolmwood's surprise turned to disbelief. "I have several notes. Are you talking about one in particular?"

"Yes. The largest one."

"Gabe—"

Gabriel shot Harrison a squelching look and he quit his objection. If he *had* to yield to the duke's demand—and he did—and if he *had* to contribute to Chisolmwood's prestige and influence—and that's what would happen if he attended his gathering—then it would bloody well be a benefit to someone. And that someone would be Harrison.

Gabriel turned his glare back to Chisolmwood. "Is my presence worth that much?"

Chisolmwood's loud bark of laughter shot through the tension in the room. He focused his gaze on Gabriel and smiled. "It's possible I underestimated your determination, Major. I will schedule the affair to be held in two weeks' time...if that meets with your approval."

Gabriel nodded. "And the note?"

"Will be handed over to Lord Etherington upon your arrival. Now, if you will excuse me, I have several appointments to keep. Lady Lydia. Etherington. Major."

An uncomfortable silence settled over the room as none of the men would be the first to drop their gaze from the other. Lydia forced the issue.

"Let me see you to the door, Your Grace," she said with a smile on her face that Gabriel thought seemed unnatural. Chisolmwood broke Gabriel's glare and held out his arm for Lydia to take.

The minute the door closed he sank back against his chair and closed his eyes. His head throbbed and his leg ached. He wasn't used to fighting any battle with the disadvantage of being confined to a chair while his opponent towered over him. *Bloody hell.*

"You didn't have to do that."

Gabriel opened his eyes to find Harrison staring out the window. He had his back to the room. His hands hung at his sides in angry fists.

"You think I did it for you?"

Harrison spun around. "Who else?"

Gabriel didn't even try to stamp down the anger roiling inside him. "I did it for *me*. Even though it was only money, at least the bastard had to give up something. If I'm lucky, some day I'll have it in my power to take away something of real value."

Gabriel dropped his head back and closed his eyes. "Now, leave me alone so I get some rest. I have two weeks to build my strength."

He waited until the door closed behind Harrison then reached for the bottle on the table beside his chair and took a swallow.

Then he took another.

CHAPTER SEVEN

Gabriel sat on a stone bench beneath one of the trees in the garden at Etherhouse and inhaled a deep breath. Although winter still ruled, the crisp, clean air gave him a sense of freedom he'd missed since he'd returned. He needed the fresh air to clear his mind. To put things into perspective.

The Duke of Chisolmwood's event was tonight. He intended to leave Etherhouse first thing in the morning and go to the small flat Austin had found for him. It was time. Since Harrison and Chisolmwood had walked in on them two weeks ago, nothing had been the same.

Being near Lydia was torture. He wanted her more than he'd wanted her before. Loved her more today than he had a year ago. And she would soon marry the Marquess of Culbertson.

He raked his fingers through his hair in frustration then grabbed the two canes Harrison had given him. He had to get through this one last night with Liddy, then he could remove himself from the frustration of being near her.

"Are you ready to go back in?"

He spun his gaze to a spot a short distance down the path and watched Liddy walk toward him.

Bloody hell, but she was beautiful.

She smiled and his heart increased the rapid thumping in his chest. Yes, it was past time he left.

"I was thinking about it."

"Harrison says you've been out here quite some time."

"The day was too perfect to waste indoors."

When she said no more, he started to rise, but she held out her hand to stop him.

"Please. Stay seated."

He remained where he was.

To come outside, she'd put on a dark maroon velvet cloak with black ermine trim. Its matching bonnet framed her porcelain cheeks and the fur around her face only made her hair seem richer, more alive. His breath caught in his throat.

"Are you warm enough?"

He smiled. "Yes. Fine."

"I wouldn't want you to catch your death. Austin would never forgive us."

"There's no chance of that. The winters in England are balmy compared to what we endured in the Crimea."

"It must have been terrible."

He refused to let his mind go back to that place and instead, slid to the edge of the bench to make room for her. "Would you care to sit down?"

"Yes, thank you."

She sat beside him and straightened her skirts. Having her so near sent molten heat waves rushing to every part of him. He turned on the bench so he could see her more clearly and clutched his hand to his thigh when a sharp pain shot through him.

"Are you all right?"

"Yes, fine. Just a twinge." He ignored the pain in his leg. "How was your afternoon?" he said finally. "Harrison said you went out."

"Yes. I had tea with the Duchess of Westwood."

"How nice."

She smiled. "We had a lovely time. Baroness Frendsdale was also there with her daughters, Emmeline and Augusta. They've both been friends of mine since our come-out." She gave him an impish smile. "I hope you don't mind, but I promised them an introduction tonight."

"It will be my pleasure."

"You're quite the hero, you know. Nearly the entire conversation this afternoon centered around you and your heroic deeds to save our country."

"I hope you dissuaded them of such a misplaced notion. I'm hardly worthy of such praise."

"Oh, no." She broadened her smile. "If anything, I embellished your noble deeds. I made you out to be even more superhuman than the rumors circulating about you. I fear I implied you'd almost single-handedly defeated the entire Russian army."

"That's frightening." He shook his head. "Then I'd best be prepared to quell such unfounded rumors. I only pray that because it's barely the first of the year, there won't be that many in attendance tonight."

"Oh, no. Members of the nobility are returning to London in droves for the opening of Parliament next month. Geoffrey...I mean the Marquess of Culbertson, has attended meetings nearly every night this week in preparation. It's a very exciting time of year."

Gabriel ignored the intimacy with which Lydia referred to the marquess. "I don't suppose I can pretend an illness of some sort between now and this evening?"

"I should say not. I daresay, the Duke of Chisolmwood wouldn't allow it."

Gabriel's fingers tightened around the handles on his canes. "No, I don't suppose he would."

She glanced at his hands, then turned on the bench until she faced him. "What happened between you and Chisolmwood? What was that about a note that you demanded in payment for your appearance tonight?"

Gabriel shook his head. "It was nothing."

"That's what Harrison said when I asked him, but I am Harrison's younger sister. He's always had an irritating habit of protecting me from things he doesn't want me to know. You, on the other hand, never considered me so fragile you needed to keep things from me, Gabriel. Please, don't start now."

He cocked his head in her direction. His gaze met hers and a warmth spread through his body that settled low in his gut. "Then I won't. I'll simply tell you it's none of your business."

"Very well." She tucked her hands inside her cloak. "If that's how you feel."

"That's how it has to be, Liddy. Nothing more. Nothing less." He placed his canes out in front of him again. "Now, we'd best go inside. You're getting cold."

"And you need to rest a bit before you face your throng of admirers."

"Yes. Harrison informed me we'd be leaving early." He stood on wobbly legs. "We don't want to cause the Duke of Chisolmwood undue anxiety by being tardy."

She stood first and turned. "Do you want me to call for help?"

He shook his head. "I'm getting quite accomplished as long as I don't have to stand too long."

He took one shaky step, then another. His leg was stiff from sitting in the cold for so long, but eventually he felt as if it would support him. He took another step and felt her hand touch his elbow. The gesture made him smile. "Don't attempt to catch me if I fall," he said with a hint of laughter in his voice, although he was serious.

"Are you afraid I'm not strong enough to catch you?"

"I think you are brave enough to try. But I don't want to risk hurting you."

"Would that you had felt that way a year ago."

Gabriel stumbled, then righted himself. For several long seconds he focused on a squirrel scampering from tree to tree. He knew he should ignore her barb. He *had* hurt her. Although the fault wasn't his, it didn't lessen the pain he'd caused her.

He tried to take another step forward but couldn't. He couldn't leave things as they were. With a heart heavy in his chest, he turned toward her and looked into her eyes. Even though it had been nearly a year and a half, the hurt was still there. He shifted the cane in his right hand to grip it in the crook of his left elbow, then lifted his hand and brushed his fingers down her silky cheek.

Her skin was soft and velvety, her cheeks cool and rosy red from the chill in the air. Or it might have been from the closeness they shared. He couldn't tell.

"I'm sorry, Liddy. If there had been any other choice a year ago, I wouldn't have hurt you."

Frown lines deepened across her forehead, the confused look in her eyes indicating she didn't understand.

"Then why did you?"

"Because I didn't have a choice."

"You mean because I wouldn't come with a dowry if we married against Father's wishes."

He didn't answer, but he didn't have to. The crestfallen expression told him she had her answer.

She stepped away from him and shuddered a small gasp. She stood there a moment, then turned her head, and Gabriel knew it was too late. It had been too late from the moment he'd walked away from her in this same garden a little more than a year ago.

On legs that trembled beneath him, he walked away from her again. Only this time the hurt was more intense than it had been the last time.

❦

He looked around the crowded ballroom and shifted the weight from his injured leg. Only two hours had passed since they'd arrived and already he felt as if this night would never end.

The ball was a resounding success. Everyone who'd crowded into Chisolmwood's elegant town house remarked on it. And the Duke of Chisolmwood preened as proudly as if the Queen were his honored guest instead of an injured army major. He hated every second he was forced to add to the duke's exalted reputation.

Even though Chisolmwood's townhouse was one of the larger, more elaborate homes on London's fashionable West End, the crowd was so huge there was hardly room to move. Everyone who was anyone was there. Those who hadn't returned to the city earlier in the month had made certain to arrive in time to attend the gala event. It promised to be an evening that would be talked about for weeks to come.

He couldn't wait for it to be over.

Gabriel pulled his attention back to the topic the growing group of men surrounding him discussed. He'd not been alone all evening. There'd been a crush vying for his attention since the first guests had arrived. For several hours he'd been forced to listen to the men expound on the virtues of a war they considered Britain had won when they didn't have the vaguest idea why they'd chosen to fight. And not one of them could fathom how horrendous the conditions had been.

He breathed a labored sigh and leaned his hip against a tall stool a footman had placed nearby. Wherever he went, a liveried servant magically appeared with a stool tall enough for him to lean against so he could keep the full weight off his leg. He preferred to think that Lydia had arranged for his comfort and not Chisolmwood.

He thought of Liddy and searched for her. She was near the double French doors talking with a group of young ladies. *Bloody hell,* she was the beauty among them.

She'd pulled her hair loosely back from her face with a dark velvet ribbon that intertwined amid the curls that cascaded down her neck. She looked stunning in a gown of the deepest green. The color made her skin glow with a pearlescent luster and the style accentuated her lush figure. The flickering candles from the chandeliers cast a luminescence around her and his body reacted as dangerously as it had two weeks ago when Harrison and Chisolmwood had walked in on them.

She laughed. Her eyes sparkled with enthusiasm and her cheeks flushed brightly, whether from the heat or from excitement, he couldn't know. None of the other females here could compare. But it wasn't just her beauty that set her apart. It was her intelligence and her strength and the way she carried herself that made her so special. She would make the perfect duchess for the future duke.

He looked for the elusive Marquess of Culbertson. Even though they'd never met, he was certain he'd recognize him. Lydia had described him often enough. Tall of stature, blond good looks, striking carriage, and the aura of authority Gabriel knew would surround him. No, he hadn't arrived yet. There were several young men hovering close by, but none of them resembled the paragon of manliness Culbertson was reported to be.

Gabriel was glad. Hearing Lydia describe him with such glowing enthusiasm was one thing. Putting a face to the man who would one day have a right to hold the woman he loved, touch her, make love to her, was another.

So, he watched her from afar, drinking in his fill of her, feasting on every perfect detail, memorizing the way she looked so he could recall her image when he was no longer able to see her.

As if she realized he watched her, she turned her head and their gazes locked. She smiled, then hooked her gloved hand through the arm of one of the other young ladies standing near her and pulled her friend toward him. Dozens of heads turned to watch them.

The young woman with Lydia was as dark as Lydia was fair. Her hair gleamed just a shade darker than rich polished mahogany. She was a little taller than Lydia and her build was perhaps a little fuller, but one couldn't help but be in awe of her beauty.

He stood as they approached, willing his screaming thigh muscle to silence itself.

"Major Talbot," Lydia said when she reached him. "Allow me to present Lady Emmeline Frendsdale. Emmeline, Major Gabriel Talbot."

"Lady Emmeline."

"Major Talbot, I can't tell you how pleased I am to meet you." She leaned forward and spoke softly. "I refuse to mention your heroism though, unless you want me to bring the subject up *again*."

He smiled. "No, I prefer you don't."

"As I thought." There was an intelligent gleam in her eyes. "I couldn't help but notice that you seem decidedly uncomfortable with the attention everyone showers upon you."

"I am forever in your debt." He smiled first at Lady Emmeline, then at Lydia.

Lydia stepped forward and nodded to a nearby footman. The liveried servant discreetly moved the stool closer to Gabe.

"Please, sit down, Major." Lydia glanced toward the stool. "I told Emmeline that you'd been monopolized long enough with talk of war and battles and the happenings in different parts of the world. You appear in need of a respite."

"You always were an astute observer." Gabriel leaned against the stool. "Are you ladies enjoying the evening?"

"Oh, yes," Emmeline replied. "I can't remember seeing such a crush except at the height of the season. The duke has you to thank for giving him the distinction of hosting the affair of the year."

Even though Gabriel knew it was true, it wasn't what he wanted to hear. Being among the first to receive the new Victoria Cross had put him unexpectedly in a small, very elite group. The Queen's medal for valor in battle still seemed far too shiny where it rested on his chest.

He clenched his jaw in frustration. "Yes, it's too bad the Marquess of Culbertson isn't here to enjoy it."

"He'll be here," Lydia said with a confident smile on her face. "He had an important meeting and was obviously detained."

Gabriel expected Lydia to be anxious for Culbertson to arrive, but only Lady Emmeline glanced toward the stairs. He thought he might comment on Liddy's lack of interest but the Marquess of Bendendine and the Earl of Canesport chose that moment to interrupt.

"The *Chancellor's Lady* docked this morning with more soldiers returning from the Crimea, Talbot. I suppose you've heard?" Bendendine said, placing one hand on his protruding stomach. "It won't be long before we have all our boys home."

Gabriel pulled his attention away from Lydia and Lady Emmeline. "Yes. Except for the young men who will never return."

Bendendine cleared his throat. "Yes, well, that is the tragedy of war. There will always be fatalities."

"But I dare say we showed them where the strength in Europe lay," the slightly inebriated Canesport slurred. "The Russians should never have been so foolish as to think they could battle us and win."

That remark was followed by the enthusiastic murmur of agreement and the nodding of heads. More onlookers joined the circle. Harrison was among them.

"Everyone knows the war only lasted as long as it did because of Russia's disregard for her soldiers' safety," a portly gentleman said.

"Our soldiers have always shown themselves well," the Earl of Hollingsworth added. "And our officers are the finest in the world. Always have been."

"Do you agree, Major Talbot?" Bendendine asked.

Of all the men he'd met this evening, Bendendine had been the most curious, had been the most interested when Gabriel was asked a question.

"No, sir. I'm afraid I don't."

A deafening stillness silenced the group, then everyone in the growing circle turned toward him with frowns on their foreheads.

"Are you saying that our soldiers didn't show themselves well?" Canesport bristled.

"Absolutely not," Gabriel began. "The soldiers who fought in the Crimea were the bravest, most noble men ever to have put on British uniforms."

"Then what are you implying, Major?"

He looked into Harrison's hooded gaze and fought the war waging within him. He wasn't sure if this was the time or place to say what needed to be said, but he owed it to the tens of thousands of men who'd died to tell their story. Finally, Harrison answered his internal debate for him.

"I think you should explain yourself," Harrison said. "Many of the men here tonight have no idea what you, or my brother, or the rest of the men we sent to fight in the Crimea endured. I think the world deserves to know."

Gabriel began cautiously, explaining in detail the conditions in the Crimea. The longer he talked, the larger the crowd of men, and even some women, grew. Mostly they listened, but a few asked questions. A majority seemed interested, and all were appalled.

"Are you saying the Russians were more concerned with their men than we were?" Canesport asked, his tone defensive.

"What I'm saying is that our men arrived on foreign soil totally unprepared, and were forced to endure hardships that were intolerable. Perhaps the next time we are so eager to send our men to fight, they should be provided military equipment that isn't outdated, and we should make sure they don't have to scavenge the clothes off their fallen comrades' bodies because their own threadbare uniforms can't keep them warm."

More eager guests crowded around them and a voice from the back of the circle encouraged him to continue. He did.

"Before we abandon our men on foreign shores, we should make sure we provide winter quarters so they aren't forced to live in the open during the freezing winters without any more covering than the canvas of their tents. And that they are at least given a heavy coat, and that we provide enough support personnel that they don't have to chop tree roots from the frozen ground after a full days' battle because that is all that is left for firewood."

"What do you suggest we do about this?" a quiet voice filled with authority asked, and Gabriel lifted his gaze.

The gentleman was tall and broad-shouldered, and held

himself in a regal stance that exhibited an undeniable air of authority.

Gabriel had no doubt he faced the Marquess of Culbertson.

CHAPTER EIGHT

So, this was the man Lydia would marry. The man who would give her a house filled with laughter and children. Who would come home to find her waiting for him with open arms.

Gabriel studied him, thinking to find some flaw. He didn't. He only saw a keen intelligence he couldn't help but admire. He could see why she was enamored of him. They were perfectly suited to each other.

"Major Talbot," Harrison said stepping between them. "Allow me to present the Marquess of Culbertson."

Culbertson inclined his head. "Major. Thank you for bringing these atrocities to our attention. Now, how do you suggest we go about crafting reform?"

Gabriel had heard enough from Lydia to know Culbertson's reputation and influence was admired throughout England. He also knew he had within hearing one of the most powerful men in London. The opportunity to bring about the necessary changes for the soldiers willing to lay down their lives for their country was here and now. No matter what his personal feelings were for Culbertson, he knew he couldn't waste this opportunity to help the men who would fight in future wars.

He rose from his stool and faced the marquess. "Thanks to the *Times* of London and the pictures they ran as evidence of what was happening, conditions improved the last year. Alexis

Soyer, the head chef of the Reform Club in London, arrived and there was finally adequate food to feed the starving soldiers. Then, Miss Florence Nightingale arrived with her forty nurses, and the wounded and dying at least had someone to make their last few hours more comfortable, or simply hold their hand while they died."

A few soft sniffles echoed in the silence that followed Gabriel's last statement. Several ladies dabbed at their eyes, and even a few of the men.

"But until legislation is enacted," he said, casting his gaze over the crowd listening to him, "there is no guarantee anything will improve for the next group of soldiers sent to protect Britain's interests."

Culbertson turned toward Harrison. "Is there any connection to this and the reason you have asked to speak before the House of Lords when it opens, Etherington?"

Harrison nodded. "After reading the horrors in the *Times*, and listening to the first-hand accounts from my brother and Major Talbot, I feel the need to reform our military system is desperate. If there hadn't been such a public outcry from the families of those soldiers who'd written of the conditions in their letters, we wouldn't have seen even the small improvements we did. It's time the government takes responsibility for the soldiers we send to war."

Applause broke out from the crowd who'd been listening to Gabriel and Etherington.

Culbertson spoke up again. "I agree. If you need someone to stand at your side, Etherington, you can count on me."

"Me, too," Bendendine said. "I haven't had a good cause to fight for in a long time. I can't think of one more worthy. Will you agree to be on hand should the need arise, Major?"

"Of course," he answered, then lowered himself to the stool a footman pushed closer. His leg ached abominably and he knew he'd be lucky if he could make it out of bed tomorrow. But he'd accomplished the goal he'd set for tonight. With Harrison and Culbertson leading the revolt for change, success was almost guaranteed.

"We'll meet at the club tomorrow and begin our strategy," the Earl of Canesport said, the rallying cry already spreading through Chisolmwood's ballroom.

En masse, the men followed Harrison to the other side of the room, leaving Lydia, her friend Emmeline, and the Marquess of Culbertson standing with Gabriel.

"Thank you, Major," Culbertson said when they were alone. "What you said tonight did more to further the cause for military reform than any of a dozen speeches Etherington or I could have given before the House."

Culbertson looked to where the men enthusiastically formulated their plan. "And we couldn't have hoped for more influential champions than the men here tonight. Every future soldier owes you a great deal."

"I'm glad I could play a part. Change is long overdue."

"Anyone with a son or father or husband over there knows how horrible it was." Culbertson took a glass from a passing footman's tray. He took a second glass and handed it to Gabriel. "But we are being terribly neglectful, Major." The corners of his mouth lifted. "We've ignored these lovely ladies unmercifully."

"Nonsense," Lydia said, answering his warm smile with one of her own. "Both your opinion and Major Talbot's are fascinating. Who better to champion such a cause than two men with your experience and knowledge?"

"Oh, yes," Lady Emmeline added, her eyes gleaming in adoration. "The welfare of our soldiers is vitally important. Those of us who don't have a voice appreciate the stand you are willing to take."

Culbertson's gaze lingered on Lady Emmeline, then moved to Lydia and his smile broadened. "Be that as it may, we've ignored you long enough. I'm sure you'd both like a glass of punch. Allow me to escort you to a refreshment table." He offered Lydia his arm.

Gabriel saw how naturally Lydia placed her hand on his sleeve and a knot twisted in his gut. He was jealous and he had no right to be. He'd given up any claim on Lydia more than a year ago.

"Would you care to join us, Major?" Culbertson offered Lady Emmeline his other arm.

"Thank you, no. I prefer to get some fresh air."

Culbertson smiled. "Of course. Being confined indoors is often difficult for a military man. We'll talk later?"

He nodded, then watched Culbertson lead Lydia and Lady Emmeline across the room.

His leg ached with more vengeance than before and he stood cautiously. He waved away the footman who stood nearby in case he needed assistance, then steadied himself on his canes and limped to the double doors that led out onto the terrace.

The air was crisp and cold, the terrace empty. In warmer weather couples would stream outside for a breath of fresh air or a secluded walk down one of the garden paths. Tonight was too chilly for anyone to venture out.

He was glad he was alone. Alone to evaluate his feelings for the man with whom Lydia would spend the rest of her life. He wanted to dislike him, wanted to consider him the enemy. Instead, what he felt was...admiration.

He rested his canes against the stone balustrade and placed his palms flat against the cool railing. He should be relieved that she would marry someone who was a perfect match for her. And he was. Culbertson was honorable and well respected, and his father was a duke. Which meant that—

Gabriel dropped his head between his hands and closed his eyes. It meant that one day Lydia would be his—

"Are you all right?"

Gabriel cast a slow glance over his shoulder to where she stood in the doorway. "Yes, I'm fine. Please, go back inside before you catch your death of cold."

She didn't leave, but took a step onto the terrace and closed the door behind her.

"I was certain I'd find you out here. Austin used to get the look I saw on your face earlier. Within minutes he could be found outside."

Gabriel looked up into the nighttime sky. "I remember a time when we both considered the out of doors enjoyable."

"Yes, well, some things change."

"Yes, they do." He wished she'd do the sensible thing and leave. Being this close to her sent waves of desire through his body.

"You accomplished a great deal tonight." She stepped toward him.

"I just brought a great travesty to the proper people's attention."

"Then it was worth attending the Duke of Chisolmwood's affair."

"Was it?"

She wasn't wearing a shawl or anything else to protect her from the cold and Gabriel noticed her shiver. Why didn't she just go inside? He wanted her with an intensity that drove him wild. He'd always wanted her, even after he knew he couldn't have her.

She made no move to leave so he removed his coat and placed it around her shoulders.

"Thank you."

She pulled the material close beneath her chin and their fingers touched. Even though she wore gloves, there was a warmth to her touch that traveled through him. "You shouldn't be out here." He dropped his hands from her and was thankful when she didn't step away from him. He wanted her near. Wanted to take in every perfect feature, wanted to breathe in the clean lilac fragrance he'd always associate with her. Wanted to have her near him for a while longer.

"Why did you come out here?"

She pulled the lapels of his jacket tighter and held them with clenched fingers. "I wanted to speak with you privately."

"You shouldn't be here. Someone might see you."

"No one will see me. No one is foolish enough to come out in the cold except you."

"And you."

The expression on her face strengthened, the look in her eyes more determined. "I wanted to thank you for coming. For bringing the hardships our soldiers endured to everyone's attention, and..." She paused. "For forcing the Duke of Chisolmwood to relinquish whatever he gave Harrison when we arrived. The expression on Harrison's face said whatever it was meant a great deal to him. I wanted to thank you before you left Etherhouse."

"What makes you think I'm leaving?"

"Do you deny it?"

He smiled. "No."

"When?"

"In the morning."

"Will you be all right?"

Worry lines etched her forehead and he wanted to brush his fingers against them to erase them. He wanted to touch her just once more, run his fingers over her features to reaffirm each small detail he'd filed to memory. He wanted to take her in his arms one last time and kiss her.

But he couldn't. One kiss would never be enough. "I'll be fine. Will you?"

His question surprised her. "What?"

"Will you be fine? Will you be happy?"

She inched away from him. "Of course I'll be happy. I'm going to marry the Marquess of Culbertson and have the home and family I always dreamed of having."

"And love?"

The expression on her face hardened. "Yes, I'll have love. More love than I would have had if I'd married you."

He staggered under the weight of her words. He couldn't let her think that. He couldn't let her think that he didn't love her.

"That's not possible," he ground through clenched teeth. "No one can love you more than I did. More than I *do*."

Her eyes filled with a sadness that broke his heart. "You're too late, Gabriel. A year ago you could have had all the love I'm capable of giving any man, but not now. I don't love you anymore."

He closed the distance between them. "Are you sure?"

"Yes. There's only room in my heart for one man and you aren't him. You never will be."

Her words acted like a knife to his heart. "If I could undo everything that happened a year ago I would. If I could take back what I said—"

It was too late. Even as he said the words, he knew it was too late. He could never win her back. But he didn't want to leave her without holding her one more time. Without kissing her one more time. Even though he knew he was making the biggest mistake of his life, he pulled her into his arms and held her close. Then, with a ragged breath, he pressed his lips to hers and kissed her.

She didn't respond and he moved his hands over her body, slowly, tenderly. Down her back, then up and over her shoulders. He cupped her head in his palm and nestled her even closer.

There was only his thin linen shirt to separate them, yet he wasn't cold. His body burned as if on fire. Just having her this near him was like living a hell more unbearable than the anguish the war had forced him to endure.

Her lack of response threw him into another hell.

Her lips were cold and unresponsive beneath his and he deepened his kiss. He opened his mouth over hers, his tongue outlining her lips, but she refused to open to him. He pressed a finger against her chin but she held firm and didn't yield.

Realizing she shared none of his passion jolted him with the force of a two-fisted punch. He lifted his mouth from hers and looked into her eyes.

"Are you finished?" She wiped her mouth with her gloved fingers and met his gaze.

Tears filled her eyes, pooling together until one wet drop silently slipped over the edge and tumbled down her cheek. With trembling fingers, she wiped it away the same as she had the imprint of his kisses.

He couldn't breathe. Couldn't find the strength to order his heart to continue beating, his mind to form the correct thoughts. "Yes, my lady. I apologize for my behavior. This will never happen again."

She didn't acknowledge his promise, but pulled his jacket from around her shoulders and handed it to him.

Their fingers touched when he took it from her and she jerked her hand away as if even through her gloves his touch burned her.

Something inside him died at that moment. He wanted to

say her reaction to his kiss hadn't bothered him, but it had—more than he thought he could live with.

He took a step away from her, then stopped when a voice from across the terrace interrupted them.

"There you are. Allow me to escort you back inside, Lydia."

"Yes, please."

The Marquess of Culbertson stepped toward them and claimed the woman he'd been given to be his bride.

When they left, Gabriel stood in the cold December air and relived another time when he'd lost everything.

CHAPTER NINE

He was gone.

It had been three weeks and she should be glad he wasn't there as a constant temptation. Glad he wasn't there to consume her thoughts every second of her day. Glad she was free to concentrate on her future with the Marquess of Culbertson.

Except in the twenty-one days since he'd moved out of Etherhouse, she'd been able to concentrate on nothing but Gabriel. And the night he'd kissed her.

Her mind constantly relived the feel of his lips against hers, the warmth of his body pressed against her, the swirling passion she almost hadn't been able to resist. It had taken every ounce of determination and willpower not to give in to him.

Oh, how she'd ached to wrap her arms around his neck and return his kisses.

She walked over to Harrison's copy of *Bleak House* and ran her fingers across the gold embossed leather. She started to take it off the library shelf, then pushed it back in frustration.

Why had he kissed her? What did he hope to prove? That she still loved him?

She doubled her fist and slammed it against the bookcase. She hoped he was satisfied. He'd ruined everything. She'd spent the last year convincing herself she hated him, that she would never feel anything for him except disdain. And with one kiss...

She leaned her forehead against the cool leather spines and swallowed hard. The second his lips had touched hers, the earth had spun on its axis. A heat unlike anything she'd ever felt spread through her and her lungs couldn't take in enough air to breathe. *Damn him!* She'd been so sure she'd destroyed every emotion she'd ever felt for him. So sure she'd be just as disappointed with his kisses as she was with the Marquess of Culbertson's.

But she hadn't been. His kiss reminded her of what she'd lost. His kiss forced her to realize that her life with Culbertson would be filled with the granting of every earthly request, yet remain devoid of the passion she could share with Gabriel.

She pushed herself away from the bookcase and pressed her hands to her burning cheeks. She fought the self-loathing that consumed her. She still loved him. No matter how hard she tried not to, she still loved the man who'd given her up when he discovered she wouldn't come with a dowry.

She touched her fingers to her lips. She could still feel the touch of his lips against hers. Could still feel his arms holding her, his hands touching her.

God help her. When would it go away? When would she wake up without Gabriel being her first thought? Or go to bed without him being her last? When would she fall asleep without being consumed by dreams of him? When would she—

"Are you ready, Lydia?"

She caught her startled gasp and turned around. Harrison stood in the doorway dressed in his finest. He was such a handsome man that she was confused as to why he hadn't chosen a wife. It wasn't for lack of eligible females throwing themselves at him.

"Yes, I was just..."

"I know," he answered when she didn't finish and she knew he was aware of whom she'd been thinking.

He took one step into the room and stopped. "He's fine, Liddy."

She put on a bored expression and prayed her brother couldn't tell how rapidly her heart was beating. "Of course, he is. Why wouldn't he be?" She brushed at an imaginary wrinkle on her gown. "Have you heard from him?"

"I dropped by the flat where he's staying to see if he needed anything."

"Did he?"

Harrison shook his head and closed the door behind him. They were alone now and she knew what Harrison was going to say before he started.

"You have to forget him, Liddy."

She put as sincere a smile on her face as she could. "I have. I'm just curious. I wasn't sure he was ready to be on his own when he left."

Her brother walked across the room and stopped before the blazing fireplace. He braced his outstretched hands against the mantel and stared into the fire. "Chisolmwood came to see me today. He wants to formally announce your engagement." He took a deep breath and turned to face her. "I think that's wise."

She felt her cheeks warm but refused to back down from her brother's intense gaze. "We will," she said with a smile on her face. "We just haven't discussed that. I'm sure that in time—"

"Time isn't your friend. It won't change anything."

"I don't know what you're talking about. Why do you think I want anything to change?"

He narrowed his gaze. "Gabe will never ask you to marry him. He can't. Father signed the papers betrothing you to the Marquess of Culbertson. There's nothing you can do to change that without causing a scandal."

Her heart plummeted to the pit of her stomach. "That was cruel, Harrison."

"I'm sorry. It wasn't meant to be cruel. I meant it in the kindest way possible."

"Then you don't need to worry. I don't want to marry Major Talbot, and he doesn't want to marry me. He made that quite clear a year ago." She walked toward the door. "Now, if you're done explaining my duty, I think we'd better go. The crush at the Biltmore Ball will be impossible if we're late."

Harrison crossed the room and opened the door for her. She silently walked through the foyer to where Hannah and their butler waited with their cloaks. The weather had turned colder this week but it wouldn't be long until spring.

She pulled her red velvet cloak closer around her neck to ease the heavy weight that pressed down on her. A painful breath stabbed inside her chest. Harrison was right. Thinking about Gabe didn't help her. In fact, it hurt her.

"Perhaps if Geoffrey is there tonight," she said as the carriage rumbled over London's cobblestone streets, "the subject of our betrothal will come up."

Harrison laughed. "What do you mean, *if* he's there? Of course he'll be there. He always attends the functions at which he knows you'll be in attendance."

"Unless he's away on government business," she added, knowing she couldn't put off giving the marquess an answer any longer. Knowing she didn't want to.

"Yes, there is that," Harrison said as the carriage came to a stop in front of the Biltmore town house.

Every window was aglow with the brilliant lights from the huge chandeliers that hung from the ceilings in every room. She hoped the festive ambiance would replace the dread she suddenly felt. Why wasn't she brimming with excitement? Why wasn't she giddy with anticipation? She would see the marquess again tonight.

She stopped at the top of the stairs and looked around the ballroom. Her gaze focused on Culbertson and her good friend Emmeline, swirling in perfect unity to a waltz the orchestra played.

It was hard to miss him. His tall physique and striking appearance made him stand out in a crowd. Add to that Emmeline's grace and beauty and only someone blind could overlook them.

She smiled. The marquess held his partner in his arms and looked down into the warm, open smile on her face. Liddy watched for several moments, wishing her own heart would race when she looked at her future husband. Wishing she'd feel something other than the unsettled turmoil that had been there since Gabriel had reentered her life.

She stared out onto the dance floor and gathered her resolve. She'd survived losing Gabriel before and she could do it again. Her father had exposed Gabriel's greed and chosen a man of exemplary character when he'd chosen the Marquess of Culbertson. No matter what feelings she still harbored for Gabriel, she wouldn't go against her father's wishes. Harrison was right. She'd avoided the inevitable long enough.

The orchestra stopped playing and she took Harrison's arm and stepped down the stairs into the ballroom. The moment Culbertson noticed her, he brought Emmeline over to where they stood.

"Lady Lydia. Etherington," he greeted, and Lydia greeted them in return. They talked for several minutes about nothing in particular and when the orchestra struck the chord to begin the next set, he asked her to dance.

He held out his arm and she placed her hand lightly upon

it, praying she would feel a shiver of excitement when she touched him.

Telling herself it didn't matter when she didn't.

CHAPTER TEN

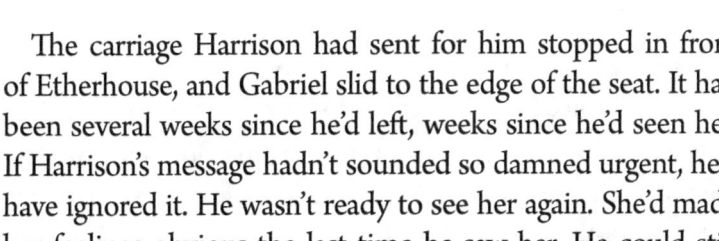

The carriage Harrison had sent for him stopped in front of Etherhouse, and Gabriel slid to the edge of the seat. It had been several weeks since he'd left, weeks since he'd seen her. If Harrison's message hadn't sounded so damned urgent, he'd have ignored it. He wasn't ready to see her again. She'd made her feelings obvious the last time he saw her. He could still feel her cold, still lips beneath his. Still hear the disdain in her voice, the rejection. She wanted nothing to do with him and he vowed to honor her wishes.

He descended from the carriage and stood for a moment until he could gain his balance. He'd improved a great deal since he'd left Etherhouse, and the intense pain that gripped his knotted muscles when he demanded too much from them wasn't nearly as severe as it had once been. He was confident the day would come when perhaps he'd even walk without a cane. Never without a limp, but perhaps without a cane. But not yet.

He took his first step, then made his way up the walk. An intense wave of unease washed over him as Ruskins opened the door. From the look on his face, something was definitely wrong.

"Good day, Major Talbot." There was a hint of strain in his voice.

"Good day, Ruskins."

The frown didn't leave Ruskins' face and as he helped Gabriel off with his cloak, the butler's usual staid and steady slowness seemed hurried.

"Lord Etherington is waiting for you in the library."

He followed Ruskins to the study door and walked inside.

Harrison stood by the crackling fireplace, his posture unnaturally rigid, his hands clasped behind his back and a deep frown darkening his features.

"Gabe."

He would have brushed aside the worry he felt if the strain in Harrison's voice hadn't been so obvious. "Harrison?"

Gabriel noticed his friend's pale complexion and the dark rings that circled his eyes. Worry and lack of sleep were evident.

"Is something wrong with Lydia?"

Harrison shook his head. "It's Austin. They have him."

Gabriel's heart clenched tightly in his chest. "Who has him?"

"The French. I just received word from the Ministry of Defense. Of course, officially our government denies they know Austin or that he has any military connection. But at least they were considerate enough to inform me that he'd been captured."

Gabe took a few steps into the room. "Tell me everything you know."

Harrison swiped his fingers through his hair. "I received a visit from one of the undersecretaries during the night. He wouldn't tell me why Austin had been sent to France, only that he was there."

Gabriel breathed a heavy sigh. "If Austin is in France, he was sent there to watch Napoleon III."

Harrison's brows shot upward. "Why do you think that?"

"It's been rumored for some time now that the emperor has ambitions as great as his uncle."

Harrison released a heavy sigh. "Yes, I'd heard rumblings along those lines but hoped they were unfounded."

"Where is he being held?"

"I'm not sure. All I know is he was last seen in Paris."

Gabriel thought of Austin being held in a French prison. He'd move heaven and earth to save him. That's what Austin had done for him. "It won't take me long to locate him."

"No, Gabe. I can't let you go after him."

"You can't stop me."

"You'd be arrested before you stepped on French soil."

"I may walk with a limp, but my injuries haven't affected my thinking, or the connections I have in France."

"But it has affected your mobility, the way you get around. Sending you over to save Austin would only get you killed."

"That's a risk I'm willing to take."

"Well, I'm not!"

"You have no choice. I have connections in France."

"If you can get to them."

"I will. I'll go ashore in Le Havre or Rouen and make my way to Paris."

"Your limp draws attention to you whether you like it or not. You can't hide. And you can't enter France from someplace else. They have every inch of French coastline guarded night and day. You'd never make it past the military."

"Then I'll sail in under their noses."

"You can't! I won't let you!"

"If you didn't bloody want me to go after Austin, then why the hell did you send for me?"

"Because I need your help. Give me the names of people over

there who can go after Austin. Names of people I can trust."

"No one! I'm the only one who can get to Austin. If the country's as unstable as I hear, do you really think I'll give you the names of the agents I know the government is looking for? No. I won't take such a risk. I'll go. Or no one will."

Etherington slammed his fist down on the top of the desk. "You can't do it! Not alone! Not with your injuries! You'd need a diversion. Something or someone who could draw attention away from you!"

"There isn't anyone who can do that!"

The door opened and both men spun around to where Lydia stood inside the room.

"I can do it."

Gabriel's heart leaped to his throat. He'd spent every day since he'd left her trying to convince himself he could live the rest of his life without her. Seeing her today undid everything he'd tried to forget—the feel of her in his arms, the way her hair smelled of lilacs and roses, the feel of her lips pressed to his.

Oh, how he missed her.

Harrison stepped around the desk to go near her. "You shouldn't be here."

Gabriel noticed the red rimming her eyes and the lack of color to her cheeks.

"I can be the diversion. I can help the major get into France without bringing attention to either of us."

"No," Gabriel answered, the thought too ludicrous to entertain.

"Yes, Major."

"No, you can't," he argued again, only this time he wasn't the only one to voice his disapproval. Harrison's negative reply brimmed with determination. It was to Lydia's credit that she didn't slink away in fear.

Instead, she lifted her shoulders and faced them. "You have no choice. None of us do. We can't sit idly by while they have Austin."

Lydia's eyes glistened with unshed tears. "We don't know what they're doing to him." There was a catch in her voice. "He could be starving, or injured. Or...worse."

One errant tear streamed down her cheek. "You asked to see Gabriel because you hoped he could help us. He can. But we have to help him, too, Harrison."

"No," Gabriel said firmly. There was no way he would endanger her. No way he'd put her at risk.

"You don't have a choice, Major. Neither do you, Harrison."

She looked from one of them to the other and Gabriel saw the depth of her resolve. He'd never been more proud of her than he was at this moment. He'd never been more afraid for her than he was now. What if Harrison actually considered allowing her to help in some way?

But he wouldn't. Harrison understood how dangerous it would be for her to go to France. He'd never allow Lydia to—

"How do you think you can help, Lydia?" Harrison asked.

Gabriel spun to face Harrison. "You can't think to consider letting her go to France."

"No, of course not. But I want to hear what she has to say."

"It doesn't matter what she says. She's not going to be involved in this."

Lydia cast a quick glance in his direction then let her final gaze rest on Harrison. "Why don't we all sit down and discuss this calmly. Please."

Harrison breathed an anguished sigh then pointed to a chair. "Gabe?"

He hesitated, knowing that whatever Lydia was about to suggest, it was probably better than anything either of them could come up with on their own. Her brothers had always underestimated her intelligence. *He* never had. He'd been in awe of it from the day they'd met.

"Now, Lydia," Harrison said, sitting in his chair behind his desk. "What do you see that we've missed?"

Gabe's heart jumped in his throat when she turned her head and looked at him.

"Do you agree that Austin is probably being held in Paris, Major?"

"That would be most likely, yes."

"If you had a way to get into the city, do you have the proper resources—the proper contacts to get him out?"

"Yes, but I can—"

She held up her hand. "I'm not doubting your ability. But don't you see, the risks are twice as great if you try to accomplish this alone. Austin's life is too important. Why not work with every advantage we have?"

"Because I don't want to put you in danger."

"But didn't you just say you had friends to help you once you reached Paris?"

"Yes."

"Then the greatest chance for failure is before you ever get to them. That is when you will be the most vulnerable."

"I'll think of something."

"What? A diversion to keep you from being suspect by the French authorities? A cover to get you into the country?"

"Yes."

"I already have a plan."

Her voice contained such confidence that a shiver throttled his spine.

"I won't allow you to be involved."

"I'm already involved, and if there's something I can do to ensure that Austin comes home safely, I'll do it."

"What are you suggesting, Liddy?" Harrison leaned forward with his arms propped on the top of the desk.

"Let me go with the major."

"No," Gabriel argued.

"Let me pose as the major's...wife. We could be newlyweds on our honeymoon."

"No!" he said louder.

Harrison rose from his chair and paced the small confines behind his desk. "Do you know what you're suggesting, Liddy?"

Gabriel couldn't believe what he'd heard. Even more astounding, he couldn't believe that Harrison would even listen to such a plan, let alone consider it. Yet he seemed to be doing just that.

"Of course, I do. The major needs to get into France without causing undue suspicion. I hardly look suspicious. As my husband, he'll hardly be considered a threat. His injury will be to our advantage. I have no doubt we can both pass as a newly married couple visiting France on our honeymoon."

Harrison came around the corner of his desk and stepped close to her. "You couldn't go without a chaperone."

Gabe threw out his hand in frustration. "Harrison! Think what you're doing. You can't let her go."

Harrison slammed his fist on the corner of the desk. "I can't let Austin die. And you're the only one I trust to save him. Which means I've got to do everything possible to ensure your successful arrival into Paris."

Harrison turned back to Lydia. "Who would you take with you?"

"I'll take Hannah. No one would expect a lady to travel without her lady's maid anyway. And Morgan will go as Major Talbot's valet. Everything will be quite proper. I won't be alone."

"What if someone discovers that you've gone with the major?"

"You can cover for me here. Say I'm ill, or that I went to the country for a few weeks. With the Marquess of Culbertson away on business, no one will think it odd that I chose this particular time to leave London."

Gabriel closed his eyes and shook his head. He couldn't believe this was happening.

If he were honest with himself, he had to admit her plan was perfect. He wasn't strong enough to make his way inland to Paris from the coast. His leg wouldn't support him that long. And he'd stand out like the proverbial sore thumb if he arrived alone. What use would he be to anyone if he were arrested the minute he stepped foot on French soil?

The disguise of newlyweds was an ideal ruse to get into the country undetected. Once they reached Paris, Jean-Paul would hide them at the inn. Jean-Paul would protect Lydia until Gabriel freed Austin, then Gabriel would bring them both home.

But there was always the chance that something would go wrong. A shiver of dread overtook him. He moved his gaze to Harrison, praying he'd see some sign that he realized Liddy's plan was too dangerous. Instead, Harrison's tortured look sent a wave of fear rushing through him.

"Harrison," he said. "Think what could happen."

"Do you think I don't know what could happen? I could lose my whole family." Harrison looked as if he carried the weight of the world on his shoulders. "I'd give everything I own for there to be another way," he whispered.

"There isn't," Lydia answered for him. "This is the only way."

A smile lit her face and she looked at Gabriel. "Nothing will happen to me, Harrison. Or to Austin. Gabriel will see to it."

A hand gripped his heart and squeezed until the air left his body. There was no doubt he would willingly risk his life to save Austin. But how could he risk Liddy's? How could he live with himself if something happened to her?

"I'll have a ship ready to sail whenever you say," Harrison said. "We'll need a ship shallow enough to navigate the Seine from Le Havre to Rouen. To avoid suspicion, that's as close to Paris as we dare go." Harrison paced a few steps then stopped. "The *Silver Star*. It will be perfect. Once it arrives in Rouen, it will remain docked under the pretext of needing repairs, and stand ready to leave at a moment's notice. Is there anything else you require?"

The bottom fell out of his world. But there was nothing he could do. "Money. I will need a substantial amount of cash. For the right sum, there isn't a guard anywhere who can't be bribed. And if things don't go as planned and we are forced to go underground for any length of time, we'll need cash to buy food and supplies."

"I'll get whatever you need," Harrison said.

"When will we leave, Major?"

Her calm voice matched her look of confidence when she focused on him. Gabriel didn't think he could bear it.

"Day after tomorrow on the tide. We need to arrive in Rouen in the middle of the day when the docks are busy. We'll draw the least attention then."

"Very well." She rose. "I'll be ready."

She walked to the door, but Gabriel couldn't let her leave without one last warning. "My lady."

She stopped and turned around.

"I won't blame you if you don't come. In fact, after your brother has had time to think over what the two of you have decided, I'm sure he'll realize the danger is too great and he'll stop you from going through with this folly."

She smiled again. "Thank you for your concern, Major. Now, if you'll excuse me, I have to get ready to leave on my honeymoon. I'll see you the day after tomorrow."

Gabriel watched her leave the room and fought the strong urge to run after her and force her to change her mind. He knew a stronger urge to grab Harrison and shake him until he came to his senses. But he could do neither.

He didn't stand a chance in hell of getting Austin out of France without her.

CHAPTER ELEVEN

Gabriel stood on the docks below the *Silver Star* and prayed that when Harrison arrived she wouldn't be with him. There were so many uncertainties with this venture. Anything could go wrong.

They could get to France only to find Austin dead. And even if he were alive, there was a chance Gabriel might be captured trying to free him, and Liddy would be stranded in a strange country, alone and unprotected.

Or, what if the French authorities implicated her in connection with his plan to free Austin and imprisoned her?

Gabriel swiped his hat from his head and raked his fingers through his hair. Bloody hell, she could even get killed trying to do this.

But most terrifying, how the hell was he supposed to survive being with her for the next week or more when he knew what it was like to hold her? When he couldn't forget what it had been like to kiss her?

He leaned against his cane and took in a deep breath. He wasn't sure he could.

"Good morning, Major."

He slowly turned and came face to face with the woman who'd haunted his dreams.

"Good morning, my lady. I hoped that you'd decide not to go through with this venture."

"I know. But I don't have any more choice than you do."

She smiled at him, the corners of her mouth lifting in a shaky smile that told him that at least a small part of her held reservations.

He faced her squarely. "It isn't too late."

"Yes, it is."

"You don't know what can happen, all the things that can go wrong."

She stiffened her shoulders, the effect as brave a front as he'd ever seen. "Bringing Austin home is worth whatever risk we have to take."

Gabriel couldn't argue. He felt the same. "Where is Harrison?"

"He stopped to talk to the captain. He asked me to find you and ask you to join them."

He looked over his shoulder and saw Etherington talking to the captain who would take them to France. He shifted his weight and turned, then offered her his arm. She didn't take it.

"Before we join Harrison, I'd like to speak with you." She stood with her hands clasped tightly in front of her and cleared her throat. "I'd like your promise that what happened at Chisolmwood's ball will never happen again."

Her cheeks turned a bright crimson and she was unable to hold his gaze. Of course she regretted him kissing her. How could she not? She'd been hand-picked by the Duke of Chisolmwood to be his son's future duchess. Why would she consider going back to a man who'd given her up when he found out she'd come without a dowry.

"You have my promise. Be assured that such a lapse in my behavior will never happen again."

He should stop there. He knew he should. Yet, something inside him couldn't keep him from revealing his feelings.

He turned his head and focused on nothing in particular. "But I don't regret it, Liddy. That's what's going to make the next week or more unbearable."

"Gabe—"

He stopped her from saying anything. "You're right. We have to have an understanding. Even though I don't regret kissing you, I won't let it happen again—because if it does, I'm not sure I can trust myself to stop."

The color left her face. He wasn't proud of himself for embarrassing her so, but it was suddenly important that she knew he hadn't given her up because he didn't love her.

"Now, I think it's time we played our assigned roles." He extended his arm. She hesitated, then took it, and he walked with her to where Harrison was talking with the captain.

"Major Talbot," Harrison said when they reached them. "Allow me to present Captain Faraday. Captain, Major Talbot."

"Major."

"Captain."

"And this is my sister, Lady Lydia."

The captain gave a curt bow. "My lady."

"Captain Faraday is aware of our reason for sailing to France," Harrison explained, "but his crew is not. They are under the assumption that this trip is no different than any other. That way, if they are questioned, they won't be able to tell the authorities anything that might incriminate you."

"Can your crew be trusted?" Gabriel asked. The grin that spread across Faraday's face reassured him.

"To the man. I would suggest, though, that you and Lady Lydia give them no reason to doubt the ruse you are playing."

Gabriel gave the captain a sharp nod, realizing that Lydia's and his role would have to start sooner than he'd anticipated.

"Then, allow me to introduce you," Harrison said as a group of sailors walked near them. "May I present my brother-in-law, Baron Talbot. And his wife, my sister, Lady Lydia Talbot."

The captain nodded. "Welcome aboard, Baron Talbot. Lady Talbot."

Liddy's hand still rested on his arm, and at Harrison's introduction, her fingers tightened. He lowered his gaze and smiled.

She met his gaze, but there wasn't a smile on her face.

He turned his attention to the sailors making final preparations for their departure. "Do you anticipate any problems sailing into Rouen?" he asked.

"No," Captain Faraday answered, "there should be no trouble. The *Silver Star* is loaded with goods bound for Paris. Once we dock, I'll return as quickly as I can."

"How long will we have?"

"I should be able to return within a week. If it takes longer than that to accomplish your mission, I'll return to England for another cargo and be back as quickly as possible. We'll work out the details before we reach Rouen so my crew and I can be of as much assistance as possible."

"That would be greatly appreciated," Gabriel said. "I have friends who should be waiting for us when we reach Rouen. They'll take us to Paris. Hopefully, we'll be able to accomplish our mission in under a week and be back to Rouen when you arrive."

Faraday smiled. "Then we should be safely back on English shores in no time."

"I hope so," he answered, knowing the chances of that happening were questionable, but refusing to say as much.

"Are you ready?" The captain cast a glance from Lydia to Gabriel, and finally to Etherington.

Gabriel nodded, then watched as Lydia stepped into Harrison's arms.

"We'll bring Austin home," she whispered. "Don't worry."

"I know." Harrison held Lydia a second or two longer, then released her. "Take care of her, Gabe. And yourself."

"I will. I'll bring them all back."

Etherington nodded then left.

Lydia and Gabriel followed Captain Faraday up the gangplank and stood at the railing while the *Silver Star* set sail.

He stood silently behind her and watched until Harrison's outline was no longer visible. Before she turned, she swiped her gloved fingers across her cheeks.

"I'm not crying," she announced.

"I know. It's the salt air. It has that effect on a person."

He couldn't help himself. He wrapped his arm around her shoulders and held her close to him. She didn't pull away from him, whether she assumed his actions were part of his role as her husband, or if she allowed him to hold her because she was frightened and needed to be held—by anyone.

For several long moments she stayed in his arms, then she slowly turned and stepped closer.

His body warmed with a soaring heat, and his heart thundered in his chest. He should stop her. He should, but...

He cradled her in his arms until a voice echoed from behind.

"Baron Talbot? Lady Talbot? Are you ready to go below?"

Gabriel turned to find the ship's steward behind him. It took him a moment to realize how superbly they were already playing their roles. From the look of surprise on Lydia's face, she realized the same.

"Yes. My wife and I would like to get settled."

He steadied himself on his cane and held out his arm. "Are

you ready, my dear?"

She placed her small, trembling hand on his sleeve and they took their first step toward their cabin.

They followed the steward as he led them through a hatch and down the narrow stairs. Out of the corner of his eye, he saw her lift her gaze to look at him. He didn't look down. Couldn't. Knew if he did, he'd realize how vulnerable she was, and he'd lose what little resolve he had left. Allowing her to go with him was such a risk.

It was all he could do to keep himself from leading her back up on deck and ordering the captain to turn the ship around and take her back where she'd be safe.

⁂

They ate their evening meal with Captain Faraday in his cabin, then went above deck. They watched until the orange glow of the sun slid low on the horizon, then Lydia walked with him down the narrow corridor to their cabin. When they arrived, he lifted the latch on the door and stepped aside for her to enter.

Hannah was inside turning down the bed. "The captain sent a tray," she said. "He thought you might like some tea before you retire."

"How nice of him."

She removed her bonnet and cloak and Hannah hung them in a narrow clothes chest affixed to the far wall.

"Will there be anything else?" Hannah asked.

"No. I'll call when I need you."

"Very well. I'll be right next door."

The door closed behind Hannah with an ominous click.

She was alone with him.

"Are you all right?" he asked.

His voice didn't startle her, but settled over her like the heat from a warm fire on a chilly night. After all, she'd heard that voice in her dreams more nights than she hadn't.

"Yes, I'm fine."

She gathered her resolve, then turned to face him.

Her heart flipped in her breast. Oh, why did he have to be so unbearably handsome? Why couldn't he be ugly, or overbearing, or ill-mannered? Why did he have to be one of the most attractive men—both outside and inside—she'd ever met? Why had he held her? Why had he kissed her? Why had he shown her what it would be like to be loved by him again?

She tried to bring Culbertson's face to the forefront. Tried to remember what it was like when he held her. But heaven help her, it wasn't anything like when Gabriel held her or kissed her.

She could never let anything like that happen again. If it did, she wouldn't be strong enough not to give in to him.

He walked across the room and sat on a hard chair next to a small table against the wall. "Please, sit, Liddy."

She sat, then watched as he rubbed his leg. "Are you in much pain?"

He smiled. "Enough. It's a great deal more difficult to keep one's balance on the deck of a rolling ship than on solid ground."

"I hadn't thought of that. Is there anything I can do?"

"No. I just need to rub the muscles. It keeps them from cramping."

He continued to rub his leg as the heavy footsteps of the crewmen made their way down the hallway outside. "I could use a cup of tea though, if you don't mind."

"Of course."

She poured him a cup of tea with sugar like he preferred, then the same for herself. When she finished she sat across the table from him. "When do you think we'll arrive in Paris?"

"Before nightfall, Tuesday."

She nodded and sipped her tea. The air outside was chilly and the hot liquid felt good going down. She closed her eyes on a sigh, and when she opened them, her gaze met his. There was a frown on his face and she felt a sudden trepidation.

"I want you to listen closely, Liddy, because you need to understand exactly what we're going to do."

She nodded, but the last swallow of tea lodged in her throat like a thick lump of cotton.

"Captain Faraday doesn't anticipate anything unforeseen happening when we dock in Rouen, and neither do I. But I don't doubt the docks will be crowded with French soldiers, so we'll have to draw as little attention as possible."

She listened closely to what he said, and nodded once or twice to indicate she understood.

"I sent a message to my friends before we left England, telling them approximately when we'd arrive. If they received the message in time, they'll be waiting for us. If they didn't, we'll have to find our own transportation."

"If they aren't there, do you know where to go?"

He moved his hand lower and rubbed a spot below his knee. "Yes, but I hope we don't have to use a public conveyance. I prefer not to involve a driver who can recall where he delivered two English newlyweds if he's questioned."

He sat back and unbuttoned his jacket, then stretched his legs out in front of him. She tried not to notice his muscular legs, or his flat, taut stomach, but her eyes continually moved to places where she shouldn't want to focus.

"Captain Faraday assures me he'll return in one week."

"Can you get Austin free in that length of time?"

"If we find out for sure where he's being held."

"If you don't?"

"Then it will take a little longer, that's all. But we'll free him. I promise you that."

She tried to keep the worry from her face but knew she'd failed. He reached for her hand and held it.

"I want you to listen carefully. This is important. We have exactly one week to get to Rouen, find Austin, and return before noon the following Monday. Captain Faraday can safely wait two or three days without drawing suspicion, but if we haven't returned by then, he'll have no choice but to set sail without us."

Her heart raced steadily in her chest, but she wouldn't allow herself to consider the worst. Gabriel had everything planned out to the last detail. She'd simply have to trust him. "Then what will we do?"

"We'll have to wait another week. The captain will pick up a new cargo and return the following Monday. He'll wait for us again until Wednesday or Thursday noon, then leave again if we're not there. He assured me he'll repeat his schedule every week until we've boarded."

She nodded, trying to show him she wasn't worried. She doubted it worked.

"If all goes well, we'll have three days to find Austin, free him, then return to Rouen by the following Monday."

"And if it doesn't?"

He lifted his hand from hers and rubbed his leg. "We'll cross that bridge when we come to it."

"Are you sure your friends won't mind becoming involved in your plan?"

He smiled and her heart stuttered. His smile still affected her like it used to.

"They won't mind. They're loyal British subjects doing

important jobs in France."

"They're taking a huge risk for us."

"It's a risk they're glad to take."

He started to say something else, then paused while more footsteps echoed outside their cabin door.

Traffic had lessened and she assumed the decreased activity meant most of the sailors had retired for the night. Which meant it wouldn't be long before the major could go to his own room without being noticed.

She clasped her hands tightly in her lap then asked the question weighing heaviest on her mind. "Do you think he's all right?"

For a long moment he didn't answer, but rubbed his leg as if he could knead his doubts away with his pain. Finally, he took a deep breath and looked into her eyes. "I don't know. I pray he is."

"So do I." She fought to hold back the tears.

Gabriel slid his chair back from the small table and turned toward her. "There's one more thing." He locked his gaze with hers. "And this is very important."

She waited.

"If for some reason something goes wrong and Austin and I don't return in time, I want your promise that you'll return to Rouen to be on board when the *Silver Star* sails for England."

"No."

"Yes. I need your word, Liddy."

She placed a stalwart expression on her face. "I won't leave you and Austin."

"You will, or you won't leave this ship. I'll lock you in this cabin and Captain Faraday will post an army of guards outside your door to keep you locked inside."

"You can't do that. You need me to—"

"I need to know that you're safe." He raked his fingers through his hair. "If something happens to me, Jean-Paul will make sure you get back to the *Silver Star*. Promise me you'll do exactly as he asks. That you'll be brave enough to leave us behind."

She fought the anger building inside her—the fear. "You don't know what you're asking."

"I do. More than you know. But I'll not risk your safety."

His shoulders stiffened and he seemed more resolved than before. "Your promise, Liddy."

She clenched her teeth and glared at him, making it plain how much she disliked his demand. He gave no quarter, but kept his gaze level with hers.

"Your promise, or you'll not leave the ship."

She finally relented. "You have my promise. I'll leave you behind when I'm certain you aren't returning."

"Thank you."

His cane sounded with each step he took toward to the door that connected her room with his. "Rest well," he said, then closed the door behind him.

Oh, how she wanted to take back her promise. How she wanted to tell him she'd never leave him.

She sat alone until the room turned dark. Hannah came in without being called and helped her get ready for bed.

For hours she lay in the darkness, telling herself it wouldn't come to that. That she wouldn't have to leave them behind.

Because if she did, it would mean that Austin was dead, and this time she'd lost Gabe forever.

Chapter Twelve

Lydia stood alone in the center of the small cabin and waited. They'd arrived in Rouen less than an hour ago, and it was time to play her role. For her, this was the most dangerous part of the plan, the only reason she'd been allowed to accompany Gabriel—to play the role of the newly married Baroness Talbot.

This was the role that at one time she'd thought would be a lifelong role—that of Gabriel Talbot's wife. This was the future she'd envisioned for herself—the only future she'd ever imagined she would have or would want. Until he so bluntly told her it wasn't her heart he wanted, but the wealth he assumed would come with her when they married.

He'd broken her heart that day and she couldn't let herself forget how easily she'd fallen for his lies. She couldn't fall for his charms again. She doubted she'd survive if she were foolish enough to give him the power to hurt her again.

She intended to marry the Marquess of Culbertson. Her father had signed the papers agreeing to the match. She was going to be a duchess one day—not because she'd chosen that role, but because that was the role assigned her. The role Gabriel Talbot had forced her into. Because he hadn't wanted her. Except...

I don't regret kissing you.

Well, she'd learned her lesson. She wouldn't risk her heart as she'd done before. They might have to spend the next few days pretending to be husband and wife, but it wouldn't be anything more. The intensity with which he'd kissed her was proof enough of how dangerous it was to be around him. She'd guard herself every step of the way or the outcome would be disastrous.

She erased any softness she felt and listened to his footsteps, the uneven gate of his walk, the muffled drop of his cane hitting just before he took another step—all the sounds she associated with him.

She turned and he was there.

He consumed the space with such a commanding presence that she was always in awe. He held himself tall and erect despite the cane, his broad shoulders back with a proud lift to his chin that was so typical. He might walk with a limp but there was nothing weak about this man.

Her gaze moved to his handsome face and her blood warmed.

"Are you ready?" he asked, the concern evident in his voice.

She nodded and he held out his arm. She placed her hand on the taut muscles beneath his sleeve.

"Come, let us face the lions." He wore the same smile she'd seen earlier, the one that only lifted the corners of his mouth.

They walked together up the narrow stairs and onto the deck of the *Silver Star*. Her step faltered the minute she stepped into the bright sunshine and looked around. French soldiers were everywhere.

"Relax, Liddy," he said, tightening his grip around her waist. He pulled her closer then slid his hand up her spine and gently touched the nape of her neck. It was a very proprietary gesture she knew he hoped would reassure her. It did. It also sent thousands of fiery sparks rushing to every part of her body. She leaned closer to him, then lifted her chin and smiled. That was, after all, what any bride would do if she were lucky enough to have a husband as magnificent as the man at her side.

"Baron Talbot," Captain Faraday said as they neared where the captain stood by the gangplank. A French officer stood with him. "Allow me to introduce Captain LeBrouche."

Lydia kept a smile on her face while she and Gabriel walked the short distance to where Captain Faraday and the French captain stood. She felt uneasy the second LeBrouche looked at her. Gabriel must have felt it too because he stepped closer to her as if he could act as a shield.

The man was small in stature but carried himself with a confidence as bold and intimidating as if he were six feet tall. His facial features couldn't be termed displeasing. He was in actuality a fairly handsome man. But there was a harsh look about him.

The severe angle of his nose and narrow cut of his jaw gave him a dangerous look. But most unsettling about his appearance was the icy coldness in his eyes. She knew at a glance he was someone to fear.

She wasn't afraid for herself but for Gabriel. He was the person the captain scrutinized most intently.

Gabriel held out his hand and shook the French captain's hand. "It's indeed a pleasure, Captain. May I present my wife, Lady Talbot."

LeBrouche slowly shifted his gaze from Gabriel to look at her.

A shiver that she tried not to let show raced down her spine. "Captain LeBrouche."

"Lady Talbot. The pleasure is mine. Captain Faraday tells me you are on your way to Paris for your honeymoon. Allow me to extend my congratulations."

"Thank you, Captain."

"Have you decided what you want to see first, my lady?"

"Oh, no. Paris is such a beautiful city I'm sure we'll never see it all. Don't you agree?"

"I do." He turned his attention back to Gabriel. "Have you been to France before?"

"No. This is my first time. Perhaps you can be so kind as to suggest some of the wonderful sights where I should take my wife."

"I would be delighted. Do you have friends here?"

A most mischievous look crossed Gabriel's face. "No, Captain. But I didn't bring my wife across the Channel to visit friends. I intend to spend as much time alone with her as possible, as I'm sure you can understand."

Lydia lowered her gaze to the ground. She felt her cheeks warm but knew it wasn't because of the mid-day sun, or the role she played as the blushing bride, but fear. Some underlying tension passed between the two men. Something she didn't understand, but instinctively knew to be wary of it.

She prayed the French captain's interest in them would fade, but it didn't. The questions continued, and every new inquiry increased the risk that they would be found out. Only Gabriel seemed at ease, as if he didn't notice the danger LeBrouche posed.

LeBrouche suggested museums they should be sure to visit, excellent places to eat, the latest entertainment. And with each comment, he threw in an inquiring question or two. With each answer Gabriel gave, the French captain's curiosity in Gabriel seemed to intensify.

Some of the questions he asked were so innocent she didn't think Gabriel even noticed how intrigued he was with him. Some were so blatant she couldn't believe Gabriel could answer them with such ease. But he did. The man posing as her husband stayed as composed as if he were among friends and family, while her knees trembled beneath her.

"Forgive me, Lord Talbot, but is it possible we have met before?"

Lydia's heart flipped in her chest. She must have moved because Gabriel's hand tightened around her waist. She forced herself to relax and take in one breath after another.

"It could be, Captain," he answered pleasantly. "Did you happen to attend our wedding? I don't think there was anyone in all of England who wasn't there. There were so many that I didn't meet even half of them."

"No, I'm afraid I did not have the pleasure." His gaze narrowed. "Were you perhaps in the Crimea? I feel as if we have met before but can't place where it might have been."

Lydia sensed a charge in the air. Gabriel slowly lifted his cane. "I was there for a short while early in the war. But I'm afraid the injury to my leg forced me to leave my fellow countrymen to fight for me."

"You were injured in the war?"

"Yes."

"It is possible that is where we met," the captain said. "Perhaps it will come to me later."

"Yes. Perhaps it will." Gabriel turned his gaze to the scores of soldiers searching the *Silver Star*. "Is it customary for each ship entering France to be given such close attention?"

The look in LeBrouche's eyes sharpened. "These are very unsettling times, Lord Talbot. We find it necessary to do everything humanly possible to make sure nothing happens that might be harmful to our government or our people."

"You have had problems?" Gabriel's tone hinted at disbelief.

"Minor problems always surface," LeBrouche added, "but

we take swift action to arrest those who brazenly disregard our laws and threaten our government."

"You have apprehended such criminals?"

"Unfortunately, yes. Several men were rounded up on suspicion of inciting against our government. They have all undergone intense questioning and interrogation. It is our intention to make sure we arrest those who so brazenly infiltrate our country and cause such an uproar. I am happy to report that the first of the executions will begin on Monday. I hope to be able to go to Paris for the hanging."

"There has been a trial?"

"Fortunately, first-hand accounts of the rabble-rousers' activities were provided to our government by loyal French citizens. We hardly need to waste time with a trial when guilt is already established."

"You say these men will be executed?" Lydia asked. A heavy weight lodged in the pit of her stomach and she felt uncommonly weak. "How ghastly."

"Try not to think about it, my dear." Gabriel kept his hold around her waist, then turned back to LeBrouche. "Where will the executions be held?" Gabriel asked, his voice sounding unnaturally calm.

LeBrouche frowned. "Do they hold some interest for you, Lord Talbot?"

"Good gracious, no! Only that as my wife and I will be touring your magnificent city in the upcoming days, for my wife's sake, I will want to avoid going anywhere close to such a horrendous sight."

"Of course. Do not worry then. The prisoners are all being kept at Mont-Valérien. It's where the crown keeps all prisoners awaiting execution."

Lydia wanted to be gone from here. She knew if she thought

about Austin chained in a prison one more minute she was going to lose her composure. Thankfully, Gabriel realized her desperation.

"If you will excuse us, then, Captain. Unless you have need to detain us?"

"No, no. Of course not. I can hardly suspect a woman as lovely as your wife of having any involvement in such activities."

"Thank you, Captain," she answered, forcing a smile to her face.

"You are most welcome, Lady Talbot."

"If there is nothing else then, I believe it's time we left for Paris. It's been a long trip and I'm anxious to get my wife to our lodgings."

"And where will you be staying, Lord Talbot?"

"On the Rue de la Beaucaire. The Hotel de Marseilles."

"Excellent choice, Monsieur. It's the most luxurious hotel in all of France. I'm sure you and your wife will be most happy there."

"I'm sure we will." Gabriel turned from LeBrouche to Captain Faraday. "Thank you for bringing us safely to France, Captain. The trip was most enjoyable."

"Yes, most," she added, trying to keep her knees from trembling beneath her. All she could think about was that they only had a few days to rescue Austin before he would be executed. And what was happening to him every minute he was in prison. A shiver raced up her spine and her flesh broke out in a cold sweat.

"Are you ready, my dear?"

She lifted her gaze. Gabriel gave her a look filled with confidence. She looped her arm through his and clung to him. She needed his strength to survive this. Powerful waves of assurance surged through her and she pasted a smile on her face.

"Thank you, Captain Faraday."

"You're most welcome."

"And Captain LeBrouche. It was a pleasure to meet you. You can't imagine how reassuring it is to know men like you are keeping France a safe place to visit."

"The pleasure is mine, Lady Talbot. I hope you and your husband enjoy your stay in Paris. It is truly a most magnificent city."

"I can't wait to see it. Good day."

On legs that trembled beneath her, she and Gabriel made their way down the gangway to where Hannah waited with their trunks.

"Hold on a little longer," he whispered. "We're almost there."

She stiffened in his arms and he gathered her more securely against him. His limp was more noticeable now than it had been this morning, but she found if she matched her gait with his, stepping with the same foot as he, they could walk as one.

It seemed to take forever to get far enough from the *Silver Star* that she felt safe. The minute they were out of LeBrouche's sight, Gabriel draped his arm around her shoulder and pulled her in front of him. She rested her cheek against his chest and gasped for air.

"Breathe, Liddy. Stay calm and take slow and steady breaths."

He rubbed his hand up and down her spine and she nodded her head because she couldn't speak. Finally she whispered, "I'm all right."

"I know." He lowered his head to kiss her forehead. "Our ride is here. Hold on a little longer."

She looked up as a carriage rumbled closer, then stopped in front of them.

"Do you require transportation, sir?" the man sitting atop the carriage asked.

"Yes, to Paris, to the Hotel de Marseilles on the Rue de la Beaucaire."

The carriage driver's face split into a wide grin before he jumped down from the seat. He waved to a man a short distance from them who rolled a wagon closer. "I will also provide transportation for your servants." He pointed to a cart that followed him. "For you and the lady, I have brought my most elegant carriage."

"How considerate." Gabriel helped her up the steps and into the conveyance. He waited until Morgan had the trunks loaded in the wagon before he climbed in beside Liddy.

His movements were clumsy, and the minute he sank onto the seat, he clutched at his leg and rubbed his thigh.

"It's good to see you, my friend," the driver said before he closed the door. "And you, mademoiselle."

"It's good to see you, too, Jean-Paul. I'll introduce you properly when we're safely away from here, but right now we need to leave as quickly as possible. Before the good captain remembers why he's so certain he knows me."

"It could be dangerous?"

"Yes."

With a sharp nod, the man jumped atop the carriage and slapped the reins. The horses lurched forward and they headed away from the docks at Rouen and toward Paris, and Austin.

As if he knew how badly she needed him to, Gabriel wrapped his arms around her and pulled her to him. She pressed her cheek against his chest and clung to him.

The carriage finally reached the peaceful quiet of the French countryside but Liddy couldn't bring herself to pull out of Gabe's arms. Even though holding him—having him hold her—didn't mean anything special, she needed his strength and comfort right now.

They rode in peaceful silence, neither of them willing to release the other. It was as if Gabe knew, as she did, that it was too late for there to be anything between them, anything except the help each could offer the other to save Austin.

By the time they reached the small auberge, the inn where they'd spend the night, Liddy was so tired she could barely keep her eyes open. Gabe took care of the rooms and she was asleep before her head hit the pillow.

They were back on the road early the next morning, but Liddy didn't mind. The sooner they reached Paris, the sooner they could free Austin.

CHAPTER THIRTEEN

"Welcome to the Hotel de Chandliere," their driver announced.

They'd made good time, only stopping once to water the horses. It was still early afternoon and the sun was high in the sky.

Jean-Paul swung open their carriage door and stepped back to let them alight.

A broad smile lit his face and Liddy suddenly felt safe. No wonder Gabriel put so much trust in him.

"I regret it is not quite as luxurious as the Hotel de Marseilles, but it does have its advantages."

Gabriel slid to the edge of the seat then maneuvered his way out of the carriage. He was in pain. It was written on his face and made even more evident by the vacant look in his eyes. When he landed on the ground a little harder than normal, his grimace confirmed her suspicion.

For a moment he stood motionless, as if he needed an extra second or two to steady himself. Then, he turned to help her from the carriage.

"We're here. You did fine, Liddy."

Her heart shifted at his words and she reached for his proffered hand, knowing his touch would send waves of heat spreading through her. Knowing she'd feel safe as long as she held on to him.

His strong, callused palm pressed against hers like a fire-brand, but she tried to tell herself that her heightened aware-ness stemmed from the danger they'd already survived and the risks that were ahead of them. Except she knew the heat pulsing through her was caused from something different, something she had to ignore.

She stepped out into a narrow Paris alley and looked up. The sun shone brightly, casting a clean tint to the row of three-sto-ried brick buildings, one butted against the other. The only opening near where they'd stopped was a weather-worn door with a wooden barrel for slop sitting to one side and a stack of crates on the other. The place where they would stay was perfect. There was nothing about it that would draw attention.

"Quickly, Mademoiselle," their driver said when the door opened and a very attractive young girl appeared. "Follow Jennie inside. It is best that no one sees you."

The heat from Gabriel's hand pressed against her back as he ushered her into the building.

They followed the girl down a dimly lit hallway and up one flight of stairs and then another. Stale smoke and ale assaulted her nose, and jovial laughter echoed below them.

Lydia knew they must be above an inn because the boister-ous voices they'd heard when they first entered gradually faded the farther they climbed.

When they reached the top floor, Jennie led them down a long, narrow hallway, lighted only by the sun streaming through two half-draped windows at either end.

"Here, my lady," she said, opening a door on the right. "I've prepared this room for you. Your lady's maid will have the room next to you. And you, monsieur. You will sleep here." She pointed to a door across the hall.

Gabriel nodded.

"Thank you," Lydia said, stepping in front of the girl and into the room. Gabriel stepped in behind her.

The room was plain, but neat and clean, with a hand-sewn quilt atop the bed and a thick comforter at the foot. Besides the bed, there was a fireplace on one wall and a small chest and a table with an oval mirror on the other. A cushioned chair sat beneath the room's only window and another chair, a straight-backed, wooden chair, sat on the other side of the bed. The furniture was roughly hewn and plain, but sturdy and serviceable.

Beside the bed was a small table with a jar of fresh flowers in the center. The thoughtful gesture caused a lump to form in Lydia's throat. In this very chaotic and dangerous world she'd entered, she suddenly found something that was normal.

"Are you all right?" Gabriel asked from behind her.

She turned to face him. "Yes, fine."

She smiled when the expression on his face relaxed.

"Would you like some tea?" Jennie asked, still standing in the doorway.

"That would be wonderful, if it's no trouble."

"Oh, no trouble at all."

The girl left the room as the man who'd conveyed them from the docks entered.

"Gabriel, my friend. How good it is to see you in the flesh."

A wide grin brightened the Frenchman's face and in a gesture that was unexpectedly personal, the man called Jean-Paul pulled Gabriel toward him. The two clasped in a heartwarming embrace that exemplified a true friendship. "The last report I received said you'd left the Crimea more dead than alive. I'm glad to see you decided to live."

"So am I, Jean-Paul."

The two friends took a step apart and Jean-Paul turned to

face her. "Do you know I owe this man my life?"

"I'm sure Lady Lydia isn't interested in—"

"But I am," she interrupted. "Rumors of his heroic deeds have circulated throughout London, but not by anyone with firsthand knowledge. Please, continue."

"Jean-Paul..." Gabriel warned.

"See how humble he is?" A glimmer of mischief brightened the Frenchman's eyes. "Only a humble man is embarrassed by tales of his valor."

"Jean-Paul," Gabe warned a second time, but she was glad his friend ignored him.

"Yes, this fool saved me not once, but twice. The second time he saved me from an ambush and took the bullet that was intended for me. He is a very brave man, this courageous fool, and I would have hated for him to die before I could repay my debt."

Gabriel patted his friend on the shoulder. "I'm afraid when we're finished, I'll be the one who's in your debt."

"No, my friend. I'm honored to help. But before we plan what we must do, please introduce me to this most beautiful lady."

Gabriel held out his hand and brought Lydia up next to him. "Jean-Paul, I'd like you to meet Lady Lydia Landwell. Lady Lydia, Jean-Paul Chandliere."

Jean-Paul bowed over Lydia's hand. "Lady Lydia, it is a pleasure to meet you." A frown deepened across Jean-Paul's forehead. "Landwell? Are you by chance a relative of Captain Landwell?"

"His sister."

"Ah, I should have realized. Bravery must run in the family. Otherwise I cannot imagine a reason an English lady would choose to go anywhere with you."

"Lady Lydia is posing as my wife to help me get past the

French soldiers. We're on our honeymoon, you see."

"Brilliant!" A grin split Jean-Paul's ruggedly handsome features. "What a remarkable plan. When I received your instructions, I feared you were attempting the impossible. French soldiers have every inch of coastline guarded. You wouldn't have made it into France had you tried. Dozens of innocent people have already lost their lives because of the official order to shoot first and ask questions later."

"And I've put you in additional danger," Gabe said.

She heard the concern in Gabe's voice and felt a twinge of guilt.

"There is danger all the time, my friend. But who would suspect a simple innkeeper of anything but serving a tankard of ale and a passable meal?"

She couldn't help but be drawn to Gabriel's friend. She guessed his age to be older than Gabriel by a dozen years or more, yet he was still enjoying the prime of life.

A thousand questions popped into her mind, but before she could ask any of them, the door opened and Jennie returned with a tea tray filled with warm bread and cheese. Jean-Paul took the tray from the girl's hands.

"This is my daughter, Jeannette Louise," he said proudly. "After her mama. We call her Jennie."

The young girl smiled and curtsied properly.

"Jennie, bring another chair so we can all sit. Lady Lydia, would you pour, *s'il vous plaît*? I see by the look on my friend's face that he is about to fall to the floor. Is it your leg?"

Gabriel sat in one of the chairs. "It's fine. Just a little stiff from the ship."

Jean-Paul gave him a look that said he didn't believe him, then sat in a chair opposite Gabriel.

She poured, handed each man a cup, then sat in the chair

beside Gabriel. "What do you know about my brother, Jean-Paul?" she asked before taking the first sip of her tea. She couldn't wait any longer. If there was any news, she needed to know what it was.

Jean-Paul's arm stopped midway in the air, and he slowly settled his teacup back upon its saucer. His gaze traveled first to her, then slid to Gabriel. Only after Gabriel nodded did Jean-Paul answer her question. His voice was soft with a tinge of hesitation, and his reply struck like a knife. "He is still alive. That is all I can say."

Tears threatened to spill from her eyes, but she held them at bay.

"They are holding him, along with another British citizen, at Mont-Valérien." Jean-Paul's gaze moved to Gabriel. "Freeing him, if that is your plan, will not be easy. He is being kept under heavy guard. The idiotic French believe they have captured two valuable English spies."

"Two?" Gabriel muttered. "Do you know the other man's identity?"

Jean-Paul shook his head. "No one seems to know who he is. But the rumors circulating suggest the authorities think they've made quite a catch. When do you plan to free them?"

"Before Monday."

Jean-Paul let out a slow whistle, then leaned back in his chair. "It can't be done. That only gives us three days."

"We don't have a choice. A Captain LeBrouche interrogated us when we arrived. He announced with a great deal of pride that the executions would begin on Monday." Gabriel stretched out his leg and rubbed his thigh. "And there's another problem."

Jean-Paul focused more closely. So did she.

"Our French captain and I have previously met. Once he remembers where, he'll connect me to Austin, and we won't stand a chance of getting into the prison without half the French army waiting for us."

Jean-Paul's eyebrows arched. "Then let us hope the captain has a poor memory." He focused on Gabriel more intently. "Do you have a plan as to how we are going to get your friend out of prison?"

The serious expression on Jean-Paul's face told Lydia how risky he considered their mission.

Gabriel smiled. "I thought I'd leave that minor detail up to you."

Jean-Paul laughed. "You know me too well."

"I know you've probably spent every waking hour since you got my message plotting a brilliant plan."

"Not brilliant, my friend. Just a simple idea that might work."

Gabriel nodded. "Are Jacque and Henri here?"

"Below, enjoying my fine ale."

"Perhaps you might persuade them to bring their ale and an extra glass to my room so we can go over this simple plan of yours?"

"Of course." Jean-Paul rose from his chair and turned to face Liddy. "It was a pleasure to meet you. If you need anything at all, don't hesitate to ask Jennie."

"Thank you."

Jean-Paul left the room and she sat without rising. Gabriel remained seated, too.

For several long seconds neither of them spoke. The air crackled with a tension she couldn't explain, yet couldn't deny. Now that they were here, she truly realized how dangerous their situation was. Complete strangers were willing to risk their lives to free Austin. How could she live with the guilt if something happened to one of them? Or, worse yet, if something happened to Gabriel?

She wasn't sure she could survive if she lost him again.

"Are you all right?"

She looked into his eyes and the knot in her stomach clenched tighter. "I'm frightened."

She hadn't meant to say the words out loud. Hadn't meant to let him know how fearful she was. But the look on his face said he understood.

"You'd be a fool if you weren't."

"What if something happens and—"

His raised hand stopped her words. "Don't," he said with a shake of his head.

His gaze held hers for a long moment, then he rose to his feet and separated himself from her. Even though she'd promised herself she'd do this without her heart becoming involved, that had been a lie. She'd never wanted to feel his arms around her more than she did right now, never ached for him to envelop her in his all-consuming strength like she did at this very moment.

A frown furrowed along his forehead as if her thoughts were obvious to him and he didn't like them. He turned his back to her and braced one hand against the wooden frame around the window while he looked down onto the alley below. The gesture was an attempt to distance himself from her. Perhaps to allow her time to dampen the feelings he knew she felt, perhaps to keep her from making a mistake they would both regret.

She suddenly felt foolish again, as foolish as she'd felt that day in the garden when she'd professed her undying love, and he'd told her he didn't want her.

He shifted his weight from his injured leg. The move didn't lessen his formidable presence. Even injured he seemed indomitable, as if no earthly force could threaten him. Yet, she knew it could. He was human, after all. He'd nearly died once before.

She closed her eyes and told herself she could not care—she

would not care.

But she did.

The love that bound her to Gabriel was an eternal love. She knew that now. She would become the Marquess of Culbertson's bride, but she would never give him her heart. She'd given that part of herself to Gabriel the first time they'd met, and he still possessed it. He always would.

She'd told herself she no longer loved him, but she did. And she didn't regret that he'd kissed her. Her regret was that she hadn't kissed him back.

What if he didn't come back to her after this mission?

She was suddenly desperate to keep him with her. "Will three days give you enough time to work out a plan to free Austin?"

He took a deep breath that stretched the material of his jacket across his shoulders, then he dropped his arm and turned to face her. "It will have to be enough."

He came toward her and leaned against the straight-backed chair. "It'll be over soon. You've done all that was expected of you. We arrived safely. The rest is out of your hands."

"I know, but—" She stopped the words mid-sentence.

Heaven help her. She wanted to tell him how terrified she was that something would happen to him. She wanted to step into his arms and lean her cheek against his chest. She wanted to wrap her arms around his waist and feel the warmth of his body seep through hers.

What was wrong with her? Hadn't the hurt he'd caused her been enough to last one lifetime? How could she consider letting him break her heart a second time?

"—I'm worried about Austin."

"I know."

He said nothing more, only pushed himself away from the chair and walked to the door. "Get some rest. I'll have a tray sent up when you wake and hot water for a bath. Is there anything else you need?"

Yes, for this to be over. For all of us to be safe. For you to return my heart.

"No, I'm fine."

He opened the door. "Rest well."

She nodded and he stepped into the hall and closed the door after him.

And she was left alone.

⁂

Lydia paced the room. After three exhausting days of planning, they were going to rescue Austin tonight.

Gabe had promised her he'd let her know when they were leaving, but it had to be ten or later and he still hadn't come.

Jennie had come up hours ago, first to build a fire in the grate, then a short time later with hot water for a bath. After Lydia bathed and dressed, Jennie brought up a tray of food. The food still sat on the small table, untouched.

How could she eat when her brother was probably starving? Or when she knew this may be the last night any one of them might be alive?

What if Jean-Paul's plan went wrong? What if none of them came back?

She wrapped her arms around her middle and held tight. She was afraid. More afraid than she'd ever been in her life. She was suddenly desperate to see Gabriel. What if he left without stopping to see her first? What if he was already on his way—

There was a soft knock and she ran to the door to answer it.

He stepped inside, then closed the door behind him. She

waited for him to speak first, but he only looked at her without moving. She couldn't stand the silence.

"Is it time?"

He nodded. "Jean-Paul and the others are waiting outside for me."

"Is there anything I can do?"

"Just be ready to leave the minute we return."

"Maybe I could help. Maybe I could go with you and—"

He held up his hand to stop her words. "Come here. We need to talk."

She sat on the chair and watched him pull the other chair opposite hers. A feeling of dread settled over her. He was going to ask her to do the impossible. He was going to tell her to be brave, to go home without him if their plan failed, to live the rest of her life without him.

She couldn't let him.

"Do you think your plan will work?" she asked in an attempt to avoid the inevitable.

"Yes."

She nodded then clenched her hands in her lap. Her heart lodged in her throat, and even though a fire blazed in the grate, she couldn't stop the shivers that racked her body. "What if—"

"Liddy," he said, clasping her hands in his.

She squeezed her eyes shut and stopped herself from rambling nervously.

"Before I leave I need you to promise you will do something for me."

"No." She pulled her hands from his grasp and bolted to her feet. "Don't ask me to leave without you. Without Austin. I won't do it."

He stood, then pulled her into his arms. "You have to. I have to know that you're safe."

"I *am* safe. I'll be safe here until you come back for me."

"I know. But if for some reason we aren't back by sun-up, I want you to go to the *Silver Star*."

She shook her head. She didn't want to hear what she was to do if something went wrong with their plan. But he wouldn't let her. He placed a finger beneath her chin and lifted until their gazes met.

"Jean-Paul left two men here who will see that you get to Rouen safely. I've already given them instructions. Tell Captain Faraday to set sail the minute you board."

Her heart thundered in her chest. "No. I won't leave you."

He lifted his hand and swiped his fingers through his hair. "You gave your word before we left."

"That was before. Because I knew you wouldn't let me come if I didn't promise."

"Don't do this, Liddy. I can't chance that something might happen to you."

"Nothing will happen to me. I'll be safe here until you return."

"You don't know that. We have to consider all the possibilities."

The earth shifted beneath her and she couldn't keep her balance. He anticipated that something might happen to him and wanted her word that she'd leave him behind.

She took a step back and glared at him. "I won't leave you behind. You can't ask me to."

He slowly took a step toward her. His eyes were dark with emotion. His pain-filled expression wrenched her heart.

He placed his hands on her shoulders, then lowered his head and touched his forehead to hers. "You've been so brave, Liddy. Very few women would have been courageous enough to leave the safety of their homes and take the risks you've already taken. Very few could have faced our French captain with such calmness. You've already had to endure more than most men are asked to endure in their lifetimes. Now, I'm asking you to do something even more difficult."

He pressed his lips to her forehead. "Promise me you'll leave the minute you realize we aren't returning."

She shook her head. "I can't."

"You have to. Jean-Paul and his family will be in danger if you don't."

She was thunderstruck. The thought of putting everyone who'd been so kind to her in danger affected her like nothing else could have, except—

He cupped one palm to her cheek. "Promise me, Liddy."

Her heart dropped inside her chest like a lead weight. She wasn't sure she was brave enough to leave them behind, yet, she knew he wouldn't give up until she gave her word that she would. She swallowed hard. "I promise I'll leave as soon as I'm convinced you aren't returning."

"That's my girl," he whispered, then leaned forward and kissed her forehead again. "I have to go. Jean-Paul and the others are waiting."

He turned and stepped away from her. Lydia felt a void unlike anything she'd ever experienced before, a loss unlike any grief she'd ever endured. She couldn't let him leave her like this. What if he never came back?

"Gabriel?"

He stopped, then turned.

Their gazes locked and what she saw in his eyes stole her breath. She took one step forward then another. And waited. She'd run the gamut of emotions since he'd come back into her life, from anger to loss to desire to raging need. She didn't want him to leave her this last time without...

She opened her mouth to speak but her words came out as a tortured whisper. "Hold me. Please."

He looked at her, then closed his eyes and sighed as if in resignation to some inner battle he'd lost. "Ah, Liddy," he answered, then opened his arms to let her in.

She rushed to him and let him envelop her.

He pulled her close, holding her as if he never wanted to let her go.

She knew the passion raging through her was real, knew the depth of emotion she felt for him was genuine. If this were the last time she'd have him, she wanted there to be more.

Lydia nestled closer and wound her arms around him.

"You don't play fair," he whispered.

When she lifted her gaze, Gabriel's eyes were dark with emotion. "Tell me you never loved me," she whispered. "Tell me you left me because you didn't love me."

His eyes closed. His breathing turned harsh and ragged. "I can't."

Her flesh burned where they touched, her chest heaved as it struggled to take in even one breath. She needed him to kiss her. She'd regret it forever if he didn't. She raised her chin and whispered a plea that he would end her agony.

His loud moan echoed in the tension-filled room and he brought his mouth down to hers.

The kiss they shared was wrought with passion, with desperation, as if it required him to surrender his soul.

She clung to him because she could do nothing else. He'd stolen every ounce of strength from her, had weakened what little resolve she had left.

"Heaven help us," he whispered, and he kissed her again.

His tongue entered her mouth and she leaned into him, gave in to him, ached to make herself a part of him. Again and again his tongue met hers, the rhythm explosive.

She was certain the desperation in his kiss held some higher meaning and searched to find it. But she'd lost all coherency.

A burning whirlpool swirled deep in the pit of her stomach, spinning, churning, then moved with molten intensity to a secret place lower inside her. A place he'd awakened when he'd kissed her before.

With a heart-wrenching moan of anguish, he pulled her closer.

She clung to him with all the strength she had.

She leaned her cheek against his chest and listened to the loud, pulsing thunder of his heart beneath her ear. This was so much more than they'd shared before—so much more than she thought there could be between Gabriel and herself. How could she ever be content with anything less?

Yet, she knew she must. And so did he.

Suddenly, the cold reality of what was expected of them loomed more menacingly. He stepped away from her and walked to the door.

She brought her hands to her mouth to stop the gasping cry, but it escaped anyway.

"If we're not back by sun-up, go to Rouen and Captain Faraday so he can take you home."

She wanted to argue with him but he didn't give her a chance.

He closed the door and was gone.

CHAPTER FOURTEEN

"We're here," Jean-Paul whispered when the wagon turned at the entrance to Mont-Valérien.

Gabriel held himself as still as possible in the fake compartment beneath the bed of Jean-Paul's wagon. If everything went as planned, the regular guard would be gone and one of Jean-Paul's men would be in his place.

"Halt," the guard demanded when the wagon stopped. "What do you have there?"

Gabriel reached for his pistol, prepared to fire. He relaxed his grip when he heard Jean-Paul's answer.

"A dozen doxies for your evening's pleasure, my friend."

The guard laughed. "A dozen? Oui! Come right in."

Gabriel breathed a sigh of relief then pushed himself out of the hiding compartment and jumped to the ground. "The guard took the bribe?" he asked, rubbing his thigh while he brushed the straw from his woolen trousers.

"Yes, but he didn't come cheaply."

"No matter. Money is the least of our concerns."

Marcel led the way toward the open door and they followed. "The guard only promised to be gone an hour so we need to hurry," he said.

Gabriel's heart raced as he followed Marcel through a small

side door. They walked past two guards lying unconscious on the floor, then to the heavy prison door that led to the area where the prisoners were held.

"There's another guard inside," Marcel whispered.

Gabriel pulled his pistol from his pocket, as did the others, and stepped closer. "I'll go first."

Jean-Paul clasped him on the shoulder. "I can lead the way. I know—"

"I'll lead." Gabriel knew his friend meant well, but he couldn't let anyone take the larger risk. "No matter what happens, get Austin out first."

Jean-Paul frowned. "We'll all get out."

Gabriel nodded then went to the door. "Ready?"

"Oui, Major."

Gabriel pushed on the thick wooden door and rushed through the opening.

The sleeping guard sat to the right of the door with his chair tipped back against the wall and his chin resting on his chest. He was a heap on the floor before he realized what happened. Gabriel grabbed the keys from the guard's belt and raced down the long line of cells until he found the one where Austin was held. He turned the key in the lock, then rushed to the corner where Austin lay.

"Austin?" He gently moved his friend but stopped when Austin moaned. *Bloody hell.* What had they done to him?

Gabriel's blood boiled. Austin hadn't only been imprisoned and beaten. He'd been tortured.

Gabriel glanced at the torn flesh on Austin's back and the burns over his arms and shoulders and was engulfed by a fury that raged out of control.

He placed his arm beneath Austin's shoulder and raised him. His face was swollen and caked with blood, and he was weak and barely conscious. But he was alive.

"Gabe?"

"Yes, it's me. Come on. Let's get you out of here."

Thankfully, Henri entered the cell and helped him carry Austin down the long hall. They made their way past the single guard, then the two in the outer room, and finally out into the open. The minute they hit the cool outside air, Austin moaned again.

"Hold on, Austin. Just a little farther."

"Thorn," Austin said.

"It's all right," Gabriel answered. He knew what Austin was going to tell him. He'd been beaten and tortured, and he'd broken. He'd told them about Thorn. "It's all right, Austin. We'll fix it."

"No...he's..." Austin grabbed Gabriel's jacket and pulled him closer. "He's...here."

Austin's words struck him like a blow to the chest. "What did you say?"

"He's here...last cell."

Gabriel settled Austin in the bed of the wagon, then raced back inside the prison. Prisoner after freed prisoner rushed past him and Gabriel evaluated each one, praying he'd recognize the man they'd dubbed Thorn.

None seemed likely.

He looked down the aisle. Jean-Paul hadn't reached the last cell. Their mysterious agent was still locked inside.

Suddenly it was important to Gabriel that he was the one to free the agent who'd played such an important role in ending the war, that *he* was the one to get Thorn to safety, perhaps as repayment for what he'd done for England.

He raced down the long corridor as fast as his aching leg would allow and met Jean-Paul as he reached the last cell. "I'll finish here. Make room in the wagon. There will be one more."

Jean-Paul left him without question and Gabriel slid the key into the lock. With a loud clang, the latch released and he swung open the door.

He looked to the huddled form in the corner of the cell. The man struggled to sit, but couldn't accomplish the deed.

Gabriel raced to his side. "How badly are you hurt?"

"I can walk, Major."

A stabbing of familiarity spiked through him and he turned his head to look at the man who'd been a mystery to him during the war. The realization of Thorn's identity nearly took him to his knees.

Gabriel halted in mid step. He'd waited more than a year to discover Thorn's identity, spent endless hours arguing with Austin over what kind of man this larger-than-life hero had to be, but the man he helped from the French prison couldn't be him. It couldn't be—because if it was, he was saving the man who would destroy any chance he had for happiness when they returned to England.

He was saving the Marquess of Culbertson.

His mind reeled. This was the man who'd masterminded every covert operation Gabriel had been sent on. The man whose daring and brilliance had saved thousands of lives. The man whose ability to discover the enemy's next moves had brought about a quicker end to the war.

The man who would take Liddy away from him.

He tried to force his feet to move but the battle inside him waged too intensely. The vow he'd made Chisolmwood more than a year ago blared with alarming hostility. He had it within his power to exact revenge on the Duke of Chisolmwood for destroying not only his life, but Liddy's, too.

If he left Culbertson to fend for himself the man would likely not survive. If he left Culbertson here…

"Have you decided if you're going to rescue me, Major? Or would you prefer to leave me to face the hangman's noose in the morning?"

Gabriel's gaze locked with Culbertson's. He saw his swollen lips and the bruises on his face. He'd obviously been beaten, but he was a strong man. If Gabriel got him to safety, he'd survive. And when they returned to England, Liddy would become his marchioness.

But that was how Gabriel always knew it would be. He couldn't live with himself if he let it end any differently. He couldn't live his life knowing that he'd taken the life of an innocent man to exact his revenge on the Duke of Chisolmwood. His conscience wouldn't allow him to be happy with Liddy, knowing he was responsible for Culbertson's death.

He didn't answer Culbertson, but lifted the agent to his knees and half dragged, half carried him out of the prison.

"Cover him with hay," Gabriel ordered when Culbertson was safely in the wagon. Marcel, Francois, and Jacques quickly covered Austin and Culbertson, then jumped in beside them.

Jean-Paul already sat atop in the driver's seat, waiting to set the wagon in motion.

Gabriel rushed to take his place beside him, but stopped when loud gunfire exploded behind him.

"Halt, Major Talbot," LeBrouche shouted as he galloped toward him.

Gabriel turned and fired. LeBrouche and a half dozen other soldiers closed in on them.

"Go!" Gabriel hollered.

The horses skittered at the explosion and Jean-Paul tried to hold them steady. But they were too frightened.

Gunshots rang through the air and Jean-Paul's frantic voice

ordered him to get in, but Gabriel knew his leg wouldn't allow him to mount a moving wagon. The only chance they had to escape was if he stayed behind to draw fire.

"Go!" he bellowed again, then slapped his hand across the lead horse's backside.

The team lurched forward and Gabriel fired his pistol until the wagon was out of sight.

He pressed his back against the wall and quickly reloaded.

Four French soldiers followed LeBrouche into the alley, but Gabe was able to keep the French soldiers pinned behind a wall of crates. He fired as rapidly as he could, then took advantage of a slight pause in the gunfire to make his escape.

He ran down the alley in the opposite direction the wagon had gone, hoping LeBrouche wanted him badly enough to follow him and give Jean-Paul the opportunity he needed to flee.

The rumble of the wagon grew fainter while the thunder of horses chasing him grew louder. He turned when he reached the end of the alley and his eyes locked with LeBrouche's. He veered to his right.

"Let the wagon go!" LeBrouche hollered. "I want the major!"

Gabriel ran faster, ignoring the stitch in his side and his leg that threatened to buckle beneath him. He ran into the Paris streets, hoping to get lost amongst the predawn vendors gathering to sell their wares. The semi-darkness helped, made him less visible. But from the commotion behind him, he knew the soldiers were gaining on him.

A bullet whizzed past his ear, hitting the side of a building. Pieces of brick chipped off. A big piece struck him above the eye. Gabriel wiped the blood from his forehead and ducked into an alley just as another bullet sang through the air. It grazed his left arm. The wound was just a scratch. His leg, however, throbbed like bloody hell.

He'd been in tight spots before and knew he didn't have much time before they caught him. He dove through the first door he could open, that of a rundown barn. It smelled of old grain and moldy hay. He limped down the aisle between the empty stalls, his leg nearly useless now. He couldn't go any further. He needed to get out of sight, needed to find someplace to hide.

He entered one of the stalls and crawled to a dark corner. Just as he reached the shadows, the door opened and a French soldier rode through the opening. Gabriel expected to see LeBrouche, but it wasn't. His adversary was a young soldier, barely out of his teens.

"Damn," Gabriel hissed as he lifted his gun and fired.

Their gunshots echoed simultaneously and Gabriel felt a sharp pain in his shoulder a second before he hit the floor.

❧

Lydia stood at the window, staring down onto the alley, waiting for Gabriel to return with Austin. The sun was already above the horizon. Sunrise had come—and gone.

"You have to get ready to leave, Lady Lydia," Jennie said from the doorway. "I promised Papa and the major that Gustav would take you to Rouen if they weren't back by sunup."

Lydia looked at the tall Frenchman standing behind Jennie, then turned to look back out the window. "Not yet."

A tension-filled silence enveloped the room. She ignored the worried glances Jennie and Gustav exchanged with Hannah. She didn't care. She couldn't leave yet. She wouldn't. Gabriel wasn't back. She couldn't leave without knowing if he was safe—if *they* were safe.

"But the major said—"

"I promised the major I'd leave when I was certain he wasn't coming back. I am far from certain." She dropped the yellow-checked curtain and stepped toward where Gustav still stood in the doorway. "Have you heard anything yet? Have any of them come back?"

Gustav shook his head. "One of our compatriots left a short while ago to find out what he could but he hasn't returned."

"We won't leave until he returns."

Gustav's shoulders lifted as if his size might intimidate her. "It's not safe to wait," he said. "The major ordered me to—"

Lydia raised her hand to stop him. "I know what the major ordered you to do, but I'm a long way from following his orders. Now, if you don't mind, I'd like to be alone." She turned back to watch out the window.

Thankfully, Hannah shooed Jennie and the Frenchman out of the room and followed them. It wasn't until the door closed behind them that the inner fortitude that held her nerves together crumbled and she sagged against the wall. She wrapped her arms around her middle and prayed the trembling would stop.

Something was wrong. They should have been back hours ago. There'd always been an innate connection between Gabriel and herself, and that connection told her something had happened. He'd have returned already if things had gone as they'd expected.

Lydia turned back to the window to keep watch. She repeated the prayer she'd prayed all night, that God would bring them all back to her safe and sound. Over and over she repeated the litany, not even stopping when Hannah came back into the room.

"Why don't you sit, my lady." Hannah pushed a chair closer. "You've stood for hours. Just rest for a bit and I'll keep watch."

Lydia shook her head then looked from one end of the alley

to the other. A sickening dread weighed heavily in the pit of her stomach, a painful pressure that pushed against her heart. She reached out to steady herself against the wall when a wave of dizziness overtook her. Worry, lack of sleep, and no food had taken its toll and she swayed again as the room swam before her eyes.

Then she saw it.

Jean-Paul's wagon rumbled down the alley and stopped beneath her window. Her heart leaped to her throat and her cry echoed in the small room.

"They're here! Oh, thank God. They're here! They're here!"

She raced out the door and down the hall. She took the stairs at an unladylike pace, but she didn't care. Her only concern was reaching the wagon where several men lifted an injured Austin out of the straw.

She scanned the area for Gabriel but didn't see him. He was probably standing guard at the entrance to the alley to make sure they hadn't been followed. That would be like him.

She breathed a sigh of relief as she rushed to her brother's side. "Austin?"

"Liddy?" he answered. "Bloody hell, Liddy. What are you... doing here?"

She reached for his hand and squeezed his fingers. "I came for you, silly. I wanted to make sure you found your way home without getting lost. Thank you for appreciating my efforts."

"Ah, Liddy," he gasped, then coughed. The effort to speak took its toll.

"Take him inside," she ordered, brushing her hand across his face.

A painful pressure tightened in her breast.

His features were gaunt as if he'd gone months with barely enough to eat, and his face was cut and bruised as if he'd endured more than his share of beatings.

The men holding him moved toward the inn and she took a few steps with them then stopped. Someone else was in the wagon. *Gabriel?*

She rushed to the wagon. "Gabriel?"

Two men lowered the second man to the ground and she could tell he was severely injured. She ran the last few steps.

"Gabriel, are you all right?"

The man they helped out of the wagon tried to stand, but failed. She reached for him as he turned to face her and stopped short. "Ga—"

"Sorry to disappoint, my lady."

"Geoffrey?" She tried to recover. "I didn't…what?…"

He tried to smile but his grin turned to a grimace.

"Take him inside," she ordered when he grabbed the side of the wagon to steady himself.

Two of Jean-Paul's men helped him into the building and up the stairs. She took note of the blood running down the side of his face and the bruises turning darker by the second.

She followed as far as the doorway, then turned. This couldn't be happening. Goeffery wasn't supposed to be here. He wasn't supposed to know she was here—with Gabe.

Gabe

She cast a quick glance over the area. "Where's Major Talbot?" she asked Jean-Paul.

"Go inside, my lady. We can't risk being seen."

She rushed through the door, then up the stairs and stopped. "Where's Gabriel?"

Jean-Paul hesitated, then answered. "He was detained."

Her heart raced faster. That was a lie. "Where is he?"

"I'm sure he'll be here—"

"Where!"

Her voice sounded shrill to her ears and filled with a sense of panic she couldn't hide. Jean-Paul's hesitation terrified her even more because she knew his first instinct was to lie. In the end he wisely chose otherwise. On a heavy sigh he said the words she'd prayed she wouldn't hear.

"He didn't make it."

❦

Austin was finally asleep. Lydia tucked the covers around him and stepped away from the bed. She'd cared for him, fed him some broth, and helped Hannah bandage his wounds. She'd done all this to keep herself busy so she didn't have to concentrate on the fact that Gabriel hadn't returned with the rest of them, that no one knew what had happened to him.

When Austin finally fell asleep, she went to the next room to check on the Marquess of Culbertson. He was lying on the bed with his left arm strapped tightly to his body.

"How are you feeling?" she asked, pushing a chair closer to the bed. She sat beside him.

"Thankful to be alive."

Every part of his body she could see was bruised with ugly purple and black marks that indicated he'd suffered the same torture as Austin. "Is there anything I can get you?"

"A glass of water, if you wouldn't mind."

"Of course."

She rose and poured some water into a glass, then helped him drink. She'd done the same for Austin just a few minutes ago.

She remembered the first time she'd lifted a glass to Gabriel's mouth. A thousand bolts of lightning had spiraled through her.

She lifted a glass to Culbertson's lips and waited for the same explosive reaction. Instead, tending the marquess was much the same as tending her brother.

She lowered Geoffrey back to the pillow and sat in the chair at his bedside. She was tired—no, more than tired, she was exhausted. She'd been awake for more than twenty-four hours and nearly every one of those hours had been filled with a nervous anxiety that bordered on fear. Now, the fear was so intense she was numb.

"How did you come to be here?"

She started, realizing for the first time that she'd been lost in thought about Gabriel, and Culbertson had caught her at it.

"I came with Major Talbot. He needed a diversion to make it into France safely. I was able to help him."

A frown pulled at Culbertson's forehead. "What diversion did you offer?"

Her cheeks warmed and she hoped they weren't as flushed as she feared they might be. "The major and I pretended to be newlyweds arriving in Paris for our honeymoon."

She looked out at the mid-afternoon sky, wondering where Gabriel was. He was such a long way from here and with his leg...

She turned back to face Culbertson's disapproval.

"Your brother agreed to let you take such a risk?"

"There wasn't any other choice."

His eyebrows arched. "And you came alone?"

"My maid, Hannah, came with me. As well as Morgan, who acted as Gabe—" She cleared her throat. "As Major Talbot's manservant."

He studied her. "I'm surprised the major allowed you to come. I would have thought he'd have refused."

"He tried, but Harrison and I gave him no choice. Allowing

me to come was the only way to assure he would make it into France."

She noticed the frown on his face and fought a wave of irritation. He'd best not question her. He'd been rescued because she'd taken the risk. He and Austin were both alive because Gabriel had risked his life to save them.

She rose from her chair and walked to the window. The sun was high in the sky. It was past noon and there was still no sign of Gabe.

"What happened?" she said. "How did you escape and Major Talbot didn't?"

He sank back against the pillow. "We made it out of the prison with no problem but the French soldiers arrived before we left the courtyard. The major held them off to give us time to get away."

Lydia's heart dropped. "Do you think he…got away?"

Culbertson hesitated. "Perhaps. Jean-Paul and his men have gone out again to search for him. Maybe they'll find him."

She heard the doubt in his voice. Waves of panic crashed inside her head. She had to believe he was alive. "Even if he didn't get away from them, it doesn't mean he's dead. Maybe the French took him captive. Maybe they're holding him prisoner."

"It's possible."

"But you don't think so, do you?"

"I think you must prepare yourself for the worst, my lady. In case the major didn't escape."

The room shifted beneath her and she reached out to steady herself.

"I know the major is very special to you," Culbertson started to say, but her pointed glare stopped his words.

"What do you mean by that?"

"I mean that before your father died, Major Talbot's name was linked to yours as a possible marriage candidate. Your feelings for him must have run deep."

"Are you asking if they still do?"

He lowered his head to the pillow and closed his eyes. "No. I think that's a question better left unasked."

A painful emptiness invaded her body, a dark void that separated her from the man lying on the bed. She didn't want there to be a chasm between them. He was the man she would someday marry, the man both their fathers had chosen for her. The man Gabriel had given her over to marry.

"Why did you agree to your father's demand to marry me?" she asked, the words escaping before she could consider the wisdom in her question.

He smiled, not a real smile, but a practiced expression she'd seen him bring up before at a moment's notice.

"Because, like you, I had no choice in the matter. It seemed terribly important to my father that you would some day be the Duchess of Chisolmwood, and I was at the age when I had to marry. At the time, there was no one I cared for any more than you." He turned his head and looked at her. "Do you regret the decision they made for us?"

She hesitated. "I could ask you the same question."

He smiled. This smile was no more real than the last. "But you won't."

"No, I won't."

He sighed. "How wise of us both."

Lydia needed to be by herself. She needed to be someplace where she didn't have to pretend that Gabriel's absence wasn't more than she could bear. "I'll return later. Get some rest." She turned away from the marquess and walked toward the door.

"We don't know that he's dead," he said from behind her.

She stopped and nodded her agreement but she didn't turn to face him. She couldn't.

"If he's still alive, Jean-Paul will bring him home."

She nodded again and reached out a trembling hand to open the door. She didn't cry though. She couldn't.

She hurt too much to cry.

CHAPTER FIFTEEN

Gabriel leaned on the roughly-hewn stick he'd whittled into a cane and limped down the alley, staying as much in the shadows against the dingy wall as he could. It had been three days since he'd killed the French soldier. Three days that he'd struggled to find enough food and water to survive. At least tonight the moon was hidden behind the clouds and he could venture a little farther to search for something to eat. Tomorrow he'd have to rest, then attempt to make his way back to Jean-Paul's. Every time he came out of hiding increased his chances of being found.

Until today, his leg hadn't been strong enough to consider walking far on it. He'd jarred it when he crashed through the boards in the stable.

He wouldn't complain though. Falling through the rotten wood in the stable floor had saved his life—in more ways than one.

When his leg went through the boards, he discovered a hollow space that led to a cellar he assumed thieves had used at one time.

He'd hidden there for three days, coming out for only a short time each night to scavenge for food and water. Garbage barrels at a nearby tavern yielded a few crusts of bread, and luckily it rained each night so he was able to catch enough water to drink. Tonight, though, he needed to find enough food to build his strength.

He pushed himself from the damp wall and walked down the alley to the nearest tavern door. Inns provided the best offerings of food. He stopped by the wooden barrel near the back door and tipped the lid that teetered atop the mound of discarded food. Then threw himself back against the wall when an alley cat leapt from the garbage with a loud screech.

He waited to be sure the commotion hadn't aroused anyone, then reached in. He found a half-eaten beef and kidney pie on top of the heap and carefully lifted it out. No wonder the cat put up such a fuss.

Gabriel caught a handful of rainwater before it dripped into a rain barrel and drank greedily, then took another bite of the meat pie. He tried to eat slowly but he hadn't eaten all day and was so damned hungry he nearly swallowed the first few bites whole. After the third or fourth mouthful he leaned back against the soggy brick building and chewed more slowly.

The meat pie, although not the best he'd ever eaten, wasn't the worst, and it might be all he found for days. Especially if his leg didn't allow him to walk far.

He wrapped what was left of his dinner in a semi-clean cloth and tucked it into his pocket, then took another drink of the cool, clean rainwater. When he finished, he leaned on his cane and stepped away from the building.

He'd only taken a few steps before he heard sounds from the other end of the alley. He looked to his right and estimated that there were at least two of them, perhaps three. From the slurred sounds of the song they sang, they were well into their cups.

Gabriel pulled the pistol from his pocket and pressed back into the shadows.

He had one bullet left. That wasn't enough to defend himself from all of them, but if he eliminated just one, his odds were better. Running wasn't an option. His leg wouldn't carry him to the end of the alley before he took a bullet in the back.

He held his breath and felt the familiar calm that always sifted through him seconds before he went on assignment. It was an inner composure that allowed the warrior in him to take over. He leaned his head back against the bricks behind him and closed his eyes while the calm seeped to every part of him.

Gabe hoped their raucous singing meant they weren't any of LeBrouche's soldiers. If they were, perhaps their lack of sobriety would work to his advantage.

He rubbed the throbbing muscles in his leg and readied himself to attack. He wouldn't fire first, but he was prepared to defend himself at the first hint of trouble.

There were more than three, perhaps as many as five. They were singing—

He listened. That tune. The words. One of the voices...

Gabriel relaxed his tense muscles and smiled.

For a second or two he listened to the familiar drinking song. Then he focused on the familiar voice singing it.

With a sigh, he dropped his pistol back into his pocket and stepped out into the alley to let the men capture him.

❧

"We should have left three days ago," Hannah muttered as she placed a tea tray on the desk behind her. "We'd be safe and sound in England by now."

Lydia ignored her maid's grumbling and kept watch at the window.

"Jeanette is waiting downstairs in the kitchen," Hannah informed her. "She made a grand kettle of soup. She's convinced that tonight her husband's search will be successful, but that's what she said last night, too."

Lydia turned away from the window and sat on the rumpled bed she seldom slept in for more than an hour or two each night. "Perhaps she's right. It's only a matter of time until Jean-Paul finds Major Talbot."

"Of course," Hannah said in a tone that indicated she didn't think any such thing. "But Captain Faraday has sailed for England already and we'll have to wait another week until he returns to Rouen."

"Then we'll wait. My brother and Lord Culbertson need the extra week of rest before being moved," she argued. "And Jean-Paul doubted he could get us out of Paris safely. After the escape of the prisoners, the French have doubled their search of the town." She rose to check the window again. "Besides, we're not leaving without Major Talbot."

Lydia ignored Hannah's raised eyebrows and lifted the curtain to look out onto the alley.

Waiting was the worst kind of torture. Worrying was the next, and the two went hand in hand. Living through the night Gabriel had left to get Austin proved that there was no greater agony than the paralyzing fear of imagining the worst that could happen.

Her heart thundered in her chest and every muscle in her body trembled. She'd gone through this torture too often in the last few days. She didn't know how many more times she could endure it or how she'd survive if Jean-Paul didn't find Gabriel tonight. She wasn't sure she could relive this nightmare again tomorrow night.

Hannah poured a cup of tea and handed it to her. She took it, but her hands shook so badly she had to set it down on the table beside her. "What time is it, Hannah? How long have they been gone?"

"It's nearly three in the morning. Why don't you lie down for a while? I'll keep watch at the window."

"I'll stay here until Jean-Paul returns."

Hannah shook her head, then busied herself by straightening the covers on the bed.

Lydia paced in front of the window, stopping every few seconds to look out onto the alley below. The minutes ticked by with agonizing slowness and she checked several more times before she had to close her burning eyes and rub them.

Please let them find him, she prayed, then opened her eyes. The sight she saw took her breath.

A wagon turned into the alley and slowed beneath her window.

"They're here," she said, straining to make out how many men returned with Jean-Paul.

With only one small lantern for light, it was too dark to see each man clearly, but there seemed to be an excitement in the way the men moved.

One by one they jumped to the ground and rushed to the back of the wagon to assist someone. Her hand flew to her mouth when she realized that *someone* was Gabriel.

He moved slowly, his limp worse than ever. But once he stood on the ground he walked by himself, with no help from the men who walked beside him.

She wanted to run down the stairs and throw herself into his arms. She wanted to hold him, press her lips to his, tell him how thankful she was that he was safe.

Instead, she walked across her bedroom and opened the door. A swarm of butterflies fluttered in her stomach as she waited for him to climb the stairs.

There was a commotion downstairs and she swiped away several tears that errantly fell while she kept her gaze riveted on the stairs. It took forever until she heard the thud of his uneven gait as he maneuvered the steps. Her breath caught and held.

The minute she saw him her heart skipped a beat, then began a rapid thump inside her chest.

His clothes were torn and bloodstained, his body cut and caked with dried blood, and his eyes filled with pain. But he climbed the stairs alone.

He made his way down the long hall toward her, using only a stick to help him. His gaze held hers every step of the way, as if he needed contact with her to continue. As if he were silently telling her how important seeing her was. Her heart raced with increasing anticipation.

Time stood still. She wanted to be alone with him, to touch him, to hold him. To have him hold her. She wanted nothing other than to tell him that she couldn't continue living if he weren't in her world. Instead, she stood in her open doorway, unable to move toward him for fear Jean-Paul or Jeannette or Austin or…Geoffrey, would realize how much he meant to her.

He walked down the hall and before he reached her room, the door opposite hers opened and the Marquess of Culbertson stepped out. He was weak and needed help to stand, but it seemed important that he speak to Gabriel.

Culbertson looked first to her, then back to Gabriel. The two men stared at each other for a long second before Culbertson spoke. "I owe you a debt." The tone of his voice sounded strangely official, not tinted with aristocratic formality exactly, but containing a military stiffness that took her by surprise.

"I'm glad I could be of service."

"I realize the risk you took. It will not go unnoticed."

"I didn't take the risks I did because I wanted recognition."

"Of course, you didn't." Culbertson's legs seemed to weaken and the servant at his side reached out to steady him. "I seem to be weaker than I thought." He nodded and the servant stepped closer. "We'll talk later, Major?" he said over his shoulder. "I'm sure there are a few matters you'd like to discuss after you've rested."

"There are," Gabriel answered.

"Thank you, again," Culbertson said before the servant took him back into his room.

Lydia watched him. For several long seconds Gabriel stared at Culbertson's closed door, then he slowly turned. His gaze locked with hers.

Her heart thundered against her ribs. She'd been sick with worry over him. Now, the inner strength she'd forced herself to rely on seemed to collapse around her. She took an unsteady step toward him, then stopped.

She wanted to rush into his arms and hold him. She wanted to press herself against him and touch him. She wanted to press her lips to his and never stop kissing him. Emotions she doubted she could control overpowered her and she took another trembling step toward him.

"I'll bring hot water for your bath, friend," Jean-Paul said, stepping between them. "You'll feel much better when you're clean and you've had a good meal."

Gabriel broke their locked gazes. "That sounds wonderful. The fare I found in the alley left much to be desired."

Jean-Paul smiled, then the smile left his face. "Do you need a doctor?"

Gabriel shook his head. "Just that hot bath and some decent food. That's all."

Jean-Paul made his way to the stairs. "It will be only a moment."

They were alone now. Stepping just one foot closer would put them in each other's arms. Yet neither of them moved. They simply stared at each other, Lydia drinking in every detail of the man she'd been afraid she'd never see again.

"Are you all right?" she finally asked.

He nodded.

"I was afraid they wouldn't find you."

The corners of his mouth lifted slightly. "So was I."

"I'm glad you're safe." She swallowed past the lump in her throat.

He smiled again and she was glad the heavy tromping of footsteps on the stairway kept her from saying more. She didn't want him to see her tears, and he would have if she had to face him much longer. Instead, she looked to where Jean-Paul came up the stairs.

"Here you are, my friend." Jean-Paul and two other men carried an empty tub and buckets of warm water toward Gabriel's room. Jean-Paul hesitated for a second when he saw her, but the spell that connected her to Gabriel was broken.

He stepped into his room with a nod of farewell, and the men followed with their buckets. The door closed behind them and she was left alone in the hallway.

She backed into her room and closed the door, then sank onto the nearest chair and said a prayer of thanks that Gabriel had come home alive.

A part of her was more certain than ever that she couldn't have survived if they'd found him dead.

✿

Once he'd bathed and eaten, Gabriel sat down in the chair beside the blazing fire and stretched his leg out in front of him. Bloody hell, but he hurt. He rubbed the muscles and put another warm, wet cloth on his thigh. Heat was all that seemed to help.

"It's good to have you back, my friend," Jean-Paul said when they were finally alone. "You look much better than you did earlier. And the smell is much improved."

Gabriel smiled. "I can imagine. The barn I hid in didn't have the most pleasing fragrance."

"Then it's as well we found you when we did."

Gabriel took the glass of whiskey Jean-Paul handed him and drank. "I didn't think I was going to make it out of this one. I was fortunate to find an abandoned stable."

"The French officer was the captain you were afraid would recognize you, am I right?"

Gabriel nodded.

Jean-Paul refilled his glass. "He must want you terribly bad, *mon ami*. French soldiers are combing every area of Paris looking for you."

Gabriel threw a swallow of whiskey to the back of his throat. "We have to leave here. Soon."

"Captain Faraday will return in a few days. We will get you to Rouen before he arrives."

A wave of frustration stabbed at Gabriel. "I didn't expect to see everyone here when I returned. I told Lydia to go to Captain Faraday if we weren't back by sunrise of that first day."

"Ha! The lady nearly had anyone's head who even suggested she leave without you. She's barely eaten a bite, or slept more than a few hours since you left."

Gabriel couldn't hide the frown from his face.

"There's no need for you to worry," Jean-Paul said with a smile. "She'll have a couple of days to rest before you have to leave. And my Jeanette will make sure she gets plenty to eat."

Gabriel felt a niggling of concern. "Will you be safe until we go?"

"Of course. The French don't know my little inn even exists."

"Let's hope it stays that way."

Jean-Paul got up from his chair. "I'll leave you alone now to get some rest."

Gabriel stayed seated with his leg propped on the pillow. "Thank you, friend. For everything."

"No, *mon ami*, it is I who thank *you*."

Jean-Paul gave Gabriel a meaningful nod then left the room.

Gabriel finished the drink in his glass, then dropped his head against the wooden rungs of the chair. He'd had so many brushes with death he wasn't sure if he was living on borrowed time or if God was sending him another warning in hopes that he'd take this one seriously. He thought of Lydia and of what could have been, what never would be.

He was glad she was asleep behind a closed door.

It was best this way. Better if she wasn't anywhere near him right now. He wasn't sure he could trust himself to keep from taking her in his arms. He'd given her up too many times already, faced death too many times. Once they were back in England their paths wouldn't cross. He'd make sure of it. Being this close was too painful for either of them.

He clamped his fingers to his thigh and rubbed his aching muscles. His movements stopped at the knock at the door. He turned to see her standing in the open doorway.

He stared at her in silence while he waited for the rapid beating of his heart to slow.

"I came to make sure you were all right." She took a step into the room and closed the door behind her.

She was dressed in white, a white robe over a white night-gown, and her hair was tied back at her neck with a white ribbon. She was more beautiful than the visions that haunted his dreams.

"I'm fine. Go to bed."

She turned and opened the door several inches. "Very well. Is there anything you need before I leave?"

He hesitated. Yes, there were a million things he needed before she left and every one of them involved touching her, holding her, kissing her, loving her. Which is exactly why she should leave his room. Now.

If he were smart, he'd tell her that. Maybe it would scare the hell out of her and she'd *run* from his room.

Instead, what came out of his mouth was, "Why the hell are you still here? You promised you'd leave when I didn't come back."

His words were sharp, his voice harsh. Anger was important right now. Any other emotion would be his undoing. From her reaction, irritation wasn't the emotion she needed or expected from him.

The door closed with a solid thud and she turned to face him. The look in her eyes seared him with a fury that seemed to match his own.

"I'm here, Major Talbot, because for some reason I don't understand, I was concerned for you. And, if you remember, I didn't promise to leave when you didn't return, I promised to leave when I was certain you *wouldn't* return. I wasn't certain of that fact that first morning." She marched toward him. "With obvious good reason, because here you are."

She swiped her hand through the air and faced him with her fists anchored on her hips. "Besides, only a fool would try to move Austin and the marquess. Neither was in any condition to travel."

She was right, but pride and some other emotion he couldn't put a name to refused to allow him to admit that to her. What he started to say was lost to him the minute he opened his mouth.

An intense pain grabbed hold of the muscles in his leg and

refused to let go. He clamped his hand around his thigh and kneaded the knotted muscles, but the white-hot pain increased until he feared he might become ill.

He growled out one agonizing moan after another while he rubbed at the gripping pain in his thigh. Nothing seemed to help. Of all the times his muscles had knotted on him, this was the worst.

Suddenly, he realized his hands weren't the only ones kneading away the pain. Liddy's were there, too, pressing down on his flesh, rubbing against the hard knots, touching him where he'd dreamed of having her touch him.

Together they worked until the pain lessened. Then, he realized his leg wasn't the only area of his body that was affected.

"Is it easing?" she asked when he straightened.

"I need to walk." He pushed himself to his feet and took his first step. He stumbled and nearly went to the ground.

"Here," she said, and rushed to his side. She placed her arm around his waist and he had no choice but to drape his arm across her shoulders. They walked from one side of the room to the other.

"Is it better?" she asked.

"Yes," he answered, but his heavy, ragged breaths weren't at all convincing.

"Keep walking," she said, and tightened her hold around his waist.

His fingers dangled dangerously close to her breast, and with each step he thought that if he'd move his hand just a fraction closer, her breast would fit in the palm of his hand. A drop of perspiration fell from his brow.

"We need to stop," he uttered with the little breath he had left.

"Are you sure?"

"Yes!"

Liddy stopped, then stepped in front of him. She looked up at him with eyes that were open wide and filled with confusion. Her gaze locked with his as if she was as aware of the connection that had always bound them, then she moved her gaze to his lips as if she was suddenly aware of where his thoughts had taken him. He wanted her. He was desperate to have her. To hold her. To make her his.

For several days he'd doubted he'd survive this mission. And he knew that even if he did, when he returned to Jean-Paul's, Liddy wouldn't be there. She'd have gone back to England where she'd be safe.

But she hadn't gone back. She was here, in his arms. The one person he knew he couldn't survive without was here.

"Ah, Liddy," he whispered as he pulled her close. He knew he was making the biggest mistake of his life, but he couldn't stop himself from making it. Then, when he held her so close she was a part of him, the heat from her body set him on fire. Every part of him ignited with a desire he couldn't control.

He moved his hands over her body, touching her, feeling her, gathering her to him. For this moment in time, this was where she belonged. Where *they* belonged—together.

He cupped his hands to her cheeks and tilted her head. The expression in her eyes was that of longing, of submission, of... desire. He knew he should step away from her, but didn't have the strength, didn't have the will.

He looked into her eyes and waited for a sign of fear. There was none. Only an intense desire that matched his own. He waited one more second before he brought his mouth down on hers and kissed her with all the passion he feared he'd never have a chance to share with her again.

Her mouth opened beneath his, her tongue skimming his lips, begging for entrance. Her fervor was more than he could take. More than he could battle against. He opened to take her in and let her find him.

Their mating was explosive. The seeking, searching, finding, exploring—all of it more powerful than anything he could have imagined. It must have been for her, too. She pressed harder against him and held on tight, all the while kissing him with an open-mouthed hunger neither of them could satisfy.

"Liddy," he whispered, gasping for breath. "Tell me to stop."

She wrapped her arms around his neck and pulled him closer. "I can't."

Her words stunned him, the impact of her admission stormed through him like a fire raging out of control. Her meaning was as dangerous and deadly as the feel of her hands on his flesh.

She loosened his shirt and pushed it from his shoulders, baring his chest to her. And she kissed him again.

He should stop her, but he couldn't. He should fight the baser needs that ran rampant through him, that consumed him. But he could no more pull away from her than he could stop his hands from loosening her gown and letting it fall to the floor. With his mouth still pressed to hers, he slid his hands across her flesh, touching her soft skin and cupping her breasts. She gasped when he held her and he took her sound of surprise into his mouth.

"You're beautiful," he whispered, kissing her cheek, then moving lower, down her neck to nuzzle against the tender spot just below her ear. "Oh, so beautiful."

Her earthy moans shot burning flames through him and he kissed the hollow of her neck.

Her chest heaved with passion, her breathing harsh and labored. He knew he should stop, but heaven help him, he couldn't. He needed to touch more of her, to suckle her and feel her tremble in his arms.

He nearly lost his composure when she arched her back and cried out his name.

"I love you, Gabriel. Even though I know I shouldn't—can't—I love you."

He kissed her mouth again, his kisses hot and wet, her response frantic and desperate. "I know."

He kissed her again and she kissed him back. Again and again he took from her—and gave to her, until both of them were beyond stopping.

If Liddy realized the risk she took, she chose to ignore it.

If she realized how impossible it would be to live with what they were about to do, she chose to disregard it.

With a desperation he couldn't restrain, he lifted her in his arms and carried her to his bed, praying that tomorrow they could both live with what they did tonight.

CHAPTER SIXTEEN

Lydia wanted to blame Gabriel for what they were doing, but the fault wasn't his. She played an equal role in what was happening. She'd known the risks when she entered his room. But she needed to see him. Needed to know he was unharmed.

When he kissed her, she told herself she would stop him. Told herself letting their passion go further was futile, even dangerous. Told herself she was in control of her emotions enough to stop him whenever she wanted. That she only wanted him to hold her once more before he was no longer a part of her life.

For a long time neither of them moved. Finally her breathing calmed to match his. He lifted his head and looked into her eyes. She knew he wanted to speak, but words had no place between them. They would only destroy the perfection of what they'd shared.

She pressed her finger to his lips to trap any words from escaping. "Kiss me again," she whispered.

And he did.

❦

Lydia opened her eyes and looked at the man sleeping beside her. His breathing was slow and even, and he seemed relaxed.

He was handsome in ways other men could only hint at. Even with the scars on his body and the limitations of his leg, he was perfect. She knew what she'd done had been foolish, but in her heart, she knew something no one else knew. Especially Major Gabriel Talbot.

She loved him.

Her body warmed when she thought of what they'd done, of what they'd shared, and her heart thundered in her breast. Loving him was so complicated.

And hopeless.

He would never be hers. She belonged to the Marquess of Culbertson. For some reason she couldn't understand, he'd handed her over when the duke had come to see her father. Handed her over as if he hadn't been given a choice.

She slid from the bed and slipped into her gown and robe, then sat on the straight-back chair near the bed. She wanted to understand why he'd told her he didn't love her when her heart told her he did. It was *her* name he'd cried out the night Austin brought him home. It had been *her* voice that brought him back when he'd given up and wanted to die. But most of all, *her* body and heart he'd claimed for his own.

She looked down to make sure he still slept. She should regret what they'd done. And perhaps she did, but not for the reasons she should. Not because she wouldn't go to her husband a chaste maiden.

She stared at the hands that had touched her with such passion, that had worked a magic that had driven her almost to a point of madness. Hands that had taken her to heights she'd never imagined.

No, she didn't regret what they'd done. She only regretted that they would never share such passion again.

She lifted her gaze to his face, and the depths of his midnight blue eyes jolted her back to reality. He was awake, studying her as intently as she studied him. Looking at her as if he were seeing her for the first time.

She couldn't hold his gaze and turned toward the door. "I have to go," she said taking a step away from him.

"Wait."

She stopped, but couldn't force herself to turn around.

"Are you all right?" he asked, his voice filled with concern.

Her cheeks grew hot. "Yes."

She heard him move behind her, knew he was up, getting dressed. She felt him come near her more than heard him. Her body grew warm. His nearness always affected her like that.

He stood behind her, his body pressed against hers. He wrapped his arms around her chest and brought her even closer.

This is what she'd always remember—their bodies molded to each other—his taller, stronger frame wrapped around her to form a protective cocoon—his lips close enough to touch her cheek. She tucked away this memory, to be able to bring it out when she needed to remind herself that she'd been loved, truly loved.

After a long moment he broke the silence. "Liddy, what happened last night was my fault. You weren't to blame. I should never have let it go that far."

She took a deep breath. "Do you regret what we did?"

He hesitated and she turned in his arms. "The truth, Gabriel. I deserve the truth. Do you regret what we did?"

His eyes clouded with something she didn't understand. Perhaps his inner struggle as he decided what answer to give her. His shoulders lifted and she knew he'd made his decision.

"If I were any kind of man, I would. God help me, I would. But I don't."

His answer shook the foundation of the fortress she'd built to protect herself after he'd left her. The fortress around her heart so his betrayal didn't destroy her. Now, she wasn't sure of anything. And she needed to be. She needed to be sure of something, at least.

She locked her gaze with his and refused to allow him to ignore her. "Why did you lie to me when you told me you didn't love me?"

He hesitated, then started to speak. She stopped him with a wave of her hand. "No lies, Gabriel. What did the Duke of Chisolmwood say or do that made Father refuse your offer?"

He shook his head and walked to the window. "Don't, Liddy. Don't look for things that aren't there."

"What's not there? The fact that you love me, but won't say the words? Or is it that you *can't* say them? What happened that day that destroyed our future together?"

"Don't torture yourself like this." He locked his gaze with hers. "I know you'd like to believe there is a way for us to have a life together, but there isn't. I can't ask you to marry me because I have nothing to offer you. Even if I did, you couldn't accept because you're not free to do so. Your father wanted you to marry Culbertson. He chose him for your husband. It's too late to think things can be different."

His words slashed through her like sharp knives that shredded her heart. The pain was suddenly more than she could bear. "What if I told you I would leave this all behind and go anywhere with you if only you'd ask?"

He reached out and clutched his fingers around the corner of the small table beside the window. It was as if he needed it as an anchor to stay upright.

"Would you ask me, Gabriel? Do you want me enough to ask?"

She stared at the tortured expression on his face. She prayed that his hesitation meant he considered her offer. Because she was serious. She would go anywhere with him. She would give up everything to be with him. She loved him that much. "Do you?"

His face paled and when she looked into his eyes, a haunted emptiness stared back at her.

"No," he whispered, and the bottom fell out of her world.

On legs that threatened not to support her, she made her way across the room and left.

This time forever.

❧

The following week was torture. Gabriel spent every minute of his days trying to forget the time he'd spent in Liddy's arms. Then, he spent every night pacing the floor so he wouldn't have to relive how his words had hurt her.

From her pale complexion and the dark circles rimming her eyes, he didn't doubt she lived the same torture. Thankfully, their wait would soon be over. Austin was nearly well enough to risk the journey to Rouen. Just a few more days.

He walked down the hall and knocked on Austin's door. When he opened the door, he found Liddy sitting beside Austin's bed, along with Culbertson.

Gabe avoided more than a glance at Liddy. They were both too adept at reading each other's looks. Instead, he looked at Austin. "How are you feeling?"

"Better each day. I was just telling Liddy that if I feel much better I'm going to run the inn short of food."

Gabe smiled. He was glad Austin was improving. Glad there was almost a smile on his face—almost. He wasn't sure what had happened to his friend while he was in prison, but it hadn't left him unscathed. Hopefully, some day he'd want to at least talk about it.

"Have you decided when we'll leave?" Culbertson asked.

"In a few days. That will give us enough time to reach Rouen, without having to hide too long outside the city."

Culbertson nodded.

"I hope you're not putting off leaving because of me," Austin said. "I'm fit enough to travel. The longer we stay here, the more danger for Jean-Paul and his family."

Gabe shook his head. "My hope is that LeBrouche will think we've already left the city."

"Maybe he's given up his search for us," Liddy said. There was a hopefulness in her tone, but Austin dispelled any chances of that happening.

"LeBrouche will never give up his search for Gabe," Austin added. "When we were in the Crimea, LeBrouche offered an illogical suggestion for an offensive maneuver. LeBrouche's commanding officer asked Gabe what he thought of LeBrouche's idea and Gabe explained why it wouldn't work. After listening to Gabe, the French commander announced that he wished he would have at least one intelligent officer like Gabe to work with instead of the imbeciles France had sent him." Austin looked at Gabe. "LeBrouche is too proud to let that insult go without exacting revenge. You're lucky he didn't recognize you when he first saw you."

"Thankfully, the beard I had in the Crimea served a useful purpose—other than keeping my face warm in the winter."

Austin sank back into the mattress and closed his eyes. "When we return to England, I'm going to go to the country and live like a hermit. I intend to let a beard grow so long I'll frighten the neighboring children if they come too near."

Everyone laughed good-naturedly—except Liddy. "You wouldn't, Austin."

A slight smile lifted his lips. "No, Liddy. I was only—"

Austin halted his words at the sound of footsteps rushing toward their room. Gabe and Culbertson rose and looked toward the door as it swung open and Jean-Paul entered.

"I'm afraid your visit has come to an abrupt end, my friend. LeBrouche and his soldiers are combing the area. They're not far away."

Gabe and Culbertson helped Austin to his feet, but before they could move with him, two of Jean-Paul's friends had him and were almost out of the room with him.

"I have a wagon in the alley. Take only what you can carry. We'll take care of the rest."

Gabe looked at Liddy. "Go. Get down to the wagon as quickly as you can."

She ran to her room. Gabe ran to his. He grabbed his clothes and a pistol he had hidden in the drawer and raced toward the stairs.

It was chaotic, with people running to straighten the rooms they'd just left so it looked like they'd been unoccupied.

Culbertson was already in the alley, and Gabe followed as quickly as his leg would allow. Jean-Paul followed him.

"Take the back alleys and get out of Paris as quickly as you can," Jean-Paul said. "Henri will lead you. He knows the short-cuts. I'm sure the soldiers will have roadblocks set for you so stay off any well-traveled roads. Follow the Seine River. It will take you directly to Rouen."

"Thank you, Jean-Paul," Gabriel said, then clutched the Frenchman's arm. "Come with us. You aren't safe."

Jean-Paul shook his head. "I'll stay here with my Jeannette and Jennie. LeBrouche has no quarrel with me."

"You don't know that."

"If it's not safe, I'll come to you later. I don't intend to be a martyr."

Gabriel nodded, then checked the wagon. Everyone was there but Liddy. She raced into the alley just as he was about to go in after her.

He reached out his arm to help her up but she raced past him to where Jean-Paul stood. "Thank you for everything," she said, then gave Jean-Paul a hug.

"Be happy, my lady. You and my friend deserve it."

She nodded, then stepped up into the back of the wagon.

"Here is some food," Jennie said, lifting a basket into the wagon. Jean-Paul lifted another basket as well as a keg of ale. Jeannette reached in with a round of cheese wrapped in a cloth. "If you're careful," she said, "the food should last until you reach Rouen. God go with you."

Liddy reached for the woman's hand. "Thank you. Be safe."

Jeannette nodded and stepped closer to her husband. Jean-Paul wrapped one arm around his wife's shoulder and the other around his daughter's.

Gabe climbed onto the wagon next to Morgan and reached for the reins. He chose that moment to look back at his precious cargo and his gaze locked with Liddy's. "Put a blanket around your shoulders," he ordered. "It's cold."

Lydia took the blanket Hannah handed her and wrapped it around her shoulders, then turned to wave at Jean-Paul and Jeannette and Jennie. Gabe slapped the reins against the horses' rumps and the wagon rolled down the alley. Now, all he had to do was get everyone out of France, and to England safely.

CHAPTER SEVENTEEN

The sun was high in the sky and they were far enough out of Paris that Gabriel should be able to breathe easier. But he couldn't. An uneasy feeling that always warned him when something wasn't right raged full force, and the voice he'd learned to listen to during the war told him to be on the alert.

He looked to both sides of the path they traveled but saw nothing suspicious. Maybe it was only his imagination. Maybe he expected the two soldiers they'd avoided on the outskirts of Paris to show up with LeBrouche.

Or, maybe it was the guilt that continued to gnaw at his conscience concerning what he and Liddy had shared. Guilt because he hadn't been strong enough to keep her out of his bed. Guilt because even though he knew it was impossible for him to marry her, he didn't want anyone else to have her either.

The thought of Culbertson holding her, touching her, making love to her was more than he wanted to consider.

He thought of the way she'd clung to him, cradled him. Remembering what they'd shared made him want to demand that the Duke of Chisolmwood give up his plan to wed her to his son. But he couldn't do that. The Duke of Chisolmwod still held too many notes. He still had the power to ruin Harrison and Austin if they didn't honor the agreement Lydia's father had signed.

He urged the team along the French back roads as his mind tried to convince his heart of the hopelessness of a life with Liddy. The Marquess of Culbertson's voice pulled him back to what was happening.

"Perhaps it would be wise to stop to rest the horses and take a bite to eat," Culbertson said from the back of the wagon.

Gabe pulled on the reins and the team slowed. He'd lost track of how long they'd traveled without stopping.

"We'll pull into that copse of trees," he answered, nodding to his right. "We should be well hidden in case any of LeBrouche's men come by."

He steered the wagon through an opening in the trees and stopped.

Culbertson stumbled to the ground with Morgan's help and held on to the side of the wagon to hold himself up. Hannah and Liddy disembarked next, but Austin was too weak to get up.

"Don't go too far," Gabe warned Liddy and the maid when he saw them walk into the woods to gain some privacy. Culbertson and Morgan both went in the opposite direction, and Gabe stayed to keep watch until Morgan returned. One of them had to be on guard at all times.

He moved closer to Austin. "How are you doing?"

"I'd be better if you'd find fewer ruts to hit. Whoever told you that you could drive a wagon?"

Gabe smiled. "I'll try to improve." He kept his gaze focused on the direction from which they'd come.

"Are they following us?"

"I'm not sure. I haven't seen any sign of them but that doesn't mean..."

"I know. I feel it, too. Do you have an extra gun? Just in case?"

Gabe reached under the seat where Jean-Paul had placed

spare guns and bullets and took them out. He loaded one of the guns and gave it to Austin. "Be careful and don't shoot yourself with it. Or me."

"Not a chance, friend. I owe you too much. I wouldn't have survived much longer in that hellhole."

"We'll be home soon. Everything will be better then."

Austin turned his face away. "I hope so," he whispered barely loud enough to be heard.

Before Austin had a chance to offer any kind of explanation as to what had happened to him in prison, Morgan and Culbertson returned. Hannah returned soon after.

"Will we leave right away or take our lunch first?"

"We'll leave as soon as we've eaten. I want to get as far from Paris as we can before nightfall."

He propped his elbow atop the side of the wagon and looked in the direction where Liddy should come from.

He heard it first—the rumbling of horses' hooves pounding the ground, the thunder of an attacking army. He spun around to see a dozen French soldiers riding toward them.

"Get down! Everybody, stay down!

He looked to the copse of trees where Liddy had gone a few minutes before. "Liddy!" He saw her running toward them and yelled again, but she was too far away. "Liddy! Run!"

She wasn't going to make it. The soldiers were closing the distance and she was a clear target.

He raced toward her and pulled her in front of him to shield her. They'd only taken a few steps before a burning sensation speared through his side. A second later he heard the muffled pop of gunfire.

When they reached the wagon, he lifted her up. "Stay down," he ordered. "Morgan! Culbertson! Get in the back! Get the guns!"

Morgan reached below the seat and grabbed the guns and ammunition Jean-Paul had sent along. He threw two of the rifles to the back and took the other with him.

"They're coming at us from both sides," Austin yelled. "I'm not sure how many."

Gabe made his way to the horses to lead the wagon deeper into the trees. The second the wagon was more hidden, he threw himself to the ground beneath the bed of the wagon and took aim. His side was on fire and he clutched the flesh at his waist to assess his injury. His hand came away wet with blood.

"They're going to rush us," he yelled over a hail of bullets. "Culbertson. Morgan. Take the ones on the right. Austin, you and I will cover the left."

Gabe looked at the French soldiers coming toward them and prayed they could handle so many. Prayed at least one of them survived this so Liddy wasn't left unprotected.

"LeBrouche is on the left," Liddy yelled.

"Dammit, Liddy! Get down. Austin, keep your sister down!"

"Austin needs me to help him," she argued.

"So help him! But keep your head *down*! And don't watch what's going on!"

He meant it. Watching someone die wasn't easy to handle, even for experienced soldiers. He didn't want Liddy's dreams haunted with the same nightmares as his.

"Hold your fire!" he ordered.

He watched the men ride closer. His heart thundered in his chest, then, just as in battle, an unnatural calm settled over him. "Not yet," he ordered again. "Let them come closer."

No one fired. He held his breath and counted to five. The French soldiers were almost on top of them.

Almost.

Almost.

"Now!"

Three soldiers fell from their mounts. Three times that many still rode toward them. Austin fired his second shot and another soldier fell. Gabriel did the same then reloaded and fired again. And again.

He didn't have time to look at the soldiers who'd ridden toward Culbertson and Morgan. He needed to reload. He rolled behind a wheel to do it. "Cover me, Austin," he yelled through the melee. Austin fired in rapid succession while he reloaded. When he finished, he rolled back into position and lifted his rifle. His gaze focused on LeBrouche riding toward them, but Gabe couldn't get off a good shot. He scrambled into the open but what he saw when he looked up made his blood run cold.

LeBrouche rode toward them with his sword drawn. But Gabriel wasn't his intended target. Liddy was.

"No!"

Gabriel lunged forward and swung his rifle high. He struck LeBrouche across the chest. The Frenchman's horse reared, throwing its rider off balance.

In an expert show of horsemanship, LeBrouche righted himself and swung his sword through the air. Thankfully, he'd turned his attention away from Liddy and to him.

LeBrouche's sword missed Gabriel's torso by inches and instead caught the tip of his rifle. The rifle flew out of his hands and landed on the ground, too far away from him to reach.

Gabe staggered. He could make a dive for his weapon, but knew he'd never reach it in time. As if LeBrouche realized the same thing, the corners of his mouth lifted to form a sadistic smile.

Gabe didn't move, but watched LeBrouche lift his rifle.

There was no place to go. No chance to escape this final attack.

The Frenchman took aim at Gabe's chest.

Before he had time to pull the trigger, a loud explosion echoed in the air. LeBrouche turned in disbelief to where Liddy stood with a rifle in her hands. He wore an incredulous expression as he focused first on her, then the dark circle staining the sleeve of his jacket. Anger changed his expression and he shifted his aim to Liddy.

Gabe lunged for his rifle, rolled, and fired. LeBrouche's chest opened and he fell to the ground.

Gabe struggled to his feet and listened. Everything was quiet.

Liddy stood in the back of the wagon, her face pale, her fingers gripping the rifle.

He walked to her and held out his hands. "Give me the rifle, Liddy."

She lowered her gaze to the gun in her hands and stared at it in confusion. She wore the same empty look he'd seen so often on the faces of young soldiers after their first battle.

"Give me the gun," he repeated.

She slowly handed over the gun. He placed it on the ground and lifted his arms. "Come down, now."

She studied his outstretched arms a second before leaning toward him.

He clasped his hands around her waist and lowered her to the ground. "It wasn't your bullet that killed LeBrouche, Liddy. It was mine."

She nodded. "I know. But...I've never shot anyone before."

"And you never will again. I promise you."

She laughed a hollow laugh. "Austin told me to squeeze the trigger but make sure I didn't hit you."

Gabe smiled. "I'm glad you followed his advice."

She looked up at him. There was a pleading look in her eyes. "Hold me, Gabe. I need you."

He nestled her close and wrapped his arms around her.

"I'm afraid when I'm not with you."

"I'm here, Liddy. I'll always be here for you. Always."

He held her closer and pressed a kiss to the top of her head. When he opened his eyes, his gaze locked with the Marquess of Culbertson's dark, knowing gaze.

Gabriel slowly pulled Liddy from his embrace and brushed the back of his fingers down her cheek. When she hesitated to step out of his arms, he said, "You need to check on Austin."

She nodded and walk around him. He was glad she didn't turn to see Culbertson standing behind her. Glad she didn't see the heated expression on his face.

"Well done, Major Talbot," Culbertson said when he was close. "This is the second time I owe you my life."

Gabe ignored Culbertson's comment. He was doing his job. Nothing more. "Are you all right?" he asked, noticing a streak of blood on Culbertson's arm.

"A scratch, nothing more."

"You'd better have Lady Lydia look at it."

"Yes, she is rather good at nursing, isn't she? She did an excellent job in your case, I understand."

Culbertson's last statement didn't require an answer and he offered none. He watched the marquess walk to the wagon then followed him. "Morgan, drag the bodies behind those bushes, then pull the wagon where it won't be seen. We'll stay here tonight."

"Yes, Major."

He watched Morgan drag the first body, then turned to where Hannah sat in the wagon. "Hannah, could I see you for a minute?"

"Yes, Major."

He found his cane and walked a few feet from the wagon, just far enough so they were out of sight. He leaned his back against a tree and swiped the perspiration from his face. Everything spun around him and he slid to the ground.

"Are you all right, Major?"

"I need you to get some water, and bandages, and that salve you used on Captain Landwell."

He lowered his head to his knees as the world shifted beneath him. He tried to hold onto consciousness but knew he was losing the battle.

⁂

He wasn't sure how long he'd been unconscious, just as he wasn't sure how he'd moved from a heap beneath a tree by the stream to close to the wagon. But when he opened his eyes, he was on a makeshift bed and Liddy was sitting on the ground beside him. Austin and Culbertson were watching from nearby.

The sun was low in the sky, its golden rays cascading around Liddy like a halo, the shimmering sunlight deepening the color of her face, and tinting her hair with auburn streaks. Even in this disheveled state, she stole his breath away. He couldn't imagine there was an angel in heaven to equal her. And the features of her face, the upward tilt of her nose, her high cheekbones, her full lips, all of her, sculptured to perfection. All except her unmistakable anger. And it was directed toward him.

He smiled. "I see I need to offer an apology," he said trying to mask the pain in his side.

Her lips pursed tighter, her eyes narrowed. "Don't you *ever* frighten me like that again."

"You're in for it now, Gabe," Austin said with a wide grin on his face. "Liddy's been in a state since they carried you back."

"I'm sorry," he whispered. "The next time I lose consciousness

I'll make sure to give you fair warning."

"I don't mean that, you…you…" She slapped her thigh in frustration. "You conceited imbecile. Why didn't you tell me you'd been shot?"

"It slipped my mind."

"Liar!"

"Actually, I was thinking about one or two other things at the moment."

"No, you weren't, Major. You weren't thinking at all! If you had been, you would have realized that you needed help. Or didn't you think I was capable of dealing with a little blood?"

"You'd seen quite enough blood already. I didn't want to add mine to your—"

"Oh, how thoughtful," she hissed, and he knew she didn't mean anything of the sort. "What do you think I am? Some hothouse flower that needs to be pampered?" She slashed an arm through the air in frustration. "Some spoiled brat who's been waited on hand and foot?"

He thought the wisest course was to not answer, but that only seemed to fan the flames of her temper more.

"Then, you don't know me, Major."

"I know I owe you an apology. I'm sorry." He lifted his gaze to where Culbertson seemed to be watching Liddy's reaction with extreme interest. He needed to shift the marquess's attention away from Liddy's concern. "Has it been quiet?"

Culbertson nodded. "Morgan's kept watch, but it doesn't seem as if any more soldiers are following."

"I doubt any will," Gabe responded, "until they realize LeBrouche hasn't returned. Hopefully, by then we'll be on our way back to England."

"We'll need to get an early start, then," Culbertson said. He moved his gaze to Liddy. "I believe Hannah's made a place for you in the wagon. It would be my pleasure to escort you there."

Liddy gave Gabe another scorching glare before she accepted Culbertson's offer.

The marquess pulled Liddy's hand into the crook of his elbow, then rested his fingers over hers. The gesture was a blatant show of proprietorship.

When they had moved away, Gabe pushed himself up and leaned against the wagon wheel. The stitch in his side ached, but he ignored it.

"Will you be all right?" Austin asked.

"I've had worse and survived."

"I wasn't talking about your side."

Gabe rested his head against the rough boards of the wagon and closed his eyes. "Leave me alone."

"Are you sure?"

"Yes. Go."

Gabe listened until it was quiet and he knew he was alone. He'd like to say he regretted their one night of passion, but he would never regret it. The memory of her in his arms would have to last him the rest of his life.

❦

Every morning for the past three days Gabriel had made his way from high on a hill overlooking Rouen to the docks to check for Captain Faraday's arrival. Each day he'd returned with disappointing news. Today would be different.

"Is the *Silver Star* there?" Austin asked the minute Gabe broke through the thick hedgerow where they'd hidden the wagon.

Gabe nodded. "Get everything together. We'll leave at dawn."

A smile lifted the corners of Austin's face and he put his arm around Liddy's shoulders and gave her a hug. "Only a few more days, Liddy, and you'll be home. Just in time to throw yourself into another Season."

"Yes, just in time."

Culbertson stepped forward. "What should we do with the wagon and horses, Major?"

"We'll take them with us."

The men stared at him as if they hadn't heard him correctly, but when he shook his head, they held their questions.

"Lady Lydia," he said, "instruct Hannah and Morgan to load everything, then get some rest. We'll leave early in the morning."

Liddy nodded and went to speak with Hannah and Morgan. When she was gone, Gabe walked through the trees to a spot where he could still see the wagon, but was out of hearing. Austin and the marquess followed him.

"Does Captain Faraday know we're here?" Austin asked.

"No. I'll go back as soon as it gets dark. It was too risky to board while it was still light."

"But there's a problem," Austin stated as if he could read Gabriel's mind.

Gabe tried to make light of their situation. "There isn't a problem," he said with as close to a smile as he could muster.

"I can read you like a book. What's wrong?"

Gabriel looked to where Culbertson leaned against a large oak tree near them and realized it wasn't wise to keep anything from either of them.

"Rouen is crawling with French soldiers. They're searching every ship that docks or sails."

"We'll just have to get past them," Austin said as if that was a simple matter.

Gabriel shook his head. "If it were just the three of us and Morgan, we'd take the risk of boarding the ship without being seen. But not with Hannah and Lydia. We can't chance them getting caught."

Culbertson pushed away from the tree. "What's your plan, Major?"

"The five of you are going to be part of Captain Faraday's cargo."

"And what about you?"

"Don't worry about me."

Austin raised his eyebrows and stared at him. "I don't like this."

"You don't have to like it, Captain Landwell," Gabe said, pulling rank when he'd never done so before. "And neither do you," he said to Culbertson. "You just have to follow orders. And your orders are to get Hannah, Lydia, and yourselves to England."

"And you?"

"I can take care of myself."

There was a long silence, then Culbertson stepped closer. "You mentioned we were to be part of the ship's cargo. Perhaps you could be more specific."

Gabriel explained his plan. When he finished, Austin released a long breath. "It's too risky."

"We've taken bigger risks before."

"Then *I'll* do it."

"No," Gabe answered him with a slash of his hand through the air. "They'll recognize you. And you." He looked at the marquess. "I'm the only one they haven't seen."

"I can't let you do it," Culbertson said, twisting a leaf that he'd pulled from the tree.

Gabe smiled. "You're not in charge of this mission, *Agent Thorn*. I am. And I'll give the orders."

Culbertson looked him squarely in the eyes. There was a harsh expression on his face, a dangerous glint in his eyes. "You know what your chances of making it out of France are, don't you?"

"No different than any mission on which I was assigned during the war. It's a risk I took many times over."

"There has to be another way," Austin said.

Gabe held up his hand to stop him from going further. "There isn't. This is the only chance we have. LeBrouche is the only one who could have recognized me, and he's not alive to point a finger."

Culbertson narrowed his gaze. "I can't approve of this."

"You don't have to. All you have to do is play the role you've been assigned."

The marquess shook his head. He knew he'd lost the argument. "Good luck, Major," he said before he turned and walked away from them.

Austin watched Culbertson leave. "If this doesn't work, she'll never forgive you," he said.

Gabe laughed. "If this doesn't work, it won't matter."

He'd be dead.

CHAPTER EIGHTEEN

Gabriel sat in the driver's seat of the wagon and kept the horses moving at a slow, steady pace. He'd waited hours for the perfect opportunity to get them to the *Silver Star*, and it was finally time. He intended to have them aboard just before the ship sailed. There was less chance they'd be discovered that way.

He wended his way through Rouen's cobbled streets, then turned toward the harbor. The smell of the sea grew stronger and his heart pounded more heavily. He checked the pistol in his pocket.

They were almost there. He looked over his shoulder at the seven kegs in the back of the wagon. Hannah and Lydia were hidden in the two nearest him. Austin, Culbertson and Morgan in the next three. And the two barrels nearest the back were filled with maggot-ridden garbage and human refuse they'd taken from heaped garbage containers and slop pails in half the alleys of Rouen. The stench was atrocious.

Gabriel prayed if they were stopped, the French soldiers wouldn't have the stomach to look any further than the first two barrels.

He turned a corner and made his way closer to where the *Silver Star* was docked. It was early afternoon and the wharf was a hive of activity, with a half dozen ships preparing to sail.

His heart pounded. He only had to get them aboard and they'd be safe. Faraday promised that as soon as they were carried on board he'd raise anchor and set sail.

Gabriel moved at a slow, steady pace until the *Silver Star* was in sight. It wouldn't be long now. He was glad. It had been more than an hour since he'd sealed the lids, and even with the air holes they'd punched in the sides and bottoms of the barrels, he knew they must be uncomfortable.

"We're almost there," he said to the kegs behind him. "There are four soldiers up ahead. Relax, and don't make a sound."

The horses kept their pace, making their way through the crowded lane until they reached the gangplank that rose to the deck of the ship. The minute he pulled back on the reins, half a dozen sailors from the *Silver Star* shuffled down the gangplank, pushing two four-wheeled carts.

Gabriel climbed down from his seat, clutching his cane in his hand and pulling his cap low over his brows. He'd let his beard grow and didn't think it was likely anyone would recognize him now, but perhaps if they had a description... perhaps if they were watching for someone with a limp...

He made his way to the back of the wagon, keeping an eye on the soldiers. One group stood around two brightly painted doxies working the docks, looking for a quick coin. Another few sat on crates, watching the loading and unloading of cargo with halfhearted enthusiasm. He gave them a second glance and breathed a sigh of relief that none of them seemed interested enough to walk toward him.

He and one of Faraday's sailors climbed onto the back of the wagon while the other sailors rolled the first cart into position. The first keg was the heaviest and they struggled to move it. When they rolled it to the cart, the lid came lose and some of the putrid slop sloshed over the side and ran down the side of the barrel. Bloody hell, but the smell was pathetic. His stomach lurched and he slammed back the cover.

"We'll dump it as soon as we get out to sea," he said beneath his breath.

"Maybe we should leave it behind on the cart as a little parting gift," one of the sailors answered and they all smiled.

When the first barrel was on the cart, they went back to get the second. Before they had it loaded, a voice stopped them.

"Halt!"

Gabriel slowly reached into his pocket and wrapped his fingers around the gun hidden there. He cautiously lifted his head and turned his gaze to six French soldiers walking toward them.

"What do you have there?"

The soldier who'd asked the question was the only officer in the group, a captain. He walked with a strut and a puffed out chest. When he stopped beside the wagon, he cocked his head as if the decoration on his uniform should impress them. Gabriel's instincts warned him to be wary.

"It's slop. The English sea captain has been hired to take it to the Channel and dump it."

The officer laughed. "That is ridiculous. Why would anyone pay someone to haul away their slop?"

"Don't ask me," Gabriel said, shrugging his shoulders as if the answer didn't concern him. "All I know is that I was hired to deliver these seven barrels of slop to the English captain so he could take them out of Rouen and dump them into the Channel."

The French officer stared at Gabriel with a frown on his face, then placed his hand on the pistol at his waist. "You know what I think, monsieur? I think you are lying. I think you do not have slop in these barrels, but something else that you don't want us to see." The French officer pointed to the barrel they'd already moved to the cart. "Open it."

Gabriel stepped forward. "It's slop. Can't you smell that it is?"

"What I smell could be in the bottom of your wagon to make us think the barrels are filled with slop. Open it!"

Gabriel stepped back with a shake of his head. "You'll regret it. The smell will make you sick."

The captain pointed to the barrel and gave Gabriel a final order to open it.

Gabriel placed his hands on the lid and pulled. "It's stuck."

"Help him," the captain ordered the nearest sailor. Together they pried until the lid was partially off.

"We almost have it," Gabriel announced proudly. The rank odor of rotten garbage and human refuse already filled the air and the captain reached into his pocket and pulled out a handkerchief to cover his nose.

With a hard tug, Gabriel removed the lid, and at the same time slammed his hip against the side of the barrel so the rancid slop sloshed over the edge.

"Damn you!" the captain bellowed as a wave of the horrific refuse splattered down the front of his neatly pressed uniform. "Damn you! I should have you—"

"A thousand pardons, Captain, but it was stuck. I didn't mean to be so careless. It was an accident, I assure you. The barrels are filled with slop as I said they were."

Gabriel pasted an apologetic look on his face as the French captain's uniform dripped with the maggot-ridden, foul-smelling slop. "I will try to be more careful with the next barrel, Captain. Perhaps this one will not be so difficult to open."

"No! Get out of my sight. Then get this plague-infested wagon out of here."

The captain spun around to the soldiers who were having as hard a time as Gabriel keeping a straight face. "Make sure this imbecile gets these barrels loaded, then get him the hell out of here. Escort him out of the city and make sure he never comes back."

"Yes, sir," they each said, struggling not to laugh as their commanding officer held his wet, putrid uniform away from his body and staggered down the dock.

Working as quickly as possible, Gabriel helped the sailors from the *Silver Star* load the kegs onto the two carts and take them up the gangplank. The French soldiers followed Gabriel onto the deck of the ship, but kept a safe distance from the barrels. When the kegs were unloaded, the soldiers motioned for Gabriel to return to the wagon.

He knew the soldiers wouldn't leave until he did, so with only a cursory nod to Captain Faraday, he walked back down the gangplank and climbed aboard the wagon. With a smart slap of the reins against the horses' backsides, he drove away from the *Silver Star*. Two soldiers rode escort until he was far away from the city and...

...from Lydia and the ship that could take him home.

CHAPTER NINETEEN

She was going to die.

Darkness surrounded her. Heavy, dank air engulfed her until she couldn't breathe. She tried to convince herself the keg where she hid was the inside of a small curricle traveling through Hyde Park on a cloudy afternoon. But the longer she was there, the smaller the barrel seemed, the more confining. She gasped to take a breath but couldn't fill her lungs. She was suffocating.

She coiled into a tighter ball and clamped her hand over her mouth to stop the scream she felt building inside her.

Dear God, let it be over.

Let them be safely aboard the ship soon. Let Gabriel lift the lid so she could see. So she could breathe. So she could fall into his arms.

The wagon stopped.

She heard Gabriel's muffled voice and counted to ten. Then twenty. Then higher. It wouldn't be long now. Her heart raced in her breast. Excitement rose to a fevered pitch.

The wagon shifted and she knew Gabriel had jumped from the wagon. Then it shifted more and she envisioned Gabriel moving the other barrels. It wouldn't be long now.

Finally, her barrel moved and she knew she was going aboard the *Silver Star*.

For what seemed an eternity, she remained quiet and scrunched in the barrel, waiting for someone to lift the lid. Finally, someone turned her barrel and pried off the lid.

Even though the sun was hidden behind a wall of clouds, the sudden brightness hurt her eyes.

"Liddy?" a voice said from above her. "Are you all right?"

It was Austin. She tried to stand but couldn't. "I can't move, Austin. My legs won't work."

Her brother laughed and reached in to help her. He picked her up as if she weighed nothing and held her close. When her legs were steady beneath her, he lifted her out of the barrel.

She looked around to find Gabriel. She just needed to see him. Just needed to make sure he was all right.

"Oh, Liddy," Austin said, swinging her around in a circle. "We did it. Gabe's plan worked."

She looked around again.

Hannah was out of her barrel and sitting on a crate, fanning her face. Geoffrey was engaged in a serious conversation with Captain Faraday. And Austin still held her around the waist, supporting her as if he was afraid she'd fall.

But Gabriel wasn't anywhere in sight.

Her breathing raced, her blood roared against her ears, her legs went weak beneath her. And the *Silver Star* rocked as the sailors released the vessel from its moorings and it sailed toward the Channel.

"Where's Gabriel, Austin?"

"Don't worry about Gabe, Liddy."

"Where is he?" she asked again, frantically combing the deck for sight of him.

"Austin?"

Austin anchored his hands at her shoulders and turned her to face him. "Gabe will be all right. He'll get to us somehow."

She couldn't believe what he'd just said. "He's still back there?"

Lydia ran to the starboard side of the ship and stared toward the harbor. "How is he going to get out of France?"

"Liddy, don't."

"Tell me! How is he going to get home?"

"Captain Faraday had one of his men hide a small boat down the coast. We're going to sail a couple of miles downstream and wait until midnight. If Gabe can get to the boat in time, he'll row out and meet us."

"But the French have every inch of coastline guarded. He'll never make it past them without getting killed."

"If anyone can make it through French lines, Gabe can."

Every nerve in Lydia's body trembled. She didn't want him to risk his life for them—not again. Didn't want him to be a hero. Didn't want to learn to live without him—not again. She wanted him here, safe, with her.

"What if he can't get to us by midnight?"

"Then he'll go inland. Captain Faraday will return in two weeks."

"But they'll be waiting for him. By then they'll know what he's done."

"Liddy, stop."

Austin held up his hand to silence her, then wrapped his arms around her and pulled her to him. For a long time neither of them spoke. When he did, his words chilled her to her bone.

"How'd you let this happen?" he whispered.

Lydia stiffened against him.

"Gabe told you he couldn't marry you. Nothing has changed. Father signed an agreement with the Duke of Chisolmwood that you would marry his son. You don't have a choice in this." Austin swiped his fingers through his hair in frustration. "Neither does Gabe. Neither of you did from the beginning."

"Why? Because Gabriel doesn't have a title?" She hardened the look she gave him. "Because you don't think he loves me?"

Austin gave a harsh laugh. "Hell. Anyone with two eyes can see he loves you. But love isn't enough. It never has been."

"Why, then?"

"Don't, Liddy."

"Why!"

Austin couldn't hold her gaze. "There are reasons. I'd give anything if you and Gabe hadn't been caught in the middle of this, but you're the ones who will pay."

"I don't understand," she said, because she didn't.

Austin ran the backs of his fingers down her cheek. "I know you don't. You have to marry Culbertson. It's been arranged. Gabe can't marry you. It's not possible."

She staggered away from her brother and leaned against the ship's railing. The French coastline was behind them, growing more distant by the minute. She searched for a small boat sailing toward them, a boat carrying Gabriel. But she saw nothing. Only the vast expanse of water, land and sky. Without Gabriel anywhere in it.

Hannah came to get her and she followed her maid to the cabin the captain had readied for her. She went through the motions, giving Hannah her dress to wash and press so she could put it on again after her bath.

They'd wait until midnight.

She smiled when Austin came to get her for the meal the ship's cook prepared for them. She pushed the food around on her plate while carrying on a semi-coherent conversation with the Marquess of Culbertson. Then, she pleaded exhaustion early with the promise to go right to bed and get a good night's sleep.

The minute the Marquess of Culbertson left her at her cabin, she wrapped a blanket around her shoulders and made her way back on deck to watch for Gabriel.

They'd wait until midnight.

She stood in the shadows for hours as she watched the passing riverbanks. Every hundred yards along the Seine there was another campfire, another guardpost. How in the world would Gabriel find a spot where he wouldn't instantly be apprehended?

Lydia concentrated on the direction from which Gabriel would most likely come toward them, but the beautiful French coastline held no promise.

Her fingers and toes grew numb from not moving, her cheeks and nose tingled with the cold, and still she kept her vigil. She had until midnight.

The full moon cast a huge, white glow upon the water. She prayed he'd sail through the light so she'd see him coming. She swore if he came back to her she'd never let him out of her sight again.

The minutes went by, then an hour, and another. She stared until her eyes burned and she couldn't feel her legs beneath her. And still she watched.

At first she didn't realize the small speck on the water might be him. But as he came nearer, she recognized the boat and the man in it. A lump formed in her throat and she blinked fast to keep the tears from falling.

The lookout signaled that Gabriel had been spotted and there was a flurry of activity on deck. Lydia pressed herself into the shadows so she wouldn't be seen.

Captain Faraday rushed out of the wheelhouse, still buttoning his coat.

Austin ran up the stairs from below with Culbertson close behind him. They all raced to the starboard side of the ship to help Gabriel aboard.

At last a half dozen sailors lowered ropes and Gabriel climbed the ladder.

His progress was slow. As soon as he made his way over the ship's railing he clutched his thigh. A gasp caught in her throat.

Captain Faraday and the Marquess of Culbertson shook his hand and Austin clasped his fingers atop Gabriel's shoulder. They talked softly and Gabriel leaned against the railing to take the weight off his leg. He was in pain. She knew it without seeing him take a step.

She stood in the shadows and watched Austin take him to his cabin. Tears ran down her cheeks, burning her skin and causing the ache in her head to worsen.

When she was certain she wouldn't be seen, she swiped at the tears that refused to stop and stepped out of the shadows.

Into the Marquess of Culbertson's arms.

⚜

Gabriel awoke from a dead sleep and knew without looking that someone was in his cabin. Whoever it was hadn't made a sound, yet he knew they were there.

Close.

Watching him.

After all the years he'd spent in intelligence, it was something he sensed.

He opened his eyes and slowly turned his head to the side.

She stood still, dressed in white, hair cascading around her shoulders, her arms hanging casually at her sides.

"Liddy?"

He started to rise, then dropped the covers back over him.

He could hardly stand in front of her naked.

She walked toward him, her bare feet making no sound on the smooth wooden floor. When she reached the side of his bed, she stopped but didn't speak. After several long seconds she breathed a heavy sigh that shuddered in the silence and reached for the belt at her waist to pull it loose. She pushed the material from her shoulders and let it fall to the floor.

He stared at her in confusion and when he opened his mouth to speak, she placed her fingers against his lips to quiet him.

In the tension-filled silence, she lifted the edge of his covers and climbed in next to him.

"Liddy?"

"Shh," she whispered. "Words have no place between us. Not tonight."

She rose above him and kissed his lips. Her kiss was gentle and he answered her tender entreaty with all the emotion he possessed. She cupped his cheeks in her palms and kissed him again, then lay down beside him.

He wrapped his arms around her and held her close. She nestled against him, forming to every curve and hollow. With his chin resting against the top of her head and one of his hands cupping her breast, they lay cradled against each other.

The hours went by far too quickly. He didn't want this night to ever end, but knew it would.

Before he was ready to give her up, she separated herself from him and slid out of bed. She gathered up her robe from beside the bed and put it on.

She was ready to leave him but he wasn't sure he was strong enough to let her go. He wanted to reach for her, to pull her back to him and hold on tight. But that wasn't possible and he knew it. Chisolmwood had purchased her for his son and he was powerless to prevent it from happening.

She took a step away from him then another until she reached the door. "Gabriel?" she whispered with her hand on the latch. She didn't turn around. It was as if she didn't have any more courage than he did when it came to doing what they both knew they must.

"Yes?"

"Is there any way we can ever be together?"

A painful silence followed. His lack of response should have answered her question, but he couldn't take a chance that she'd harbor any hope. Through a pain that was more agonizing than he could bear, he gave her the only answer he could. "No."

She nodded as if she'd anticipated his response, but her hand trembled as she lowered the latch.

She opened the door and stepped into the corridor.

He didn't know how it had come to this. He shouldn't have let her stay the night with him. He shouldn't have held her in his arms. He shouldn't have let himself dream that every night could be like this one. But he had no control where she was concerned.

And for the rest of his life he would have to live with this and every other memory they'd shared...and lost.

Chapter Twenty

Nothing was real from the time they stepped off the ship in London. Harrison waited for them at the docks with four carriages. One for Hannah and Morgan. One for Austin, Harrison and herself. One to take the Marquess of Culbertson to his residence. And one to take Gabriel away from her.

She pressed her fist against her stomach. She hurt. Oh, dear God, but she hurt. This time when he left her there would be no reason to come back.

They reached Etherhouse and Harrison kept her close as they made their way up the walk. Ruskins opened the door and for the first time in her life the butler wore a smile on his face.

"Welcome home, Lady Lydia," he said with a respectful bow.

"Thank you, Ruskins. It's good to be home."

Harrison gave the order to bring tea, then led them to the morning room. "Why don't we sit down? After such a long day, I believe a brandy is in order for both Austin and myself."

Harrison went to the sidebar and poured Austin a brandy. Ruskins opened the door and a servant entered with tea and sandwiches that she set in front of Lydia.

"Ruskins," Harrison said before the butler could leave. "Have Cook kill the fatted calf. I've listened to my brother's stomach growl for more than an hour now. Please, warn Cook that he'll undoubtedly devour everything she puts in front of him."

"Very good, sir."

"A toast," Harrison said after Ruskins closed the door behind him.

Austin and Harrison each had their brandy, and Harrison poured Lydia a small glass of sherry so she could join his toast.

"To my brother, who gave me the worst scare of my life, and who I'd miss more than life itself if he hadn't come back to us."

Harrison and Lydia raised their glasses.

"To Liddy," Harrison continued. "Who put herself in danger, not because she was asked, but because she's the true hero of our family."

Lydia blushed as her brothers raised their glasses to toast her.

"And to Major Gabriel Talbot," he added. "A dear friend. One who's not present to hear this, but to whom I owe more than I'll ever be able to repay. He had in his care the two most important people in my life and he brought them back safely. This isn't the first time he's made an immense sacrifice for our family and we will forever owe him more than we can repay."

A knowing glance passed between her two brothers and with eyes that glistened with emotion, they drank a toast.

Lydia wasn't sure what Harrison meant when he said this wasn't the first time Gabriel had made a great sacrifice for their family, but she assumed he meant the times he'd saved Austin's life during the war. That had to be it. And yet...

"Now," Harrison said, refilling the men's glasses. "I want to hear this brilliant plan of Gabe's that got you safely out of France."

Austin related every detail of how they'd hidden in the barrels that Gabriel passed off as refuse. Then, when he feared they'd be discovered, Gabriel had jostled one of the barrels of slop.

Lydia knew if Gabriel were here he'd stop Austin from

making him out the hero, but without his interference, it was impossible to lessen his ingenuity and bravery. He *was* a hero. His heroism came out more clearly with every detail Austin revealed. But Gabriel wasn't here to be a part of their celebration. He'd chosen to make their break clean.

Lydia thought of the nights they'd spent in each other's arms. Was it possible that his world hadn't changed as drastically as hers?

Was it possible that what they'd shared had meant nothing to him?

A niggling wave of trepidation gnawed away at her, causing an uneasy feeling to sit in the pit of her stomach and refuse to go away.

He'd meant it when he'd said there wasn't any way they could ever be together, but somehow she knew separating himself from her hadn't been his choice. She knew he didn't intend to see her again. But the reason wasn't because he didn't care for her enough. She would know if that were the case. If there was one thing she was certain of, it was that Major Gabriel Talbot cared for her. No, not just *cared* for her.

Major Gabriel Talbot *loved* her.

Lydia smiled—not a small grin she could hide behind the cup of tea she'd raised to her mouth, but a wide, euphoric smile that made her want to shout with glee. Gabriel loved her just as she loved him, injured leg included. But there was a reason he'd walked away from her, and it had nothing to do with the dowry he'd used as an excuse not to marry her.

An explosion of light ignited somewhere inside her breast. She wasn't sure what it meant, but it gave her a glimmer of hope. If she could discover the reason he thought he couldn't marry her...

"Why did Gabriel refuse to marry me a year ago?"

Her question couldn't have had a greater impact if she'd dropped a cannon ball in the middle of their sitting room. The glass in Harrison's hand stopped mid-way to his mouth and Austin sputtered as he tried to swallow the sip of brandy that suddenly seemed to have difficulty going down.

"Would you like me to repeat my question?" she said, watching the color fade on both her brothers' faces. "What was the *real* reason Gabriel—"

"We heard you," Harrison interrupted.

Of her two brothers, he seemed to recover first. Austin, however, kept his gaze focused on some insignificant spot on the other side of the room.

"You know what Gabriel told you," Harrison said.

"I know that what he told me was a lie. My dowry meant nothing to him."

"What would you have lived on?"

Lydia smiled. "I have Southerby Manor."

"Do you think that would have been enough?"

Lydia wanted to laugh. "Yes, it would have been enough. We loved each other," she said, rising from the sofa. "Love and Southerby Manor would have been more than enough."

She moved her gaze from one brother to the other. "What happened when Gabriel met with Father? You were there. What did Father say that forced Gabriel to tell me he didn't love me?"

A soft knock on the door prevented her brothers from having to answer her question.

"The Duke of Chisolmwood is here," Ruskins announced. "I suggested that now was not a good time but he was quite insistent."

Harrison and Austin exchanged uncomfortable looks, then Harrison rose from his chair. "Show the duke in, Ruskins."

"Very well."

The Duke of Chisolmwood walked in without being announced.

"Your Grace," Harrison said stepping away from his chair.

"Etherington."

The greetings were stilted. When they'd finished with the required pleasantries, the duke turned his attention to Lydia. A chill ran down her spine.

"I'm glad to see you are no longer missing." He studied her with an assessing glint.

"I was hardly missing, Your Grace. I was visiting a friend."

"Whom were you visiting?"

Lydia tried to make her lie convincing. "I spent last month in the country."

"How interesting, then, that you were seen disembarking from the *Silver Star* just a few hours ago along with your brother, Captain Landwell, and Major Talbot."

Lydia fought the warning that caused her blood to rush to her head. "Then you also know that your son, the Marquess of Culbertson, disembarked from that same ship."

"Yes. I just left my son and heard some fabrication that doesn't bear repeating. I thought perhaps you might be able to enlighten me as to the real reason you went to France."

"I'm afraid I can't. Where I've been isn't open for discussion."

The Duke of Chisolmwood's eyebrows narrowed. "Then perhaps we should move on to a topic that *is* open for discussion."

"And what might that be?"

"The announcement of your engagement to my son."

Lydia's breath caught in her throat. "I—"

His Grace held up a hand to stop her from continuing. "I just informed my son that I will schedule a celebration to announce your engagement a week from today."

"Your son agreed?"

"Of course. He knows his duty. He's known for more than a year that he's required to marry you."

Lydia clasped her hands in front of her and faced their guest. "Because it's his *duty*?"

"Liddy," Harrison said, his voice filled with warning.

She ignored him. She was tired and frustrated and her nerves were stretched to the limit. The man she wanted to spend the rest of her life with had just walked away from her for the second time. Now, the Duke of Chisolmwood was explaining that his son would marry her 'because it was his duty' and she would marry him for the same reason. Well, she didn't care a fig about *duty*.

She glared at the duke. "Perhaps," she said louder than she intended, "I prefer to have a *choice* in selecting the man I'm to marry."

"You don't *have* a choice. You never did. Your year of mourning allowed you a postponement, not a reprieve."

"Because my father signed some paper?"

"Yes. Because your father signed some paper. A legal agreement, signed by your father and witnessed by your brothers."

Lydia's gaze darted to Harrison, then to Austin. She couldn't believe they'd had a hand in her betrayal. They both knew how much she and Gabriel loved each other. "How could you?"

"Oh, don't blame them," Chisolmwood said. "They had no more choice than your father."

Her blood ran cold and she took a step closer to the Duke of Chisolmwood. "What did you say that made my father sign your agreement?"

"Nothing, really. I simply gave him a choice he couldn't refuse."

"What choice?"

Chisolmwood's brows arched and he looked toward Harrison, then back to her. "Your father didn't tell you?"

Lydia couldn't hide her surprise. "Tell me what?"

Chisolmwood smiled, then gave a bitter laugh. "He took our secret to his grave. How like him."

"What secret was there between you and my father? And what choice did you give him?"

Chisolmwood hesitated, then answered her with a staggering degree of haughty confidence. "I gave him the choice of making you the Duchess of Chisolmwood, or, allowing you to marry a penniless major and bringing about the total ruination of himself and your brothers."

Lydia swayed and Harrison's arm was there to support her. "You threatened to ruin Father?"

She looked up and saw a dark, angry stain in Harrison's eyes. Austin hadn't moved from the center of the room but the glare in his eyes was even blacker than Harrison's.

"And Gabriel? Is that why he told me he didn't want to marry me?"

The room filled with a deadly silence as she looked from one brother to the other, then finally focused all her bitterness on the Duke of Chisolmwood. "Why is it so important that I marry your son?"

Chisolmwood took a regal step forward and breathed in a breath so huge it lifted his shoulders. "Because you were born to be a duchess." He slashed his hand through the air. "Just as your mother was. Until *he* stole her from me."

The hostility in Chisolmwood's voice shocked her. She opened her mouth to speak but no words came out.

"You were in love with our mother?" Austin said.

"And she was in love with me! Until your father forced her to marry him!"

Lydia looked first at Harrison, then Austin. The shocked expressions on their faces told her Chisolmwood's revelation was as complete a surprise to them as it was to her.

Lydia shook her head. The duke was mistaken. Her mother and father had been more in love than any two people she'd ever known. Obviously, though, Chisolmwood had never recovered from loving a woman he couldn't have. "So you decided if you couldn't have my mother, your son would have me?"

Chisolmwood smiled. "You're so much like her you could be my Genevieve in the flesh. If only I could have saved her from the life she had, married to *him*."

Lydia stepped out of the protective cocoon Austin and Harrison had formed around her and walked to the other side of the room.

She kept her back to the duke and for several long seconds stared at the lifeless logs in the grate. When she couldn't stand the anger raging through her any longer, she slowly turned to face him.

"What did you use to blackmail my father?"

"His debts."

"How much?"

The corners of Chisolmwood's mouth lifted. "More than your brothers and Major Talbot could begin to pay. Although they've made a valiant effort to do so."

She remembered Gabriel's demand for the largest note in exchange for his presence at the ball Chisolmwood hosted.

Her world shifted around her. To keep her father and brothers from being ruined, Gabriel had told her he didn't love her. Then he'd demanded the largest of her father's notes. She focused her gaze on Harrison. "How much is left to pay?"

The expression on Harrison's face turned hopeless. "More than we could pay if I sold everything we own."

Lydia's heart plummeted to the pit of her stomach. "And if I refuse your son's offer?" She faced Chisolmwood bravely even though a feeling of dread overwhelmed her.

"Everything that isn't entailed will be mine, and everything that is entailed will fall to ruin in a matter of a few years."

Lydia fought the thundering of her heart. This was the same choice Gabriel had faced. "You're that desperate for your son to marry me?"

"I'm that desperate to make your mother's daughter a duchess. I'm that desperate to give you everything I wanted to give your mother but couldn't."

"Even though you know I don't love your son but love someone else? The same as my mother loved someone else and didn't love you?"

"No! Your mother loved me. She always loved me. Always!"

Lydia suddenly realized that the Duke of Chisolmwood had lived with the delusion of her mother's love for so long his fantasy had become a reality. Which meant there were no lengths to which he wouldn't go to see her married to his son.

"My son will come to see you shortly."

Lydia tried to meet the duke's threats with a courage she far from felt. As if he realized the threat she was about to make, he held up his hand to stop her words.

"You'll accept his offer. You are too much like your mother to do anything different. You will make whatever sacrifice is necessary to save your brothers from ruin."

"Is that what you think my mother did?"

"Of course. With never a word of complaint."

Lydia stared at Chisolmwood and searched for the words that would make him believe her mother had been happy with her father. But she suspected anything she said would fall on deaf ears.

She let her gaze move to where her brothers stood together. The soldier in Austin faced her with his jaw clenched tight, his shoulders squared, with the forced bravado of a man facing a firing squad. In contrast, Harrison studied her with the quiet strength that had always been his forte. Oh, how she loved them.

She knew how much they hurt for her, knew how much they wanted things to be different, but nothing could change what she had to do.

"Liddy—" Harrison started to say but Lydia held up her hand.

"Don't. You've known all along how this had to end."

Lydia faced the duke. "You may tell your son I shall be expecting him to call."

She turned away from him before she had to see the superior gloat of victory on his face, and walked toward the door. She couldn't stand to be in the room with the man who'd just destroyed her chance for happiness, and yet...

She stopped when she reached the door. She couldn't leave without telling the Duke of Chisolmwood something she hadn't told another living soul, something even her brothers didn't know. She turned.

"I was with my mother when she died. She was very weak and in a great deal of pain. But at the end, she wouldn't take any more laudanum because she said it muddled her mind. I sat beside her on the bed and she took my hand and pulled me close. She wanted to make sure I heard her last words."

"What did she say?" The look on Chisolmwood's face filled with hopeful anticipation.

"She said, 'Take care of your father. Leaving him behind is the hardest thing I've ever had to do.'"

Lydia didn't wait to see Chisolmwood's reaction but stepped

out of the room and closed the door behind her.

She thought of her life without Gabriel and understood what her mother had meant.

Chapter Twenty-One

Lydia made her way through the crush in the Plunkett's ballroom on her way to the terrace. The crowd was unbelievable tonight, with nearly all of Society back for the start of the Season.

It had been nearly a week since they'd returned from France, and each night she'd gone to either a ball, a musicale, or the opera.

As everyone in Society had noted, the Marquess of Culbertson had also been in attendance.

She glanced to an alcove at the back of the room near the door that led outside and studied him. He was deep in conversation with her friend Emmeline. The two seemed to get along very well so Lydia didn't feel guilty about leaving him.

She left the ballroom and breathed in the cool night air. With a heavy sigh, she rubbed her fingers against her temples. She was as tired as she'd ever been. And as confused.

Culbertson had come to see her as his father said he would, and he'd asked her to marry him. She'd accepted because she had no choice. Not if she wanted to keep her brothers from losing everything. She didn't doubt for a second that the Duke of Chisolmwood would follow through on his threat.

Lydia took in a huge gulp of air and hugged her middle. If only she'd never met Gabriel. If only she'd never fallen in love with him. If only they'd never made love. Then she wouldn't know how wonderful love could be. Or how much she would always miss him.

She felt like a fragile string being pulled so tightly she was ready to snap. She'd never considered herself as having a delicate disposition. Never thought she might fall apart at the slightest provocation. But that's how she felt now—as if the next step she took might not be on solid ground and she'd fall into a pit so deep she'd never be able to climb out.

And it was all his fault. Gabriel's. Twice she'd thought she'd lost him in France, but even that hadn't been as painful as when he'd walked out of her life the day they returned. She knew then that he'd never come back and she wasn't sure she was brave enough to survive on her own.

She wanted to laugh. This was his fault, too. She desperately wanted to be alone with him, to sit with him someplace quiet and talk, to let him hold her and kiss her and make love to her.

She thought of the Marquess of Culbertson talking to Emmeline in the candlelit alcove and wondered how long she could be gone before they'd miss her. She knew not long, and took a step toward the doorway, then stopped when a voice whispered from behind her.

"Have you come out to enjoy the beautiful evening?"

The earth shifted beneath her. For just a second she was afraid to turn around in case the voice didn't belong to Gabriel. In case there was someone else in the world whose nearness sent shivers down her spine. In case there was someone else with the ability to cause her heart to thunder in her breast.

But she knew there wasn't.

She prepared to show him she hadn't given him a thought since he'd left, and slowly turned around. It only took one look for her breath to catch in her throat and her heart to soar. She had to force herself to breathe.

"Gabriel."

"Lady Lydia." He bowed politely. "How are you?"

"Very well, thank you. And you?"

He smiled. "I've been well."

His gaze didn't leave her face. It was as if he was memorizing every feature. She felt the same, as if he might have changed in the last week. She studied him to make sure he hadn't.

"I'm rather surprised to see you here. I don't remember that you were especially fond of crowds."

"I'm not."

An uncomfortable silence stretched between them and she filled the gap with the first words that came to mind. "I was just returning to Lord Culbertson. He's waiting for me. Would you care to join us?"

Gabriel shook his head. "I came to talk to you."

She hesitated. "I don't think—"

"It won't take long."

When she hesitated longer he finished with, "It's important, Liddy."

He stepped closer and leaned against the stone railing.

She knew from experience it was his habit to take his weight off his injured leg when it ached. "How is your leg?"

He lifted his cane and smiled. "Getting stronger. I won't be a threat on the dance floor any time soon, but now I can walk across a ballroom floor without making a spectacle of myself."

"At least you have an excuse. I danced with Lord Bingly earlier this evening. Looking at him, you'd think he had two perfectly good legs. My toes found out how deceiving appearances can be."

She was glad her comment elicited a small chuckle. She suddenly felt somewhat uncomfortable. "Harrison tells me the

Queen has requested to see you. Have you been yet?"

"I have an audience with her tomorrow."

Lydia thought how exciting it was that the Queen had asked to see him and wished she could be there when he returned to hear every word Her Majesty said to him. She suddenly recalled how the two of them had shared every event with the other, every thought.

Her heart gave a sudden lurch, then settled into a soft ache because she knew that would never happen again.

She almost wished she'd never discovered why he'd lied to her when he'd said he wouldn't marry her without her dowry. She wished she didn't understand how difficult it had been for him to walk away from her that day.

"Has the Marquess of Culbertson asked for your hand yet?"

Lydia's heart shifted painfully in her chest. She reached out to steady herself against the stone railing. After she composed herself, she took a deep breath and turned to face him with a broad smile on her face. "Yes, Geoffrey asked me to marry him."

Gabriel paused, but in the dim moonlight she couldn't tell if his expression changed.

"Did you give him an answer?"

"Of course. Haven't you heard? The duke is hosting a gala affair tomorrow night to announce our engagement. All of London will be there. I'm surprised you weren't invited. In a way, you *are* responsible for the two of us getting together."

"I am, aren't I."

She dropped her hand from the railing and gave him her back. Before she had time to move she felt him step up behind her. His body towered over her, big and warm, all strength and power, and her breath caught in her throat. She waited for him to touch her, praying he would, fearing he wouldn't.

Ever so lightly, he placed his hands atop her shoulders, gently pulling her back against him, back to chest, hips to loins, legs to thighs. An explosive heat surged through her and she leaned more snugly against him.

She didn't want to be separated from him, didn't want to think of having to step out of his arms.

She leaned her head back against his chest. "I know now what happened the day Chisolmwood came to see Father. I know why you lied to me."

His muscles stiffened around her.

"Damn," he whispered.

"It's not your fault, Gabriel. I know that now. I would have made the same choice if our roles had been reversed."

He nestled her closer. "I know you would have, but I hoped you'd never find out."

"I'm glad I did. At least now I know you love me. Even when you told me you didn't. And I can tell you that I'll always love you."

He moaned a sigh of anguish that shattered her heart.

"I'd give anything if things could be different," he whispered, then lowered his head and placed a soft, gentle kiss in the crease where her shoulder began its rise to her throat.

Her tiny moan escaped into the nighttime sky. "But they can't."

He kissed her again, then dropped his hands from around her. A huge gulf of emptiness washed over her.

It was over. Now she'd have only this last memory to add to the others.

She took a big breath that hurt going in, then stepped away from him. "I have to return. I'm sure Lord Culbertson wonders where I've gone."

She put one foot in front of the other and walked away from him this one last time.

"Are you with child?" His voice was little more than a whisper.

She stopped as if she'd come upon a brick wall. She hurt, more than she thought it was possible to hurt.

Oh, how she'd love to be able to look him in the eyes and tell him she was. If the Duke of Chisolmwood hadn't ruined their lives, having Gabriel's baby would have been the most wonderful event of her life. Instead, she'd cried for days when her monthly courses proved that she'd lost all connection to Gabriel forever.

She didn't turn around, she couldn't face him.

"No, there's no child. We can both walk away this time with no regrets."

And Lydia walked away from him.

Somehow she made her way across the terrace with her head high. She placed a smile on her face before she stepped into the ballroom, then stopped short when she collided with the Marquess of Culbertson.

He looked at her a long time, then held out his arm. When she placed her hand on it, he rested his fingers atop hers and patted her hand in a reassuring, yet somehow understanding gesture.

He looked down at her the same time she looked up, and he smiled. "Perhaps before tomorrow night, you and I should talk."

❧

Gabriel walked at Harrison's side as they left the Queen's private rooms. His cane hit the hardwood floor with a resounding echo, his uneven gait, now familiar to his ears, was more pronounced as they walked through the great halls. First one, then another bewigged footman opened doors as they made their way through the maze of corridors. Gabriel's heart skipped a beat as a strange hitch pulsed inside his chest.

He'd expected Her Highness's gratitude for the role he'd played in the Crimea. He hadn't expected the rest.

A footman opened the last door and bright sunshine hit his face, a sign that perfectly matched his mood. He and Harrison walked across the red brick drive to where their carriage awaited them. Harrison climbed in first, with Gabriel following after him. Gabriel sank down onto the plush burgundy leather and closed his eyes in disbelief. He had everything he'd always dreamed of having.

If only he had someone to share it with.

"I thought Her Highness was in a very good mood today," Harrison said when they were on their way.

Gabriel's loud laughter echoed inside the carriage. "Good mood? Good mood! Bloody hell! I'm afraid that before I reach my small, dingy flat she'll realize what she's done and take everything back."

Harrison laughed. "Oh, you mean the two country estates she gave you—both of which are extremely profitable, I might add. And the London town house. Quite an enviable piece of property. I know a number of men who've had their eye on it for a long time to no avail."

"It was too much."

Harrison focused his gaze on Gabriel. "How much would you put on even one of the lives you saved when you took those papers from that Russian general?"

"I didn't do it because I thought I'd be rewarded."

"No one thinks you did."

Gabriel sat back against the seat and tried to digest the vastness of what the queen had bestowed on him. He was a rich man. Far wealthier than he'd ever dreamed of being.

Oh, not in coin. Her Majesty hadn't given him a monetary

reward of any great sum. But in time, the land she'd given him would make him wealthy.

He closed his eyes to block out Lydia's image. His wealth no longer mattered without her to share it with.

He knew he shouldn't ask, yet he couldn't keep from finding out. "I hear tonight is the ball to announce your sister's engagement. I'm sure the Duke of Chisolmwood is pleased his plan is finally fulfilled."

Harrison turned to look out the window. "I'm sorry, Gabe. I tried to get father's debts paid before Lydia had to marry Culbertson but the amount was just so damned huge. How Father could have been so irresponsible is beyond comprehension."

"Lydia said he wasn't the same after your mother died."

"No, he never got over her death." He turned back to face Gabriel, his expression filled with amazement. "Do you know the reason Chisolmwood went to such lengths to force Father to sign the betrothal agreement?"

Gabe shook his head. This was a part of the mystery he couldn't understand.

"Chisolmwood was madly in love with Mother. He spent his whole life thinking she loved him, too. In his demented mind he's convinced Mother was unhappy with Father."

"Hell," Gabriel hissed through his clenched teeth. He knew there was a hidden reason why Chisolmwood had gone to such lengths, but nothing as unbelievable as this. "So, Liddy is your mother's replacement."

For several long minutes neither of them spoke. Finally, he heard Harrison's whisper. "It's not too late, Gabe. Take Liddy and run. You love each other. You deserve to be happy."

Gabe shook his head. "How long do you think either of us will be happy knowing you and Austin have been ruined? Or do you think Chisolmwood won't exact revenge if we run off together?" Gabriel laughed. "He will. Don't doubt it for a second, Harrison, or you'll lose everything!"

"I know." The carriage turned the corner to Etherhouse and slowed.

"Would you care to come in and have a drink to celebrate your visit with the Queen?"

Gabriel shook his head. "Another time. I think I need to go home. It's been a long day, and you'll need to get ready for Liddy's engagement ball tonight."

"I'd rather not go."

Gabriel knew that was how he'd feel if he were in Harrison's place, but staying away wasn't an option. "This is Liddy's future you're celebrating. She needs you to be there for her."

The carriage stopped and Harrison disembarked. "What are you going to do now?" he said before closing the door.

"Her Highness just gave me a London town house you tell me will make me the envy of half of London, plus two country estates. I think after a good night's sleep I'll see exactly what I own. I'd like the use of your carriage for a few days if you don't mind."

"Use it as long as you like."

Harrison started to close the door and Gabriel stopped him. "Take good care of her."

"I will," Harrison said, then gave the driver Gabriel's directions.

The carriage took off down the street and Gabriel leaned back into the seat. This was it then. As close as he would ever be to her again. As far away as he would always be from her.

After tomorrow, he'd leave for the country. That had always been his dream, as well as hers, and he'd make the best of the opportunity he'd been given.

Without her.

Without the half of his heart he needed in order to do more than simply exist.

The carriage stopped in front of the small flat he'd rented, and Gabriel scooted toward the door. Bloody hell, but his leg was stiff. The hours he'd had to stand before the Queen made his leg ache as much as trying to hold his balance aboard the ship had. He couldn't wait to get inside and rub his knotting muscles.

He maneuvered down the steps the Etherington driver lowered for him and stepped to the ground. His footsteps halted when he saw a shiny black carriage with the Marquess of Culbertson's emblazoned crest on the door in front of his rooming house.

An austere-looking gentleman walked toward him carrying a small leather-bound folder that he held guardedly near his body. Another gentleman accompanied him.

"Major Talbot?"

"Yes."

Gabriel arched his eyebrows and waited. After a short silence the man looked toward the rooming house door.

"We've been sent by the Marquess of Culbertson on business. Could we go inside?"

Gabriel nodded, then led the way into his ground-floor flat and stepped inside the small, sparsely-furnished room. He closed the door behind the two men and turned to face them. "What do you want?"

"My employer, the Marquess of Culbertson, sent me with the express purpose of delivering a parcel. I believe his exact term was…gift."

"And the reason for this…*gift*?"

"A repayment of sorts, for services rendered."

Gabriel felt his temper rise. After tonight, Culbertson would have the only *gift* that was important to him, and no bloody substitute would make what he'd taken away from him hurt any less. "Tell your employer I won't accept his gift. I want *nothing* from him, or from his father."

"Lord Culbertson explained you might feel this way, but he insists you open the folder before you make a final decision."

Culbertson's secretary held out the leather packet he'd been guarding since he'd arrived.

Gabriel lowered his gaze to the man's outstretched arm, hesitated, then took the folder.

Using his cane to help him to the small table in the center of the room, he placed the folder on the scarred surface and opened it. He reached inside and—

"What the hell is this?"

"It's payment in the amount of—" Culbertson's secretary stopped and handed Gabriel a slip of paper he'd retrieved from his jacket pocket. "It's a gift in that exact amount. We can count it if you'd like to make sure—"

"No."

Gabriel stared at the amount on the paper and let his heart race in his chest. It was the exact amount Harrison told him remained of his father's debts. Culbertson was gifting him the money to pay Lydia's blackmailer. "Why?"

"Lord Culbertson has his reasons."

"What does he expect in return?"

Culbertson's secretary smiled. "Lord Culbertson said you would know the answer to that."

The two men looked at each other for several long seconds. "There is one more item," Culbertson's man said, reaching back into his pocket and taking out a smaller envelope. "I'm to give you this."

Gabriel took the envelope and opened it. It was an invitation to the ball the Duke of Chisolmwood was hosting tonight to announce Lydia's engagement to his son.

"My presence is requested?"

"I don't believe Lord Culbertson used the term 'requested', Major Talbot. I think he has something more definite in mind."

"I see."

"Lord Culbertson thought you would."

The man walked to the door and stopped. "Until tonight, then."

Gabriel showed his guests out, then sank down on the chair beside the table and stared at the folder filled with an astronomical amount of money—the same amount Harrison and Austin still owed on their father's notes. Culbertson must have discovered his father's blackmail plan and didn't want to start his marriage with such a dark cloud marring his future happiness. After all, what groom wants to know his bride was blackmailed into marrying him? But why was it so important for Gabriel to be at the engagement ball tonight?

Gabriel read the invitation again, then leaned back against the rough rungs of the chair and smiled a bitter smile. Of course. Appearances were everything to the Duke of Chisolmwood, as they must be to his son, the marquess. How better to put the stamp of approval on his engagement than for his betrothed's former suitor to be there?

He swiped his hand over the rough planes of his face. If that's what it took to get Austin and Harrison out from under Chisolmwood's thumb, he'd do it.

What choice did he have, after all?

He tied the leather straps that sealed the folder and tucked it under his arm, then walked out to the waiting carriage. He needed to give the money to Harrison. Maybe if he were lucky, he'd be there when Harrison threw the money in Chisolmwood's face.

"Take me back to Etherhouse," he said, climbing in.

He rode through the city streets silently praying that when he reached Etherhouse, Lydia wouldn't be there. It was one thing to know he'd have to pretend to be happy for her tonight when the Duke of Chisolmwood announced his son's engagement.

He didn't think he was strong enough to fake such a reaction twice in the same day.

CHAPTER TWENTY-TWO

Gabriel didn't arrive at the engagement ball early. Hell, he almost didn't arrive at all. If he could have, he'd have sent Culbertson's invitation back with a message of his own, and he doubted either Culbertson or his father would have enjoyed reading what he thought of their manipulations. But what purpose would that serve? He'd played this game of theirs for more than a year, and when tonight was over, he'd be finished with them forever.

After all, this was no different than some of the missions on which he'd been sent during the war. More than once he'd wanted to quit in the middle and give up, but that hadn't been an option. Quitting wasn't an option now either. He'd see this through to the end, and that meant standing in view of all of London as one of the well-wishers when the duke announced Lydia's engagement to his son. Then he would have completed his final mission for the man he'd discovered to be the elusive Thorn.

He relaxed his tightened grip around the handle of his cane and looked over the crowd one more time. He spied Harrison against the far wall and headed in that direction.

"I was afraid you wouldn't come," Harrison said when he reached him.

"I almost didn't."

There was a serious expression on Harrison's face. "When will you leave London? Yet tonight? Or will you wait until at least tomorrow?"

Gabriel smiled even though he didn't feel like it. "It depends on how long my presence is required here."

"Or how drunk you get after you leave?"

Gabriel didn't answer. The less said the greater success he'd have of concealing how much he hurt.

"Mind if I join you?"

"I make a lousy drunk but you're always welcome."

"I'll bring Austin. You'll seem pleasant company by comparison. Have you given Chisolmwood the money?"

Harrison patted his jacket pocket. "Culbertson met me when I arrived and asked that I wait to pay his father until after he announced his engagement."

"Did he give a reason why?"

"No, and I didn't ask. I don't care when I pay Father's debts, as long as I get the bastard out of my life."

"We'll offer a toast to that happy occasion later."

"Until later," Harrison said. "I need to find Austin. He's no doubt outside. I don't know what the bastards did to him in France, but since he returned, he doesn't last but a few minutes confined indoors."

Gabriel followed Harrison through the crowded ballroom. They met Austin as he came in from outside. His eyes contained the same haunted look Gabriel had noticed often since they'd returned from France.

"Just in time," Austin said, swiping at the sheen of perspiration on his forehead. He pulled at the cravat at his neck, then nodded toward the makeshift dais placed against the wall and decorated with several huge bouquets of flowers. "The performance is about to begin."

Gabriel followed Austin's gaze. Lydia stood amid several other young ladies, each of them dressed in their finest. But none of them compared. Lydia sparkled like a diamond in sunlight.

The ache inside his chest hurt even more. He reminded himself that he didn't have to watch when Chisolmwood announced his son's betrothal, that he didn't have to see the look of elation on Culbertson's face when he claimed his future bride. He only had to remain in the crowded ballroom until the announcement was made, then he could leave before the festivities started.

Gabriel watched Culbertson walk to where the Duke of Chisolmwood waited. When Chisolmwood saw his son approach, the older man's face lit with a glow that caused the pain in Gabriel's stomach to tighten. He wanted this over. He wasn't sure he could watch what he knew was about to take place.

"It'll be over soon," Austin said as if his feelings were obvious for all to see.

Gabriel didn't show that he'd heard his friend but stared at the spot where Lydia would join the Marquess of Culbertson when their betrothal was announced.

As people pushed closer, Gabriel felt their excitement grow in anticipation of the momentous event. Tonight's happenings would undoubtedly be retold in every sitting room in London for weeks to come.

The clenching knot in his stomach made him want to walk away as fast as he could. Instead, he leaned against his cane and waited for his world to end.

He looked at Lydia, at the expression on her face, praying to read her innermost thoughts. Was she happy? Was this as difficult for her as it was for him? Was that a look of pain in her eyes, or was she secretly hopeful as she considered her future as the Marquess of Culbertson's wife?

He wanted her to look at him, thought she would *feel* his presence as was usual when they were near each other. But she didn't search him out. She continued her conversation with the other young ladies as if she were enthralled with whatever they said.

Maybe it was just as well. He wasn't sure he could survive if she looked at him and he saw…happiness.

He turned away from her. The Duke of Culbertson stepped onto the platform with his son at his side. This was it, then. The final Chapter. The last time he would have to give her up.

There was a loud murmur from the excited crowd followed by a cacophony of shushing sounds. Finally the room stilled enough that one could hear the proverbial pin drop to the floor. Chisolmwood stepped to the center of the stage and held up his hands.

"Friends, thank you for coming. This is indeed a joyous occasion. I'm glad you are here to share in my happiness. I had an exceedingly long, and monumentally impressive speech prepared for tonight's event." He paused while the crowd tittered and guffawed. "But my son convinced me my glowing accolades would only serve to embarrass us both."

There was another round of laughter and applause, followed by a gradual quieting before the duke continued. "I intended to tell you how pleased I was that my son had finally chosen a woman with whom to share his life—"

He held up his hands when several in attendance started to clap.

"…but he informed me that news of this magnitude should be his to make."

There was general laughter at that.

"So, I'll let my son, the Marquess of Culbertson, announce his intentions and say nothing more, except to state for all the world that I couldn't be happier with his choice of a wife. Not only is his future bride a vision of loveliness and the perfect choice to be the future Duchess of Chisolmwood, but she is the woman with whom I've dreamed my son would share his life since the day she was born."

The crowd broke out in applause as the duke stepped back to allow his son to take the stage.

The man who was about to announce his engagement to Lydia stepped forward.

Gabriel couldn't watch this. He'd had to give her up time and again and it had hurt more each time, but this was the worst. Before, when he'd separated himself from her, she'd still been free, there'd still been a glimmer of hope that he could win her back. After tonight, she'd belong to another man.

He stepped back, preparing to barge through the bodies pressed behind him in his attempt to escape. As if Austin realized his intent, he moved closer.

"Soon," Austin whispered just loud enough for Gabe to hear. It was the voice of reason he needed. For Liddy's sake he had to put his stamp of approval on her match. For Liddy's sake his presence was necessary so no one would think there were any lingering feelings between them. For Liddy's sake—

Gabriel forced his mind to concentrate on the Marquess of Culbertson's speech.

"Welcome friends. As my father said, you have been invited here tonight to be a part of a celebration. This is indeed a most joyous occasion, especially for my father, who despaired that this day would ever come."

A brief tempest of laughter spilled from the guests. When they quieted, Culbertson turned to face his father. "Your Grace, thank you. For everything. Especially for declaring publicly how pleased you are with my choice of a bride. Your acceptance and approval has always been of the utmost importance to me."

The Duke of Chisolmwood smiled with fatherly pride as the

crowd erupted into a lengthy applause.

After several moments, the Marquess of Culbertson held up his hand for silence. "Everything my father said about the woman I have chosen as my bride is true. She is an exquisite vision of beauty. Her grace and elegance make her the perfect woman to be my marchioness. But those are only physical attributes and not what is important when choosing a woman with whom you will spend the rest of your life.

"Finding a woman who captures your heart and soul is much more complicated. Many of you know finding a love such as this is often as elusive as capturing the mist. But when you have found that other part of your heart, you are the most fortunate of men. My father, more than anyone, knows what I mean…" The marquess turned to face his father. "…because he once found a woman he loved with all his heart and soul, as I have."

There was a rush of sighs from the crowd and Gabriel fought the urge to leap onto the small dais and stifle Culbertson's declaration of love. How could he profess such a love when the woman he claimed he couldn't live without didn't share that same passion? Or had Liddy told him she did? Gabriel gritted his teeth and listened while the marquess continued.

"I consider myself the luckiest of men because I have found a woman I love with all of my heart."

After a series of sighs, the crowd exploded into a thunderous ovation.

"Thank you for accepting my offer of marriage," he said, turning his gaze to the corner beyond the small dais where Liddy stood amongst a group of her friends. "You have made me exceedingly happy. I will always be humbled that you found it in your heart to return my love."

Everyone knew the marquess intended to marry Lady Lydia Landwell, and they strained to catch a glimpse of her. But Gabriel didn't look. He didn't want to see her expression when she smiled at Culbertson. He didn't want to see the glow in her eyes, whether real or not.

"The love of my life," Culbertson said, walking toward the gathering of females with his arm extended and a broad smile on his face. "Lady Emmeline Frendsdale."

Gabriel's heart skipped a beat. Amidst the explosive gasps of surprise that came from the crowded room, he wasn't sure if it had resumed beating or had forever stopped.

Strong fingers grasped his arm and he looked first at one brother, then the other. Their expressions turned from ones of surprised shock to elation. Their held breaths erupted in peals of laughter as they realized the ramifications of Culbertson's announcement.

"Congratulations!" Austin yelled out, and from all around them hundreds of voices echoed his salutation. Within seconds, the room exploded in thunderous applause and boisterous shouts of approval.

Had the Duke of Chisolmwood known his son intended to marry Emmeline Frendsdale? Gabriel looked to where the duke stood and realized at a glance he hadn't. Although there was a smile frozen on his face, anyone with an inkling of what had just happened knew the look of happiness was for the sake of appearances. His sallow complexion and the blazing glare in his eyes said this was as big a shock to him as it was to everyone else in the room. Everyone except Lady Emmeline Frendsdale, whose eyes brimmed with adoration as she focused on the man who'd publicly declared his love for her.

Gabriel searched for Liddy. He found her adding her enthusiastic applause to the loud cheering in the room. She stood close to Lady Emmeline, and a moment before Culbertson reached them, she gave the marquess's betrothed a warm embrace.

The room seemed fixed on the scene before them, watching

the interaction between Lydia and Lady Emmeline with rapt attention.

When Culbertson reached them, he brought Liddy's hand to his lips as a show of affection, then turned to his betrothed and took her into his arms.

The onlookers broke into thunderous applause.

"Follow me, Austin." Harrison patted the money in his pocket. "We have an appointment with the Duke of Chisolmwood and I don't want to be late."

CHAPTER TWENTY-THREE

Lydia leaned against the low cement balustrade on the terrace and waited. The muffled roaring of excited voices still echoed from behind the patio doors as the guests offered their congratulations on Culbertson's announcement. It had indeed been a shock to everyone.

Especially Gabriel.

She watched him as Culbertson made his announcement and recognized the restrained fury he kept from escaping. His years in the military had trained him to take charge of any situation, to accept nothing less than victory, so she knew how helpless he felt having to stand by while another man announced his engagement to her.

If the roles had been reversed, she wouldn't have acted nearly so nobly.

Her breath caught and she clamped her hand over her mouth to stop the nervous laughter that wanted to escape. She couldn't believe things had turned out the way they had. Only a few days ago she thought she was the one Culbertson would announce as his future wife. And last night in the dark, she'd told Gabriel goodbye for the last time. Until Culbertson saw her and told her his plan for both of them to escape a life separated from the person they loved.

God did indeed answer prayers, and the Marquess of Culbertson realized he was as loathe to spend the rest of his life apart from the person he truly loved as she was.

If everything went as Culbertson had planned, this would be the last time she'd ever have to go through a night like this.

She paced from one end of the flagstone terrace to the other, stopping before the open doors to listen for his footsteps. The longer she waited, the more anxious she grew. She clutched her fingers around the cement railing and—

The ballroom doors opened and excited voices from inside spilled into the nighttime silence. She took a deep breath in anticipation, then turned around when the determined thud of his cane hit the flagstones behind her.

"Have you finally come for me?" she asked.

"Yes, my lady. I've finally come for you. And I don't intend to ever let you go again."

"Good." The tears she swore she wouldn't shed ran down her cheeks and she quickly swiped them away.

He took several steps toward her and stopped when he reached her. "How long have you known Culbertson was going to announce Lady Emmeline's name instead of yours?" he asked.

"Since last night."

"I see." He breathed a heavy sigh. "I should be exceedingly angry with you."

"You should?"

"Exceedingly. The torture you put me through took several valuable years off my life."

"I have suffered more," she said as a rebuttal. "Your discomfort doesn't come close to matching the torture you put me through when you told me you didn't love me and left me a year ago. Then when Austin brought you back more dead than alive. Then again when Jean-Paul returned with Austin and

Geoffrey but you weren't with them. And once more when you delivered us safely aboard the *Silver Star* and we sailed without you. And last night when you told me goodbye a final time. When I tally the score, you owe me far more in years than I owe you."

He smiled. "Let it never be said that I don't pay my debts. I intend to devote the rest of my life making up for my rudeness."

"You most assuredly will. I intend to make sure you do. You may start this moment."

He arched his brows in a devilish gesture. "Of course. What service may I offer?"

"You may begin by holding me."

"It would be my pleasure."

He gathered her in his arms and his warmth enveloped her. She sighed with relief. "How do you think Chisolmwood will take his son's announcement?"

She heard his chuckle beneath her ear. "Publicly? Joyous elation."

"Privately?"

"I don't know. Your brothers can fill us in on the riveting details when they return."

She lifted her head in alarm. "The money! Do they have the money to repay His Grace?"

"Yes. Culbertson sent Harrison the amount to pay their debt."

A heavy weight lifted from her. "Oh, it seems I'm more indebted to Lord Culbertson than I thought."

"We're *all* indebted to him. Especially me." He placed his finger beneath her chin and lifted until her gaze locked with his. "I love you, Liddy."

"And I love you. I always have. But what I feel is more than love. It's... it's..."

He ran the backs of his fingers down her cheek. "What do you feel, Liddy?"

She thought a moment then said the only word that came to her mind. "Consumed."

"Consumed by what?"

"Not what," she said. "By whom. By you." She nestled her face against his chest. "Do you know what it's like to be consumed with thoughts of you day and night? It's been more than a year since you walked away from me that first time and there hasn't been a day— No, there hasn't been an *hour* that I haven't wondered what you were doing. Where you were. If someone else was taking care of you, talking to you, laughing with you..." She stopped and swallowed hard. "Holding you."

"You're the only woman I'll ever hold—day, night... anytime."

An errant tear spilled from her eye and she wrapped her arms around him and held tighter.

"Ah, Liddy. I love you so much I nearly died that first time I had to give you up. Then, I missed you so much I didn't care if I came back from any of the missions I was sent on because what did it matter? Life wasn't worth living if you weren't a part of it."

"Oh, Gabriel."

He lowered his head and kissed her gently. "Do you know how I survived the trip to England from the Crimea? I survived because every day Austin told me when we got home you'd be waiting for me. I fought to stay alive so I could see you just once more. Then I fought to stay alive because I couldn't bear the thought of leaving you. And tonight..."

He held her close. "Tonight was the hardest of all. Standing there while I thought Culbertson intended to announce he was going to marry you.

"I searched the room, knowing if it were possible to steal you away, I'd do it. I love you, Liddy. More than I have a right to."

She cupped her palms against his cheeks and brought his

mouth down to hers.

He lifted his lips from hers. "How soon will you marry me, Liddy?"

"Tonight?"

He laughed, then kissed her again.

Oh, she'd missed the feel of his arms around her and his lips against hers. Missed feeling the warmth of his body against hers and the surety of knowing she'd spend the rest of her life with a man who loved her as much as she loved him.

For her, love was enough.

It always had been.

See all of Laura's books on her website at
www.lauralandon.com

About Laura Landon

Laura Landon enjoyed ten years as a high school teacher and nine years making sundaes and malts in her very own ice cream shop, but once she penned her first novel, she closed up shop to spend every free minute writing. Now she enjoys creating her very own heroes and heroines, and making sure they find their happily ever after.

A vital member of her rural community, Laura directed the town's Quasquicentennial, organized funding for an exercise center for the town, and serves on the hospital board.

Laura lives in the Midwest, surrounded by her family and friends. She has written thirty Victorian historicals, eighteen of which have been published by Prairie Muse Publishing and are selling worldwide in English, one in Japanese, and several in German. Two are Scottish historicals.

Always beautifully set and with a mysterious twist or bit of suspense, Laura's books average a million pages a month read by her loyal readers.

LAURA LANDON IS A PRAIRIE MUSE PLATINUM, KINDLE PRESS, AND AMAZON MONTLAKE AUTHOR

www.lauralandon.com
Laura's Amazon Author Page:
www.amazon.com/Laura-Landon/e/B004GANR1O

Also from Laura Landon
by Prairie Muse Publishing

SHATTERED DREAMS
WHEN LOVE IS ENOUGH
BROKEN PROMISE
A MATTER OF CHOICE
MORE THAN WILLING
NOT MINE TO GIVE
LOVE UNBIDDEN
KEEPER OF MY HEART
THE DARK DUKE
CAST IN SHADOWS
CAST IN RUIN
CAST IN ICE
CAST IN SCANDAL
(novella in Her Majesty's Scoundrels boxed set)
JADED MOON
THE DEVIL'S GIFT
ONE MYSTICAL MOMENT (novella)
BEWARE THE RICH MAN
BEWITCHED BY THE POOR MAN
BETRAYED BY THE BEGGAR MAN
BEHOLD THE THIEF
WINTER'S COLD HEART
SPRING'S TENDER HEART

From Laura Landon
by Montlake Romance

SILENT REVENGE
INTIMATE SURRENDER
INTIMATE DECEPTION
THE MOST TO LOSE
A RISK WORTH TAKING
BETRAYED BY YOUR KISS
RANSOMED JEWELS

From Kindle Press
THE SECRET ROSE
DARK RUBY
DECEPTION IN EMERALDS
THE TRAITOR'S CLUB
Ford | Hugh | Jeb | Caleb

From Wolfbane Publishing
A VOICE ON THE WIND

WHERE THE WOMAN BELONGS
NOVELLA

COMPANION BOOKS (series)
by Laura Landon

THE BROTHERHOOD
When Love is Enough | Broken Promise

RANSOMED JEWELS
Ransomed Jewels | Jaded Moon
Dark Ruby | Deception in Emeralds

THE REDEEMED
The Most to Lose | The Dark Duke

CAST IN SCANDAL
Cast in Shadows | Cast in Ruin
Cast in Ice | Cast in Scandal

THE TRAITOR'S CLUB
Ford | Hugh | Jeb | Caleb

RICH MAN POOR MAN
Beware the Rich Man | Bewitched by the Poor Man
Betrayed by the Beggar Man | Behold the Thief

SEASONS OF THE HEART
2-Hour Reads
Winter's Cold Heart | Spring's Tender Heart
Summer's Distant Heart | Autumn's Wild Heart

REVIEWS
BEWARE THE RICH MAN

★★★★★   Fantastic! Different

November 12, 2019

Finally a book with its own story, loved it.

★★★★★

October 22, 2019

I absolutely loved book 1 of this series, Blake and Willow's story! A different kind of hero and heroine than the usual historical romance brings. Well written storylines and wonderful characters. Captivating from the very start.

Laura Landon is an amazing writer, and I always find her style to be such a comfortable and rewarding read, with so much to offer. Next up, Bewitched by the Poor Man.

BEWITCHED BY THE POOR MAN

★★★★★

January 4, 2020

I had just started reading Laura Landon's series and to tell you I couldn't put it down till I read all 4 books, I loved every one of them from the Rich man to the Thief, I especially loved, how she describes the beginning of the ready made clothing, plus the Warehouse and the materials used for the clothing back then, what a pleasure. I will have to get more of her books.

★★★★★

October 25, 2019

Quinn and Ali's is a wonderfully written love story that captures the reader's attention from the very beginning. These two had so many heartaches, and trials on their road to happiness, but it was very rewarding to experience the strength and courage they had as they grew to know and trust each other. Another great read by Laura Landon.

BETRAYED BY THE BEGGAR MAN

★★★★★ Lovely story

December 30, 2019

Five stars because of the way they suffered and yet were able to change their lives. The love and caring that brought them home.

★★★★★

October 30, 2019

Another winner in this series! Liam is not from nobility but from the filth and poverty of London's Whitechapel. Despite his harsh and loveless childhood, with the help of a friend, he works hard to make a good and honorable life for himself. When Lady Millicent comes asking for his help to find her sister, Liam is drawn to her immediately and risks all, even his very life. A beautiful bond forms as their feelings grow and they support each other through hardships that continuously challenge them. So much going on in this book with a wide host of characters, good and bad. A wonderful love story with lots of action, surprises and romance.

BEHOLD THE THIEF

★★★★★ Wow. Amazing

December 30, 2019

Five stars because of the way they were handling the situation and how much heart Lilly had as far as helping abused wonen. Enjoyed that part in the story.

★★★★★

November 5, 2019

Loved Reading this book just much as I've enjoyed reading all of Laura Landon's books. Just enough romance and intrigue to keep your attention throughout the book. Laura has a way of writing a book that makes you feel like you're a part of the story and you can't wait to see how it ends.

★★★★★ Absolutely Loved It!

November 2, 2019

I love the world Laura Landon created in this series and am sorry this is the last book. Each and every character has captured my interest, and the adventures and even the trials faced have brought so much entertainment with them. What a talented writer! I highly recommend all her work.

Jack and Lily's story was amazing! Had to reach for the tissues often with this one.. but that was a good thing. Just couldn't put it down! An awesome read!

Linger in the pages of a great love story